Hannah Dennison was born in England, relocating to Los Angeles with her daughter and two cats in tow to pursue a career in screenwriting. Along the road to publication she has served as an obituary reporter, antique dealer, private jet flight attendant and Hollywood story analyst.

Hannah is currently serving on the judging committee for the 2012 Edgar Allan Poe Awards for the Mystery Writers of America. She teaches mystery writing and social media at UCLA in Los Angeles and still works full-time for Davis Elen Advertising, a west coast advertising agency.

Although California is where she currently lives, Hannah's heart will always be in the English countryside. She enjoys hiking, horse riding, skiing and seriously good chocolate. Hannah is married to a fellow writer.

Website: www.hannahdennison.com

Blog: www.hannahdennison.blogspot.com

Twitter: @HannahLDennison

Facebook: www.facebook.com/VickyHillMysteries

Vicky Hill's Facebook page:
www.facebook.com/pages/Vicky-Hill/84329298565

The Vicky Hill Mystery series

A Vicky Hill Exclusive!
Scoop!
Exposé!
Thieves!

Thieves!

HANNAH DENNISON

CONSTABLE • LONDON

CONSTABLE

First published in the USA in 2011 by The Berkley Publishing Group,
a division of Penguin Group (USA) Inc., New York

First published in Great Britain in 2012 by Robinson,
an imprint of Constable & Robinson Ltd

Reprinted in 2017 by Constable

3 5 7 9 10 8 6 4 2

A CIP catalogue record for this book
is available from the British Library.

ISBN 978-1-78033-065-5

Printed and bound in Great Britain by CPI Group (UK) Ltd, Croydon CR0 4YY

Papers used by Constable are from well-managed forests
and other responsible sources.

MIX
Paper from
responsible sources
FSC® C104740

Constable
is an imprint of
Little, Brown Book Group
Carmelite House
50 Victoria Embankment
London EC4Y 0DZ

An Hachette UK Company
www.hachette.co.uk

www.littlebrown.co.uk

For Brenda Dennison,
the best mum in the world

Acknowledgements

Writing can be a lonely labour of love, which is why treasured company, helpful guidance, selfless encouragement, and endless snacks fed by family and friends make each book a team effort.

I'd like to continue to acknowledge my wonderful friend and mentor, Claire Carmichael.

My IOU tally has gone beyond the purchase of a small island to an entire galaxy.

Mark Davis, chairman of Davis Elen Advertising and my long-suffering boss, whose constant refrain is 'this *is* your last book, isn't it?' but who continues to give me paid days off to meet my deadlines.

Linda Palmer, who finds time in her own busy writing and teaching life to boost my morale and provided the spark that inspired the plot in this, Vicky's fourth adventure.

Credit and a special thanks go to my daughter Sarah and her sister Emily for creating a new character for Gipping-on-Plym. May Phil Burrows live on.

A huge thank you to kindred spirits Carolyn Hart, Rhys Bowen and Marcia Talley, who are all inspiration personified. Thanks to Gail Elen for her innovative spirit and creative PR strategies, and to Cam Galano's friendship and endless generosity.

Heartfelt thanks to Natalee Rosenstein, my wonderful editor at Berkley, along with Michelle Vega, a multitasking superwoman, and to my amazing agent, Betsy Amster. Thank you for everything you do.

And last, but foremost in my heart, my husband, Jason, who had no idea what he was letting himself in for when he encouraged me to follow my dream. Jason – without you, none of this would be possible.

1

'**Y**ou can't leave *now*!' Barbara Meadows cried as I drifted nonchalantly towards her front door to make my escape.

'It's nearly one in the morning,' I protested. *How many more hen parties can the human body take?* 'I'm really tired.'

'You'll miss all the excitement.' Barbara readjusted her glittering tiara – HERE COMES THE BRIDE – that had slipped rakishly over one ear. 'You youngsters have no stamina.'

It wasn't that I begrudged our receptionist her newfound happiness at the grand age of sixty-plus. This was the third hen party of Barbara's that I'd been to in the last two weeks, and I knew of at least three more in the works.

'Olive bought the director's cut of *The Full Monty* on eBay,' Barbara burbled on. 'We're in for a real treat.'

That settled it. There are some things a young woman should never be subjected to – and full-frontal nudity in a room filled with members of the Greying Tigers Society was definitely one.

I grabbed my safari jacket from the hall coat stand and pulled it on. 'Sorry, I've got to be at St Peter's the Martyr Church at eight tomorrow.' It was only a tiny white lie. The service didn't start until nine thirty.

1

'Why bother? No one will go to Gladys Trenfold's funeral,' Barbara said with scorn. 'She was a horrid old bag.'

'Maybe not,' I said. 'But the *Gipping Gazette* does have a reputation to keep up.'

Obituaries were my area of expertise, and it was my responsibility to make sure that no funeral went unreported and no mourner was left out. 'Unless you'd like to have a word with your fiancé and ask for an exception?'

'Oh no, dear,' said Barbara quickly. 'Wilf is a stickler for tradition.' She stretched out her left hand and gazed rapturously at the solitaire diamond ring on her finger. 'I still can't believe he proposed.'

I couldn't either! I was still grappling with the idea that after years of working together, Barbara was marrying our illustrious – and intimidating – editor, Wilf Veysey.

It had all happened so suddenly – but at least it gave me hope. It was never too late to find love.

Olive Larch emerged from the kitchen accompanied by the raunchy sounds of Donna Summer's 'Hot Stuff' starting up for the fourth time. Perched atop her sleek grey bob was a pair of striped cat's ears. She carried a silver tray of tumblers decorated with slices of fruit and was moving toward us at glacial speed.

'Good grief, Olive,' said Barbara. 'We're all dying of thirst. What took you so long?' She turned to me and mouthed, 'She's always *so* slow.'

'Vicky, you're not leaving, are you?' said Olive aghast. 'You can't!'

'Sorry, I hate to go, but I really must.'

'Well, you shouldn't—' Olive started to titter nervously. 'Tell her, Barbara.'

'It wasn't my idea,' Barbara declared.

'Tell me what?'

'Someone – and we won't say who – added a teensy weensy bit of vodka to the fruit punch,' said Olive.

'The punch was *spiked*?' I was flabbergasted, particularly as

2

I'd had five glasses. 'I could lose my job!'

Spearheaded by the odious Detective Inspector Stalk, Gipping Constabulary was in the midst of an aggressive campaign to clamp down on driving while intoxicated. What's more, he was working closely with the *Gazette*. Every week, names of Gipping citizens who had been stopped by the police and ordered to take a Breathalyzer test – often in broad daylight and without due cause – were listed in MOTORIST MENACE OF THE WEEK.

'So you'll stay?' said Barbara hopefully. 'We'd love a youngster's opinion.'

Opinion on *what*? 'I'll take the back road via Mudge Lane,' I said firmly. 'We haven't had that much rain, so the ford won't be deep.' As a shortcut linking Lower Gipping to Middle Gipping, access was through a shallow stream that could be unpredictable at times.

'Don't you mean *Smooch* Lane?' Olive tittered again. It was a notorious place for romantic trysts. 'Are you having a secret rendezvous?'

'Not tonight.' *Or any other night for that matter.*

Realizing that I meant business and after promising to attend Olive's Butler-in-the-Buff buffet on Friday in Barbara's honour, I said my goodbyes and left.

As the cool night air of summer hit me, I had to admit to feeling a little light-headed.

I made it a rule to never drink alcohol and drive. The risk was too high. Besides, you wouldn't catch my heroine Christiane Amanpour arriving at the front line tipsy in a taxi.

I'd recently traded in my moped for an old but nippy blue Fiat Panda Sisley 4x4. It was hardly a flashy silver BMW like that of fellow reporter, roommate, and bane of my life, Annabel Lake – but it was mine, and not a gift for services rendered, like hers.

The Fiat's engine started the first time. Apart from a bit of rust on the doorsills and a juddering clutch, I was thrilled with my purchase for which I paid cash, naturally. As the daughter of a notorious silver thief – nicknamed The Fog – I never used bank accounts or credit cards in case they could be traced. Old habits die hard.

Moments later, I headed for open countryside, leaving the sounds of Donna Summer and the comforting lights of The Marshes housing estate behind me. The night was black as pitch – rather like the sudden wave of depression that hit me hard.

Barbara was getting married. Even coy Olive Larch was living in sin – a thought I didn't want to dwell on too long given the man in question – and here was I, an ancient twenty-three years old with no boyfriend and no prospect of finding Mr Right, either. Gipping-on-Plym was rather sparse on the bachelor front.

I reached the entrance to Mudge Lane, marked by two triangular road-warning signs. They were both graphically clear. One showed a vehicle being submerged in water; the other, a cyclist being knocked over by a car. The first didn't concern me because my Fiat had four-wheel drive, and the latter was highly unlikely given the hour of the night.

Mudge Lane wasn't one of my favourite shortcuts. The narrow, high hedge-banked road was twisty, steep and impassable in winter.

My mood darkened. What if the ford *was* running high? My Fiat would be swept downriver and my bloated body – when it was finally discovered somewhere in the English Channel – impossible to identify. And who would notice? I had no real friends to speak of. Even my parents seemed to have disowned me.

Get a grip, Vicky! I hated it when I got maudlin and administered a sharp pinch to my inside thigh. It really hurt but always did the trick. Who cares about love! Who has time for love anyway? What I needed was a frontpage scoop to cheer me up. A nice juicy murder would do nicely and – *blast!*

I slammed my foot on the brakes and swung the steering wheel sharply to the left as a vehicle, blazing with a row of white

4

lights atop a safari roof, flew around a blind corner and came barreling toward me. I managed to pull into a concealed farm entrance signposted MUDGE COTTAGE and flashed my headlights, but the vehicle didn't even attempt to slow down.

There was a hard thud. My right wing mirror was torn off, followed by the sickening sound of metal screeching on metal as a green Land Rover scraped by. I caught just a glimpse of a figure in a woollen hat fly past without so much as a second glance.

Furious, I leapt out just as the Land Rover's tail lights were swallowed up in the darkness. Pulling my Mini Maglite from my safari-jacket pocket, I braced myself for the worst and went to inspect the damage.

I was gutted. The wing mirror could be repaired, but a deep gouge along the entire length of the driver's side would need an expensive trip to the body shop.

Damn and blast! I was absolutely trembling with rage. I'd used every last penny to buy my car and intended to hunt down the driver – no doubt a farmer, given the make of vehicle – and make him pay for the damage. I couldn't even report the incident to the police because of that wretched 'fruit punch'.

I set off in the Fiat once more, drawing to a stop at the brow of a hill where a third triangular road sign warned of the almost-vertical drop below. Among the many skills I learned under Dad's 'advanced driving course', which I eventually realized focused on handling a getaway car, was navigating obstacles. These included railway lines, ditches, and small rivers. The key to success, Dad said, was in the approach.

Engaging the four-wheel drive, I took a deep breath and began a slow descent, stopping only when I reached the edge of the water at the base of the hill.

I couldn't believe it! That wretched Land Rover had dumped a pile of household rubbish in the middle of the ford and – *good grief* – was that a *bicycle*?

Fly-tipping was illegal and culprits faced huge fines of

thousands of pounds. It was also on the increase thanks to Gipping-on-Plym County Council's ridiculous 'bonsai bin system' – supposedly to encourage homeowners to cut the amount of rubbish they put out. People drove miles to dispose of old refrigerators or mattresses. I made a mental note of talking to our chief reporter, Pete Chambers, first thing in the morning. I even had a headline – BABY BINS BALLS-UP: FLY-TIPPING FIASCO!

Since I could hardly turn around, I'd have to move the stuff aside.

I cut the engine but left the headlights on so I could keep both hands free to see what I was doing. According to the wooden-posted depth reader peeping above the water line, the water was seven inches deep. I always kept a pair of Wellingtons in the boot of my car and swiftly switched footwear.

I passed the short flight of steps up to the 'kissing bridge', which was basically a wooden walkway on stilts that straddled the stream for pedestrians. The drop had to be about eight feet. There was no handrail, and I would imagine if things got hot and heavy, it could prove quite dangerous for lovers. I could think of much better locations to steal a kiss – on a cliff top overlooking the ocean, or perhaps around a campfire deep in the woods under a sky filled with stars. He'd be playing a guitar and – *focus Vicky!*

A gentle breeze rustled the leaves in the surrounding trees. I waded into the ford, making for the bicycle, but almost fell over. My feet were caught up in some kind of debris. I pulled out my Mini Maglite for a closer look.

Wrapped around my Wellingtons was an octopus-like creature with long, thick black tentacles. Puzzled, I gingerly poked at it and, to my surprise, realized it was a wig.

My heart began to thump. Something felt wrong down here. I trained the flashlight over the rubbish just a few feet away. Were those *curtains*?

The wind suddenly picked up and tore through the trees

above, making my skin prickle. Edging closer, I lifted my foot and nudged the mound of material. It toppled over heavily with a loud splash.

Captured in the harsh white light was the grey face of a partially bald woman. Her eyes were wide open, caught in an expression of horrified surprise.

I would have screamed, but there was no one – no one alive – to hear. Instead I gave a muffled whimper and began to back away, falling heavily in the water with the sudden thought. Mum was right when she said, *'Be careful what you wish for.'*

2

'Glad you rang me first, doll,' said Steve Burrows, Gipping's paramedic and my most ardent admirer. Unfortunately for Steve, the feeling was not mutual. I hadn't 'rang him first', either. All 999 calls were routed to Emergency Services, as Steve was perfectly aware.

'Here, let Steve help you get out of those wet jeans,' he said, holding up a grey hospital blanket. His cherubic face was etched with concern.

'I was only in the water for seconds,' I said, although I was beginning to feel a distinct chill around my nether regions.

In vain, I tried to shake the image of the woman's face out of my head and shivered.

'You're in shock, doll. Let me give you a hug.' Steve put his arm around my shoulders.

'I wonder who she is,' I said. 'Or was.'

'That's for the police to find out.' Steve pulled me closer. I wouldn't describe him as fat, but he was certainly cuddly. Inhaling his scent of Old Spice and antiseptic, I felt strangely comforted.

'I'm a reporter,' I said. 'It's *my* job to find out.'

The poor woman couldn't have been more than forty and certainly wasn't one of my mourner regulars. What was she doing in Mudge Lane at this hour of the night? Was it a romantic tryst that had gone terribly wrong? Had they quarrelled on the bridge and she'd fallen and drowned? In a panic, he'd fled the scene in a Land Rover.

'I really think you should sit down.' Steve gestured to the campstool he'd set up just for me.

'No. I'm fine.' In fact, I'd never felt better. Despite being banished to the sidelines the moment Detective Inspector Stalk turned up, I was riveted by the activity going on in the stream. It was just like on the telly! The area was ablaze with lights, adding an eerie stagelike effect to the small white tent erected over the woman's body, which still lay in the water to await the arrival of Coroner Cripps.

I already had a couple of headlines up my sleeve. MUDGE LANE MYSTERY: A VICKY HILL EXCLUSIVE! Or better still, RIVER OF DEATH SHOCKER!

'What's your expert opinion, Steve?' I said.

'To be honest,' said Steve, 'when you hadn't returned my phone calls, I thought you had given up on us.'

Good grief! Here we were at the scene of what could be, at worst, a fatal accident or, at best, manslaughter, and all Steve could think about was us. But since he had proved to be a valuable informant in the past and would be taking the body to the morgue, I needed to be tactful.

'You know I don't have time for relationships, Steve,' I said gently.

'I know, I know,' said Steve. 'You want to take things slow.'

'Not slow. Not anything. I want to focus on my career.'

'And so you should, doll,' said Steve, patting my arm. 'We've got our whole lives in front of us. Don't worry so much. Steve's not going anywhere.'

Which was exactly my problem.

He kissed the top of my head. A frisson of electricity shot

through my body as it always did around Steve – a phenomenon that utterly baffled me every time. I did *not* fancy Steve Burrows.

'Let Steve get you some hot tea,' he said. 'We could be in for a long night since Stalk wants to take you down to the station.'

'He wants *what*?' My stomach flipped over. I had an inherent fear of police stations. 'Why? I've already told him everything.' But even as I said it, I knew the real reason. Stalk wanted to give me the Breathalyzer test.

'You're right, Steve. I do feel a little wobbly,' I said, struck with one of my brilliant ideas. 'Do you have anything stronger than tea? Brandy perhaps?'

'Anything for you, doll.' Steve ruffled my hair – causing another tingle to surge through my loins – and disappeared into the rear of the ambulance, returning a few moments later with a small paper cup filled with amber liquid.

'This is just for medicinal purposes, you understand,' he said. I thanked him and drank the lot.

Several cheerful beeps announced the approach of the coroner's metallic-red Freelander GS 2.

Coroner Cripps flung open the driver's door, collected his black case from the passenger seat, and strode past us with a nod of acknowledgement. Dressed in his regulation white jumpsuit and Wellingtons, Cripps exuded an aura of confident professionalism. He plunged into the ford, oblivious to hidden hazards, and vanished inside the white tent.

Moments later, Stalk appeared, accompanied by a reed-thin, fresh-faced copper who couldn't have been more than nineteen.

In his late forties, Detective Inspector Stalk was built like an Aga, with a neatly clipped beard and piggy eyes. As an active member of Gipping Boxing Club, he was not a man to be trifled with. Stalk was very unpopular at the *Gazette*. Pete Chambers often said he'd rather spend the night with Jack the Ripper than five minutes in Stalk's company.

I took a deep breath and waited for the two policemen to join us. 'Do you have an ID on the victim yet, Inspector?'

'No,' Stalk snapped.

'Could it be a romantic tryst gone wrong?' I said. 'Or perhaps a hit-and-run?' I hadn't considered that possibility. 'She was on a bicycle. Maybe he didn't see her?'

'No comment,' he said.

I took out a business card – I'd had some cheap ones made at Gipping Railway Station – and handed it to him. 'If you find out the owner of the Land Rover, at least let me know. Not only did he leave the scene of an accident, he hit my car.'

'We're perfectly aware of what went on here.' Stalk studied my card and handed it back to me with a sneer. 'But if I want to talk to the *Gazette*, it won't be with a rookie.'

'But I saw the Land Rover!' I protested. 'I found the body.'

'Which is exactly why Detective Constable Bond, here, will be taking you to the station.'

'Why? I already gave you my statement.'

'To give you a Breathalyzer test,' Stalk growled. 'There is only one reason why you would be in Mudge Lane at one thirty in the morning – if you were *drunk* and hoping to avoid the police.'

Damn and blast!

'There is another reason.' Steve stepped forward and threw his arm around my shoulders once more. 'This is Mudge Lane, Officer. Surely you know what *that* means?' He wiggled his eyebrows.

'No,' said Stalk.

'Vicky and I had a romantic rendezvous.'

'That's right,' I said with relief.

'When I got here, she was in a terrible state. I remember when I saw my first body. It was a farming accident. Bloke got mangled in the thresher. Couldn't sleep for weeks. Even hit the bottle myself for a while.'

Good old Steve! 'It was a terrible shock,' I chimed in. 'I was shaking—'

'So I gave her a medicinal shot of brandy.'

11

'Just a small one. I am perfectly capable of driving home.'

Stalk regarded us both with suspicion.

Steve stuck out his jaw. 'Ms Hill needs to be out of those wet clothes and tucked up in bed, not hauled off to a cold police station.'

I had to admit Steve was impressive when angry and, despite my feelings, was deeply touched. If only I *could* fall in love with him.

'Inspector?' said a familiar voice. 'A word please.'

Startled, Stalk swung around. 'Probes! What the hell are you doing here?'

I gasped and, without thinking, shrugged Steve's arm off. This was not Detective Sergeant Probes's beat. He worked with the Plymouth Drug Action Squad, a good forty-minute drive away. What's more, I hadn't heard or seen his car arrive, and we were in the middle of nowhere.

Mobile phones did not work down in the dell, either – as I found out when I'd had to run up to high ground to make the emergency call to Steve. Considering that Probes's lightweight raincoat hardly covered his red-and-white-striped pajamas, it was as if Probes had simply teleported in from his bedroom.

Wait! Why was Probes wearing his pajamas? Surely he couldn't be the third member of the love triangle?

With barely a nod in my direction, Probes led Stalk out of earshot, closely followed by DC Bond.

'Okay, I get it. I'm not blind,' said Steve, arms akimbo. 'What's going on between you and that redheaded copper?'

'Nothing. I don't know what you mean,' I said, flustered at seeing Probes so unexpectedly. It had been weeks since we'd tried to enjoy a celebratory dinner over my last front-page exclusive, but that magical evening had been cut short when he got a phone call. Probes's promise that we'd make it another time came to nothing. Frankly, it was embarrassing seeing him again, and it was obvious that he felt embarrassed, too.

'Stalk's right,' said Steve. 'What *were* you doing in Mudge

12

Lane at one thirty in the morning?' Steve's expression darkened. 'I noticed his pajamas. And yet you tell me you want to focus on your career?'

'I was at Barbara's hen party. For heaven's sake, Steve,' I said. 'A woman is lying dead not twenty feet from where we stand. This is hardly the time to discuss our relationship.'

Steve brightened. 'So we *are* having a relationship!'

Fortunately I was saved from answering by the return of Stalk and Probes. Without even bidding a hello or goodbye, Probes stepped up onto the wooden walkway and was swallowed into the darkness as quietly as he had appeared.

'You're free to go, Vicky,' said Stalk, who had never addressed me by my first name before. 'My colleague speaks very highly of you.'

'Oh yes, I'm sure he does,' muttered Steve.

'We won't need to talk to you again,' said Stalk. 'It's clear what happened here tonight.'

'Probes knew the victim?' I said, feeling an inexplicable stab of jealousy.

Stalk made a strange chuckling sound. 'Nothing like that. The poor woman was riding her bicycle on the walkway, slipped off, hit her head, and drowned.'

I looked at him with disbelief. Did he think I was born *yesterday*? 'What about the Land Rover with all those fancy lights?'

'Coincidence,' said Stalk. 'Anyway, she's most likely a vagrant. There is a small group of gypsies camped in Upper Gipping—'

I'd heard the rumour. 'But that's miles away!' I said. 'What would she be doing down here?'

'Frankly she's no loss,' said Stalk. 'Those gypsies are a menace to society.'

Didn't Mum say that her side of the family had Romany blood in their veins? Stalk's inflammatory comments made my blood boil. 'She still deserves justice,' I said coldly.

13

'I'll say it again' – Stalk's voice hardened – 'it was an accident, and that's official. Now, you'd best get home unless you want to continue this conversation down at the station with a Breathalyzer test.'

I mumbled that it wouldn't be necessary. Stalk turned on his heel and left.

'I'd offer to take you home, doll,' said Steve apologetically, 'but I've got a body to deliver to the morgue.'

'Don't worry. I'm off.'

After Steve had successfully turned my Fiat around in an impressive eleven-point turn, I headed for home.

Let the police think what they liked, but something bad had happened here tonight. Gypsy or not, there was no way I was going to accept Stalk's diagnosis.

Tonight's events had all the makings of another Vicky Hill exclusive!

3

Barbara was right about Gladys Trenfold's funeral. There were only three mourners at her graveside – her brother, Bill; the Reverend Whittler; and me.

The service was simple. There were no flowers. No hymns sung. Even Gipping's funeral directors, Ripley and Ravish – DUST TO DUST WITH DIGNITY – had seemed to simply drop the coffin off en route to another job in Plymouth.

Bill Trenfold shed no tears and kept checking his watch. He was a shifty-looking man in his early sixties with severe bandy legs. Dressed in his navy blue with red piping Royal Mail uniform, and black, polished peaked cap, Bill wasted no time in telling us that he was on his tea break and had to resume his postal rounds as soon as possible.

Poor Gladys Trenfold. She may have been unpopular, but it was at times like this that I was proud to write the obituaries. If it weren't for the *Gipping Gazette,* lives such as hers wouldn't be recorded at all.

As we returned to the car park, Reverend Whittler pulled out an envelope from the folds of his cassock. 'Would you mind taking this envelope with you, Bill? It's already stamped.'

15

Bill glanced at the address on the letter and promptly gave it back, saying, 'Can't do that, Reverend.'

I'd always been able to read upside down: WINDOWS OF WONDER, ROYAL PARADE, PLYMOUTH, PL4 9TD.

'It's the final deposit for our stained glass window,' said Whittler, gesturing to a five-foot placard – SAVE OUR STAINED GLASS WINDOW AND GOD WILL SAVE YOU – that had stood outside the church lych-gate for as long as I'd lived in Gipping. A crudely drawn barometer marked in thousand-pound increments revealed there was only three thousand pounds to go to make the goal of twenty thousand.

'This Saturday's Morris Dance-a-thon at The Grange will close the gap,' beamed Whittler. 'Such a clever idea of your Barbara's.'

Nearly every fund-raising event in Gipping-on-Plym had been to raise money for the Trewallyn Trio. Named after its benefactor – the late Sir Hugh Trewallyn's father – the three-paned stained glass window had stood in St Peter's Church for more than a hundred years until a tree fell through it during a bad storm.

'Windows of Wonder agreed to start work on Monday,' Whittler went on, 'and with all these postal problems recently—'

'Sorry,' said Bill firmly. 'It's against company policy.'

'Don't worry,' I said. 'I'll post it, Vicar.'

'It's not my fault that the village post offices are closing down,' grumbled Bill. 'I've already had my wages cut. Did you know that they're trying to force me into taking early retirement?'

What's that got to do with posting a wretched letter? I wanted to say and would have done so had we not just buried his sister.

'Come back to the vicarage for some sherry and cake. Let's give your Gladys a good old send-off.' It was traditional in Gipping to have an after-service shindig following a funeral.

'Can't,' said Bill. 'I've already taken longer, than I should. Better get back to my job while I still have one.'

We watched Bill get into his red post van – a 1973 Morris Marina, bearing the Royal Coat of Arms – and drive away.

'Poor man.' Whittler shook his head. 'I know I shouldn't speak ill of the dead, but that sister of his left him in a bit of a financial mess. Rather too fond of snail racing, I'm told.'

'I'd better go, too.' It was already ten, and I was anxious to get to the *Gazette* to see if Stalk had spoken to our chief reporter.

Of course, I'd wasted no time in contacting Pete first thing this morning. I was worried he might give the Mudge Lane scoop to Annabel Lake – my senior by a mere three months – especially as their on-again, off-again flirtation was back in full 'on' mode.

Consequently, I'd left a long and detailed message on Pete's mobile phone making it quite clear that it was *me* who'd found the body, that it was vital we find the Land Rover, and that I suspected police corruption.

'The Victoria sponge with homemade strawberry jam was only made this morning,' said Whittler. 'Are you sure you won't change your mind?'

I hesitated. Perhaps I could just pop in for a quick slice.

Back in the warmth of the rectory kitchen, a plate of Victoria sponge sat on the pine kitchen table. Two bone china cups and saucers and a pot of tea covered with a hand-knitted, green-and-white-striped tea cosy were set alongside a jug of milk and a bowl of sugar.

Upstairs, a vacuum cleaner droned on over our heads. My landlady, Mrs Evans, ran a housekeeping service called Doing-It-Daily and counted Reverend Whittler as one of her many customers.

'Ah, Mrs Evans must have seen us walking over from the church,' said Whittler, removing the tea cosy and feeling the pot. 'Nice and hot. It's just been made.'

A quick survey of the kitchen showed that Whittler was a

very busy man – and hopelessly disorganized. Mrs Evans often complained that she was forbidden to touch his work area.

Every available surface was piled high with files and papers. A wall calendar was crammed with scribbled notes and stuck with yellow Post-its. In one corner of the room was an old computer and a fax machine surrounded by a sea of paper. According to Mrs Evans, he had been married a long time ago but after his wife died, never remarried, claiming, 'Constance was irreplaceable,' which I thought very touching.

I sat down and played mother, pouring the tea and cutting large slabs of cake that were still warm to the touch. Whittler retrieved a bottle of Harvey's Bristol Cream from a cupboard and two dainty sherry glasses.

'I should think you'd welcome a quick snifter after finding that body last night,' said Whittler, handing me a glass.

'Just a small one. I'm driving.' I wasn't surprised that he'd already heard the news. There were no secrets in Gipping. 'Who told you?'

Whittler chuckled. 'Mrs E. is great friends with Betty Bond. Her son, Kelvin, was called out to the scene. He was pretty shaken up.' I recalled the poor young constable last night. 'I'm sure he hadn't seen a dead body before.'

Nor had I, for that matter, and the expression on the woman's face still haunted me this morning.

'What did Kelvin make of it?' I intended to grill Mrs Evans later on.

Whittler took a sip of tea. 'I always say, there's nothing like the first sip of a freshly brewed pot of tea.'

'Did Kelvin mention the police thought she could be a gypsy?'

Startled, Whittler looked up sharply. He must have inhaled a cake crumb because a violent fit of coughing followed.

I jumped up. 'I'll get you some water.'

'No need,' he croaked, eyes bulging. Spluttering, Whittler reached for the sherry and drank straight from the bottle.

18

Gradually he recovered his breath. 'Goodness. Well, I never. We haven't had gypsies in these parts since I was a teenager. Barbara caused quite a scandal, I recall.'

This didn't surprise me. Barbara had been notoriously wild in her youth and never let anyone forget it.

'Stalk said a few gypsies had arrived in Upper Gipping.' I cut myself another slice of Victoria sponge.

'I only hope the poor dead woman isn't a gypsy.' Whittler dabbed his eyes with a paper napkin, adding darkly, 'For your sake.'

'What do you mean?'

'Do you know anything about gypsy funerals?'

I shrugged. 'No. Why?'

'My colleague officiated at one in St Jude's in Teignmouth a few years ago,' said Whittler. 'Over three hundred gypsies turned up.'

'Three *hundred*?' I squeaked. The *Gazette* prided itself on being one of the few newspapers in the country that recorded the names of every single mourner. How would I ever cope?

'Oh yes. It was like an invasion,' Whittler said with relish. 'Gypsy funerals are quite something. It's traditional for relatives from all over the country to come and pay their last respects. Festivities can go on for days. My colleague told me that after the service, they even dug a hole in the church car park and roasted a whole pig.'

'A *pig*!' I gasped. 'I suppose it will make a change from the usual sherry and fruitcake.'

'One of their customs is to burn the wagon of the deceased with all their possessions in it,' said Whittler. 'They perform a ritual destruction. I'm told it's quite astonishing to watch.'

'Even now? With modern trailer caravans?'

'Oh yes. Imagine if my parishioners decided to do the same?' Whittler chuckled. 'There would be fires burning in Gipping every single day.'

I believed it. I went to at least seven funerals a week.

'They're all dreadful thieves,' Whittler went on cheerfully. 'Steal anything not bolted down. She'll be buried at St Peter's naturally. You'd better prepare yourself.'

And with that worrying thought, I said, 'I really must go.'

'Wait! I almost forgot,' said Whittler. 'We must toast Gladys. More sherry?'

'I'm fine.' Mine was still untouched. I still couldn't get used to the tea-sherry-cake mixture of flavours first thing in the morning. Whittler refilled his glass and offered up a little prayer. I drank it down in one go and got to my feet. 'Don't forget to post that envelope, Vicky,' he said. 'There's a very large cheque in there.'

Reassuring him that I'd physically take it to the main post office in the High Street, I bid the vicar goodbye and walked back to the car park to collect my Fiat.

It sounded as if things were soon going to get very lively in Gipping-on-Plym.

4

To my disappointment, there wasn't a gypsy to be seen in Gipping-on-Plym. It was business as usual.

Knowing the four-space car park behind the *Gazette* would already be full, I left my Fiat in the alley adjacent to The Copper Kettle across the street. Topaz Potter, who owned the café as well as The Grange, charged me one pound – paid in advance – for the privilege. It was easier than having to use the free car park half a mile away.

To my surprise, there was no sign of Topaz's red Ford Capri and, emerging from the side passage, I noted that the café blinds were at half-mast. On the front door was a sign saying CLOSED UNTIL FURTHER NOTICE.

How odd. I'd only seen Topaz yesterday, and she hadn't mentioned she was going away. I stooped down to peer under the blinds and saw the wooden chairs turned upside down on the Formica tabletops.

'She's gone, then,' came a hard voice.

I jumped up to find two of my regular mourners, Florence Tossell and Amelia Webster. 'It certainly looks like it,' I said.

'I knew she couldn't keep that place going,' said Florence, fiddling with the wart on her chin. 'Didn't I tell you, Amelia?'

Amelia nodded. Both ladies wore crimplene summer dresses and hand-knitted cardigans, but Amelia had added a large straw-coloured floppy hat despite the fact the day was overcast. 'People prefer The Warming Pan,' she said. 'And her food was overpriced and tasted dreadful.'

I had to agree with her on all counts. I ate at the Kettle only out of a misguided sense of loyalty.

'We were hoping to bump into you,' said Florence. 'Is it true that the gypsies are back at The Grange?'

'*Back* at The Grange?' It would certainly explain Topaz's sudden absence. Having inherited the estate from her uncle and aunt – Sir Hugh and Lady Clarissa Trewallyn – Topaz must have dropped everything and gone to protect her birthright.

Topaz didn't live at The Grange. She didn't use her real name, either – namely that of Lady Ethel Turberville-Spat. For reasons that still remained a mystery to me, Topaz fancied herself as Gipping's local vigilante, adopting the pseudonym of Topaz Potter and doing a terrible job of running a café as a front.

'Oh yes. In Sir Hugh's day, they used to camp there every summer,' said Florence. 'Remember all that scandal with Barbara?'

Barbara again. Here she was more than forty years later and still unable to escape her past.

'We're awfully worried about Saturday's Morris Dance-a-thon,' Amelia said. 'My husband, Jack, is the Ranids's squire this year.'

'Squire?' I said.

'It's the squire's job to run the programme and call the dances,' said Amelia. 'Jack threatened to burn down all their caravans if they weren't gone by Saturday.'

Amelia's hand fluttered to her floppy hat. She pulled the brim down, hard. Jack Webster was notorious for his temper, which often turned violent after a few glasses of lethal Devon scrumpy. I took a closer look at Amelia's face and fancied I saw a yellowing bruise above her right eyebrow.

'When Jack came to pick you up last night from Barbara's,' I said, 'did he take the shortcut through Mudge Lane?'

'Jack didn't show up,' said Florence, throwing her arm protectively around her friend's shoulders. 'Eric and I had to take her home.'

'It wasn't that he forgot,' protested Amelia. 'He'd been drinking at the Three Tuns and didn't want to lose his licence.'

'Doesn't he drive a green Land Rover?' I said.

'All the farmers round here have green Land Rovers,' snapped Florence.

'Was he out shooting rabbits?'

'Why are you asking all these questions?' Amelia sounded upset.

'Just curious.' It dawned on me that news of the woman's demise might have reached the vicarage but not the High Street. Yet.

'If anyone was shooting rabbits, it would be those gypsies poaching. Mark my words. We don't want thieving gypsies in Gipping, with their filthy children and rabid dogs—'

'And all the nasty rubbish they leave behind,' said Amelia. 'They don't use toilets, you know.' She pulled a face. 'They just go number one *and* number two in the woods.'

'Don't be silly,' said Florence sharply. 'These days they have all the mod cons and demand equal rights. My sister lives in Brighton, and she said they had some gypsies passing through only last month, and one of them drove a flashy silver Winnebago with a satellite dish! Imagine!'

At the sound of clopping hooves, Amelia turned to Florence and said, 'Mod cons? Just look at that!'

A pretty green-and-yellow-painted bowtop wagon, drawn by a glossy-coated skewbald pony in a gleaming harness, trotted on by. Bells tinkled cheerfully, and the *clink, clink* of metal pots

23

and pans fastened to the guardrails seemed to play a magical melody of their own. So much for the dirty old vans!

At the reins stood a handsome man in his late twenties looking very Pirates-of-the-Caribbean. Dressed in black jeans and a white shirt with balloon sleeves, he sported a moustache and wore his long dark-brown hair tied back in a ribbon.

Catching my eye, the man gave me a stunning smile that made me blush. On impulse, I waved.

'What are you doing?' hissed Florence. 'Don't encourage him, you stupid girl.'

'I was just being friendly,' I said, gazing after the departing wagon and wondering if there was a real bed inside. Frankly, I found gypsy life fascinating and romantic – life on the open road. Singing around a campfire. Sleeping under the stars.

Two women followed on foot. One looked a few years older than me, with long dark hair and a hard face. Dressed in a traditional ankle-length skirt and white peasant long-sleeved blouse, she carried an open basket.

'Lucky heather?' she said, walking up to us. 'Keep you safe from the evil eye.'

'Shoo!' said Florence, flapping her hands. 'Go away.'

'I'll take one,' I said firmly. If I had to report on this funeral, I couldn't afford to upset the mourners.

'That'll be three pounds, and don't ask for change.'

Three pounds! The young woman thrust a tiny bunch of lilac heather tied with a red ribbon into my hands. I noticed her nails were long like talons. I took out my wallet, annoyed that I only had a fiver, and handed it over. She snatched it and headed off for another unsuspecting member of the public.

'You got ripped off,' scoffed Florence. 'Three pounds!'

'Five, actually,' I grumbled.

'No, thank you,' said Amelia as a second gypsy woman in her late sixties limped over with a stack of flyers peeping out of a canvas shopping bag. 'Please go away.'

The woman had obviously been a beauty in her heyday. She

wore her grey hair coiled on top of her head and enormous hoop earrings. A long, red dirndl skirt, matching blouse, and fringed shawl completed her outfit.

'Can I have a flyer?' I said.

'Bless you, me angel,' said the woman, shooting Amelia a venomous look and adding, 'And you should watch that husband of yours. One day he'll go too far.' She limped after the disappearing wagon.

My stomach turned over. *Perhaps he already had!*

'What a horrible woman,' gasped Amelia. 'What a thing to say!'

I studied the flyer ROAMING RIGHTS FOR ROMANIES! WE CAMP BECAUSE WE CAN! with Florence – smelling strongly of cooked bacon – reading aloud over my shoulder. '"Shortage of residential and transit authorized sites, retrospective planning permission holdups, lack of health care and education, poor environmental conditions, unemployment" – blah, blah, blah. I told you so!' she said, stabbing the paper with her finger. 'They're playing the human rights card. They're here to stay. Just you see.'

'Oh dear,' said Amelia. 'Jack is going to go berserk.'

Realizing I'd wasted precious minutes chatting, I said, 'I really must get to work.'

'Can you ask Barbara when she intends to finish the window?' said Florence. 'The Morris Dance-a-thon is only a few days away.'

I looked across the street and saw newspaper still taped up inside the show window.

'Jack wanted me to make sure the Ranids's mascot was in the centre,' said Amelia. 'It's so unlike Barbara. I suppose she's too busy with her wedding plans.'

Promising them I'd find out, I bid my goodbyes and left.

Life was certainly never dull in Gipping-on-Plym.

5

'Oh, I'm so glad you're here,' said Olive Larch, looking distinctly frazzled. Three large cardboard boxes were standing at the foot of the padlocked wooden shutters that screened the display window.

'I don't know what to do with them. Or *that* thing.' She pointed to a man-sized hobbyhorse standing by the entrance to the nook. A long, black cape enveloped the wooden pole reserved for the rider. Atop was a garish white horse head sporting a highwayman mask and jaunty black tricorn hat. The model horse's mouth was permanently open in a macabre smile, revealing an impressive set of teeth.

'That's not the mascot for the Gipping Ranids,' I said, knowing full well our local Morris dancers had a giant green frog.

'It's the Turpin Terrors,' said Olive. 'Phil insists I put it in the window, and all this stuff, too.' She kicked the box with her patent-leather pump.

'Where's Barbara?' I said.

'No one knows.' Olive wrung her hands. 'Wilf called and told me to come in.' Olive occasionally worked in reception

26

when we were extra busy, but her excruciating slowness was more of a hindrance than a help. 'I rang her house and left two messages.'

'Perhaps Barbara had too much fruit punch and overslept?' I said – though that would be a first in *Gazette* history. Barbara liked to boast that she'd only taken two days off sick in all the years she'd worked for the newspaper – and that was because she couldn't ride her bicycle to work because her ingrown toenail had flared up.

'Phil wants all this in the window *today*,' said Olive.

'I saw Amelia Webster outside wondering why the window wasn't done yet.'

'I can't do it without Barbara. You know how she is.'

I certainly did. Along with the archive room, it was her pride and joy. Barbara refused to let anyone interfere in her themed window displays and kept the shutters padlocked just in case someone silly enough was tempted.

'Since Barbara keeps the key with her, there is not much you can do about it,' I said. 'And anyway, who is Phil?'

'You don't know?' Olive's jaw dropped. 'Phil Burrows is a famous Morris dancer.'

I shook my head. 'No. Can't say I've ever heard of him.'

'He used to dance with the Gipping Ranids until he was poached by the Turpin Terrors,' said Olive. 'They're based in Brighton and dance all over the country. Phil is making a guest appearance. It's very exciting. I knew him as a lad. Even then I knew——'

'I'm sure Barbara will be here soon.' Time was moving on, and I was anxious to get upstairs to the reporter room. 'Just tell Phil he'll have to wait, and in the meantime, take a look through those boxes.'

'But they're Phil's,' said Olive. 'Oh, I forgot to tell you that Pete called an emergency meeting in his office. You'd better hurry. You're already late!'

Cursing Olive under my breath, I tore upstairs.

27

6

Luckily for me, Pete was on the phone. I managed to slip into his office unnoticed and stood at the back of the room. There was an air of excited anticipation. I knew my instincts had been right about the bald woman. *Accidental drowning? My eye!*

My fellow journalists – court reporter Edward Lyle; sports go-to man Tony Perkins; and, of course, Annabel – were squashed on the tartan two-seater sofa seemingly riveted to Pete's 'conversation', if you could call it that.

Gripping the receiver in one hand, Pete was hunched over his desk, scribbling furiously into his notepad and uttering the occasional grunt.

Pete slammed down the phone. 'We're on!' He threw his pencil onto his desk, where it promptly rolled off and fell to the floor.

Annabel leapt from the sofa. 'I'll get it!' She bent down to pick it up – making sure that Pete got an eyeful of cleavage in her plunging V-neck, pale-yellow T-shirt before putting the pencil back onto his desk. 'Looks like we've got some action here this week, folks,' said Pete, all business.

'That was Detective Inspector Stalk at the police station

putting us on red alert. We're about to be invaded by some hundred-plus gyppos.'

'It's politically incorrect to say the word *gyppos*, Pete,' reminded Annabel. 'I believe the term these days is *travellers*.'

'They'll be coming for the funeral,' I said. 'Do we have a name yet?'

'Belcher Pike,' said Pete.

'That's a strange name for a woman.'

'Belcher is not a woman, silly.' Annabel swivelled around to face me, draping her arm along the back of the sofa. Her V-neck gaped open to reveal a lace-trimmed, pale-blue bra. 'He's some important gypsy king who has come to Gipping to die.'

'What about the dead woman in Mudge Lane?'

'Accident,' growled Pete. 'Can we move on?'

'Let me fill her in, Pete.' With an exaggerated sigh, Annabel turned to me again. 'The police said she was cycling across the kissing bridge, wobbled off the edge, hit her head, and drowned.'

'That's ridiculous!' I cried. 'What about the Land Rover that hit my car?'

'Don't know anything about that, do you Pete?'

'Are you quite finished?' snapped Pete, unwrapping a fresh stick of gum and folding it into his mouth. Sometimes I wish he still smoked. His mood had seemed better in the good old days.

'I was just filling her in,' said Annabel, adding, 'since she *was* late.'

'I went to Ms Trenfold's funeral, actually.'

'Are you feeling all right?' said Edward. 'It must have been a terrible shock to find the body.'

'It was, thank you, Edward.' I shot him a grateful look, unwilling to say that last night I had suffered nightmares about drowning in a sea of hair. 'All I'm saying is that I have a feeling I might know who is responsible, and I don't believe it was an accident.'

'Well, believe it,' said Pete.

29

'But even Stalk originally hinted that it was a suspicious death, but then Detective Sergeant Probes turned up—'

'Oh! Colin is such a cutie-pie,' gushed Annabel.

'Enough!' Pete slammed his hand down on the table. 'The woman drowned. End of story.'

'The less of those bloody gypsies, the better,' Tony declared. 'Thieving beggars.'

'She'll *still* have a funeral,' I persisted. 'We *still* need to know who she is.'

'We forget, Pete,' said Annabel sweetly. 'Vicky takes her job as an obituary writer very seriously.'

'Why would the ruddy gypsies pick Gipping?' Tony said bitterly. 'They've never been here before.'

'Actually, Tony,' said Edward, 'my mum told me they used to come here years ago. They camped up at The Grange.'

'And that's where they're going now,' Pete said. 'Apparently Belcher Pike has decided to spend his last days on this earth in Gipping-on-Plym. Aren't we lucky?'

'They're sticklers for tradition and highly superstitious,' said Edward. 'Apparently the dying gypsy's wagon must be pitched away from the main camp in an isolated spot. He must never be left alone day or night. Gorgers – that's the name they give for non-gypsies – are forbidden to cross the threshold, as it's believed their presence can send the Romany's soul to hell.'

'How pathetic!' said Annabel.

'Did you know that there are between two and three hundred thousand gypsies living in Great Britain at the moment?' Edward went on. 'Of course, it's impossible to be accurate because they are always on the move.'

'That's why they're called travellers,' Annabel insisted. 'Because they are always on the move.'

'Ah, but *that's* where you're wrong,' Edward said cheerfully. 'Many people make that mistake. Both are legally recognized as distinct ethnic groups and have the protection of the law. Romanies are the real deal. Travellers tend to be dropouts from the seventies, old hippies, and people unwilling to work. Now, the *Irish* traveller is a different breed all together. He's disliked by—'

'Romanies, travellers, who cares!' shouted Pete. 'We've got a bloody important gyppo about to kick the bucket here in Gipping-on-Plym, and hundreds of the buggers are heading for The Grange just in time for this Saturday's Morris Dance-a-thon.'

There was a chorus of dismay, especially from Tony. 'Bloody hell. It'll cause a riot.'

Pete leaned back in his chair and flung his feet up on his desk. 'And that means *trouble*. And trouble means *news,* and news means *readers*!'

'Why can't we just evict them?' said Annabel. 'The Grange is private land. Surely it's illegal.'

'Technically, yes,' said Edward. 'I believe there is a public right-of-way from Ponsford Ridge. But even if the site is unauthorized and perceived as an official transit pitch, the law stipulates they can stay put for thirty-five days – actually, it takes a good ten to file an eviction notice, so you're looking at a minimum of—'

'A bloody long time,' said Pete. 'We get the picture.'

'And since the old boy is dying, we've got the Human Rights Act to deal with,' Edward said. 'They can't be thrown off the land.'

'It's true,' I said, taking the flyer out of my safari-jacket pocket. 'One of the gypsy women gave this to me today.'

Pete snatched it from my hands and skimmed the contents with a groan. 'Bloody hell!'

'A gypsy told my fortune once,' said Annabel with a seductive wriggle. 'She said men would always fall in love with me and to be careful of the married ones.'

'They're all crooks.' Tony stuck his jaw out belligerently. 'The bastards mended my roof, and the first time it rained, water poured into the attic and brought the ceiling down. It cost me

31

hundreds of pounds. If it were up to me, I'd set those caravans on fire and burn the lot of them.'

'Not helpful, Tony,' barked Pete. 'Who lives at The Grange now?'

'It's supposed to be empty,' I said. 'The place belongs to—'

'Lady Ethel Turberville-Spat,' said Annabel smoothly. 'Inherited it from her aunt and uncle—'

'She usually lives in London,' I said, wondering why I was continuing Topaz's lie.

'Not anymore. My sources tell me she's back at The Grange.'

'Good,' Pete nodded, seemingly deep in thought. 'Do you still have your contacts with Westward TV?'

'Why?' Annabel said.

My heart sank. Shortly before Annabel's fall from grace, she'd persuaded Westward TV that she had the biggest exposé of the century, namely that she'd located the daughter of one of the most notorious criminals in England – ie, me. Since Annabel ended up with egg on her face and it all came to nothing, I'd be surprised if they were willing to talk to her again.

Pete jabbed his finger at Annabel. 'Call Westward. Do whatever it takes to get a camera crew. Go and interview the Spat woman—'

'Omigod!' squealed Annabel. 'I'm going to be on camera at last—'

'Get her reaction. How does she feel about her home being invaded? Is she frightened? You know the deal.'

I raised my hand. 'Actually, I sort of know her ladyship. Why don't I handle her? She can be a little unpredictable.'

'No, Vicky,' said Pete. 'You'll have your hands full with Belcher Pike's funeral if we're to believe Edward's prediction.'

'But he's still alive,' I protested.

'So get a head start.'

'She won't get very far,' said Edward ruefully. 'Gypsies don't like talking to gorgers – especially the press.'

'We'll run the Spat piece on this week's front page,' Pete

32

declared. 'That should get a few angry letters to the editor.'

Annabel clapped her hands. 'How about this for a headline – SPAT'S SPAT WITH THE PIKEYS!'

'You can't say *pikeys*,' said Edward. 'Politically incorrect.'

'But the gypsy's name *is* Pike.' Annabel sounded smug. 'Belcher Pike. Get it?'

I cringed. Annabel was appalling at headlines.

'PIKE'S PLOT IN PERIL,' I said suddenly. 'Or, GRIEVING GYPSIES—'

'Silence!' Pete slammed his hand on the desk. 'Just get on with it.'

'I'll come with you, Annabel,' said Tony.

'I don't need anyone to hold my hand, thanks.'

'Don't flatter yourself.' Tony had asked Annabel out on a date once and still hadn't gotten over being rejected. 'These people can cause a lot of problems with the environment when they leave a site. You know how strict our recycling rules are. I want to take a few photos before they wreck the place.'

Tony was an avid supporter of Greenpeace and had sympathies with Eco-Warriors, Gipping's environmental watchdogs.

'A fly-tipping piece?' Pete nodded eagerly. 'I like it.'

'I thought I'd get a few quotes from Ronnie Binns about the challenges he faces as a garbologist.'

'Good luck,' Annabel and I chorused. We'd never agreed before – though in this instance, Ronnie Binns's personal hygiene problem was legendary. His pungent aroma of boiled cabbages could be smelled a mile away.

Pete's phone rang. He snatched it up, listened for a brief moment before slamming the receiver back into the cradle. 'Vicky, Olive wants you downstairs. Phil Burrows is in reception.'

'He's got some nerve showing up here,' said Tony grimly. 'Guest appearance! What a bloody cheek.'

'Get over it, Tony,' said Pete. 'You would have done the same. You just weren't good enough.'

'Personally, I think Morris dancing's silly,' Annabel declared. 'Grown men in silly hats with bells strapped to their arms and legs, waving sticks around. It's stupid.'

'I'm sorry to hear you think it's stupid,' came the voice we all knew and dreaded. Everyone leapt to attention. Our illustrious editor – and now Barbara's fiancé – stood in the doorway.

'I'll have you know that Morris dancing has been in existence since the sixteenth century, young lady,' scolded Wilf, who had never liked Annabel at the best of times. 'William Kempe, the Shakespearean actor, was one of the first to dance the Morris.'

'We all dance the Morris,' Edward chipped in. 'If you're local, you dance the Morris. In fact, I only gave up because of my knee injury. Wilf still does the odd event, don't you, sir?'

'That's right.' Wilf removed his trademark Dunhill pipe from the pocket of his brown tweed jacket and clamped it between his teeth, unlit. 'It's a real coup to snag Phil.'

'Burrows shouldn't have signed on with the Turpin Terrors,' said Tony stubbornly. 'Remember the outcry when David Beckham went to play for the Los Angeles Galaxy?'

I hardly thought world-famous footballer David Beckham and Morris dancing were in the same league but kept quiet.

'You're only jealous because you're stuck in this boring dump,' said Annabel.

An awkward silence descended on the room.

'I didn't mean the *Gazette* was boring,' mumbled Annabel.

'How is Barbara feeling, sir?' I said, neatly changing the subject. 'She's never off work.'

'That's very nice of you to ask, young Vicky,' said Wilf. 'She's got a migraine.'

'Migraines are brought on by stress,' Annabel declared. 'She should lie down in a dark room.'

'I'm sure Barbara knows what to do,' Wilf said stiffly and swung around to face me, his one good eye, sharp and bright. 'Were there many people at Ms Trenfold's funeral this morning?'

'I'm afraid it was just the reverend, her brother, and myself, sir,' I said. 'Seems she wasn't very popular.'

'That's why the *Gazette* obituaries are so important,' said Wilf, swelling with pride. 'We are recorders of history and keepers of the truth. Another newspaper may not have bothered with Ms Trenfold. With no husband or children to continue her line, it would have been as if she had never lived at all.'

'Quite right, sir,' I said. 'Which makes me wonder about the dead woman in Mudge Lane last night. No one seems to care about who she was.'

'Bollocks!' muttered Pete.

'Pete?' said Wilf sharply. 'A word in my office. *Now.*'

Pete shot me a filthy look and followed Wilf's departing figure.

'That wasn't very clever,' said Annabel.

'It was an innocent question,' I protested, but I felt sick. I would never knowingly throw our chief reporter under the bus. 'Why am I the only person who cares around here?'

The phone rang in Pete's office again. Annabel picked it up. 'It sounds like Olive is having a nervous breakdown. You'd better hurry downstairs.'

7

Pausing at the reception door, I pulled a comb and small mirror from my safari-jacket pocket and dragged it through my shoulder-length bob. Unlike Annabel, I wasn't vain, but since I was about to meet a mini celebrity, I wanted to look my best.

I'd inherited the famous Hill sapphire-blue eyes. They were my best feature but – being so unusually distinctive – had almost brought about my downfall. As a result, I pretended to wear coloured contact lenses, which Annabel liked to point out whenever I received a compliment.

I stepped into reception to find a tall, heavy-set man leaning over the counter.

Olive heaved a sigh of relief. 'Here's Vicky now.'

'Hello. You must be Mr Burrows,' I said. 'Vicky Hill.'

The man turned around and rewarded me with a smile of blinding white caps. Frankly, I'd been expecting a rustic farming type and was taken off guard by his orange fake-tan complexion and designer-spiked dirty-blond hairstyle.

I guessed he was only a few years older than me, though it was hard to tell. Fake tan can be deceptive. I noticed his hair also sported telltale orange tints, confirming my suspicion that Mr Burrows had been overzealous with Sun-In hair-care products, too.

'So! Here is the famous Vicky Hill.' Phil Burrows was dressed in expensive clothes. Designer jeans – something I knew all about thanks to Annabel's obsession with labels – and a black silk shirt, which was open halfway down his chest, where a fuzz of brown hair exploded over a gold button. 'Call me Phil,' he said. 'I've heard a lot about you.'

'All good, I hope.'

'Oh yes.' He gave a knowing wink.

'Shall we go somewhere private?' I was considering the nook in the corner of reception, away from Olive's adoring gaze. She was already on the phone telling her friends he was here.

I caught a snatch of 'Phil and I had a lovely chat' and 'autograph'. It was then that I noticed a stack of professional headshots of Phil Burrows on the counter and – *good grief* – a Phil Burrows look-alike doll dressed in Morris dancing attire. Bells, ribbons, et al.

'The nook, eh?' Phil's brown eyes twinkled. 'Not sure if I'll be able to trust myself in there with someone so beautiful.'

Stifling a groan, I mumbled a gracious, 'Thank you.'

'Wow,' he said, studying my face. 'He told me you had the most incredible sapphire-blue eyes and—'

'I wear contacts,' I said firmly.

And then, with a sinking heart, I just *knew*. There was something extremely familiar about Phil, *and* his last name was Burrows.

'You're not related to Steve Burrows by any chance?' I said.

'Little Steve's my baby brother,' said Phil with a laugh. 'I know all about the gorgeous Vicky Hill. Let's take a look at you.' Phil took several steps backward and gave me an admiring once-over. 'Very nice.'

God! He even sounded like Steve. I deliberately slumped

over in the hope of looking deformed. 'Thanks, but shall we get on?'

'I meet a lot of girls in my profession,' Phil said. 'Fame attracts groupies and, not meaning to brag, I'm never short of a bedfellow or two, but Steve's right. You're a catch. He's a lucky man.'

'That's very nice of Steve to say that,' I said, not surprised that Steve continued to regard me as his girlfriend. 'But I'm not caught by anyone. I'm too busy with work.'

'In that case—' Phil took my hand and brought it to his lips. I braced myself for the Burrows tingle, but thankfully, Steve's brother didn't have the same electric touch.

'All's fair in love and war.' Phil wiggled his eyebrows – he even had Steve's mannerisms. 'I've got a suite at Gipping Manor. Why don't you come over tonight for a drink?'

How typical. 'Working. Sorry.'

I heard Olive gasp. 'Oh, Vicky! You should!'

Steve's ardour was easy to manage. If anything, it was rather innocent and touching. Phil was a different animal. Fame had given him a sense of entitlement and an ego to match.

I gestured to the opened cardboard boxes on the floor. 'Presumably all these are yours?'

One box contained items – tankards, black sweatshirts emblazoned with TURPIN TERRORS, and tricorn hats – sealed in plastic bags. The other box had SILENT AUCTION written on the inside flap. It seemed to contain a mixture of what looked like used clothing and objects normally relegated to a charity shop.

'All this needs to go in the window today,' said Phil. 'Just wait until you see the stuff for the silent auction. Everyone wants a bit of Phil.'

'What about the horse mascot?' Olive said.

'That's Beryl.'

Given that the Turpin Terrors had a highwayman theme, I said, 'I thought Black Bess was the name of Dick Turpin's horse.'

38

'No. She was called Beryl,' said Phil.

I saw no point in arguing.

'I was trying to ex-ex-explain to – *Phil*.' Olive looked uncomfortable. 'Our Gipping boys only want *their* mascot in the window.'

'Let Barbara sort that out when she gets here.' I sat down in one of the leatherette chairs. 'Phil, take a seat.'

'Is there a problem?' Phil sat down. He leaned back and put his arms behind his head, pulling the fabric of his shirt tight across his chest. Although he and Steve were about the same build, Phil's thin shirt outlined solid muscle instead of flab. There was even a hint of a six-pack. 'My agent told me I'd get full use of the window display.'

I thought this highly unlikely. 'Do you have anything in writing?'

'My agent handled it.' Phil's expression hardened. 'I waived my appearance fee for this as a favour to the Women's Institute. I even cut short my training in Brighton. My fans *expect* to see my stuff in the window, *and* I've already announced it on Facebook.'

Celebrities! I took a deep breath. *Patience, Vicky!* 'Perhaps one of the members of the Women's Institute said you could use the window and forgot to tell Barbara?' I suggested. 'Since we can't reach Barbara, can we talk to your agent?'

Phil looked at his watch. 'He's in Los Angeles and won't be up yet. They're eight hours behind.'

'Los Angeles!' said Olive directly behind me. I hadn't heard her creep up to eavesdrop. 'Hollywood! I bet he knows Paul Newman.'

'I doubt it,' I said. 'Paul Newman died three years ago.' I remembered it well. My mum cried.

'I'm working on a deal with an American dance show,' said Phil. 'It's a bit hush-hush at the moment.'

'I won't say anything,' Olive said, enthralled. 'Is it *Dancing with the Stars*?'

'I'm not allowed to say which one,' said Phil, feigning modesty. 'But put it this way: the Hoff and I are friends.'

'*The* David Hasselhoff?' Olive clung to the back of the chair. For a moment, I thought she might swoon. 'How did you meet him?'

'I was dancing in the Brighton International Folk Festival, David saw our performance and we got talking.' Phil reached for his man-bag and unzipped it. He took out a colour photograph of two figures standing arm in arm. The man on the left was definitely David Hasselhoff.

'Is that you?' Olive peered over my shoulder. I caught a whiff of her perfume – Elizabeth Arden Blue Grass – my grand-mother's favourite. 'It's hard to tell.'

Phil cut a dashing figure dressed as a Turpin Terror complete with red tatter three-quarter coat, tricorn hat, and highwayman mask. 'Being a Terror is a different ball game from dancing with the Ranids. Presumably you'll want to interview me for the day-in-the-life feature?'

I hadn't considered it, but it wasn't a bad idea. 'Yes, of course.'

'I'll have to check with my agent,' said Phil, 'but plan on coming to the Manor tomorrow night. By the way, where are the extra headshots?'

Olive looked blank. 'I don't know.'

I hadn't realized just how much we all relied on Barbara's efficiency.

'You should have gotten them by now.' Phil's tone was mild, but I sensed a flicker of irritation. 'My agent posted them last week.'

'We've been having a lot of problems with the post, haven't we?' said Olive. 'It's the cutbacks.'

'If they've gone missing—'

The signature tune from *Flashdance* erupted from Phil's man-bag just in time. Phil pulled out his iPhone. 'Yo! What's happening?'

'It's probably his agent,' whispered Olive as Phil wandered over to the front door and stepped outside.

'Do you think I should talk to Phil's agent about Barbara's party on Friday night?' Olive went on. 'I was going to ask Phil to make a special appearance as a surprise.'

'I would just ask Phil.'

'I wish someone had thrown me a hen party,' Olive said wistfully. Having been a spinster for most of her sixty-five years, Olive's first attempt at marriage had lasted less than a week. For the past month, she and the pungent Ronnie Binns were a hot item – a thought that I could not dwell on for too long without feeling ill.

'Perhaps if I can find a way to put Phil's things in the window, he'll agree?' she said.

'I should check with Barbara first. In fact, I may as well go and see her on my way back from The Grange.'

Phil reappeared. 'Sorry, ladies; I've got to run. I'll be back tomorrow to check on that window; otherwise' – he looked grave – 'I might have to pull out of the show.'

Reassuring Phil that all would be well – even though I had serious reservations – I was relieved when he disappeared.

'Did you say you were going to see Barbara?' said Olive. 'I've got something for her. Wait a moment.'

Olive went behind the counter, muttering, 'It's under here somewhere.' After what seemed like ages, she produced a small, rectangular package covered in brown paper with lashings of tape.

'Isn't that Phil's?' I said exasperated.

'Of course not.' Olive tapped a perfectly manicured frosted pink nail at the crudely written name in black marker pen: BARBARA MEADOWS, OPEN BY ADDRESSEE ONLY! EXTREMELY CONFIDENTAL. There was no postage mark. 'And whoever sent it can't spell.' She picked up the package and shook it. There was a dull thud. 'I wonder what it is. Would it be naughty to open it?'

41

My thoughts exactly, but I had no intention of doing so in front of Olive. 'We shouldn't. It's personal.'

'It could be anthrax!' Olive dropped it onto the counter and sprang back, terrified.

'Hardly.' Although I had to admit that the package did look sinister. 'Who delivered it?'

'I only left reception for a moment to use the little girls' room. When I got back, it was on the counter. Should we call the police? What if it's a bomb?'

Olive could be so dramatic! 'I'll take care of it.'

Fortunately, the phone rang, and Olive had to answer it, giving me the perfect opportunity to grab the tape dispenser off the counter – marked in black Sharpie DO NOT REMOVE FROM RECEPTION – and slip it into my pocket. I was going to need that.

Olive had a point. The contents of the package could be dangerous, and I would hate for something to happen to Barbara.

Grabbing it, I hurried off to my car.

Someone needed to check.

42

8

The package was heavily taped but no match for my Swiss Army penknife. I sliced through the bindings and removed the brown paper to find an old, battered shoebox.

Inside was an object wrapped up in a torn sheet of yellowing newspaper. With surprise, I saw it was none other than an obituary page from the *Gipping Gazette*! It was dated August 26 – Dad's birthday – 1963. There was no note.

I lifted out the package with care and unwrapped it to find a single white-leather Mary Jane with a peep toe and honeycomb cutouts.

Perhaps the shoe was connected to Barbara's wedding day? Wasn't the bride supposed to wear *something old, something new, something borrowed, and something blue*?

This was certainly old. I wasn't a shoe expert, but it looked like something my grandmother would have worn, but it didn't look exactly *bridal*.

For a start, the two-and-a-half-inch heel had brownish stains – Devon was known for its rich red clay, which was used to make the terracotta pots from which the Torquay terracotta industry began in the late nineteenth century – but it was the circular metal object that had been jammed into the toe of the shoe that was most puzzling.

It was an old steel bicycle bell, with a starburst on the top and a crown on the bell pusher, stamped MADE IN WEST GERMANY. Of course, everyone knew that Barbara owned a bike. Hers was pink and she was very fond of it. Baffled, I returned the bell, which still worked and emitted a bright *ding-ding,* back inside the shoe.

There was something weird about it that gave me the creeps. Why mark it confidential? Where was the other shoe? Was the date on the newspaper significant, and what could this possibly have to do with Barbara?

I smoothed out the newspaper. The headline read, MILDRED MOURNED BY MILLIONS!

A sharp rap on the window made me jump. *Blast!* Steve, dressed in his white paramedic uniform, was standing there, clutching a bunch of pink carnations.

I opened the window.

'Morning, doll,' he said, wheezing heavily. 'I ran. Got five minutes?'

'Not really. I'm just leaving.' But Steve appeared not to hear. He walked around to the passenger side. I made a mad scramble, rolled the shoe up in the newspaper, shoved it into the box, and placed it on the seat behind me. I'd have to tape it up again later.

'Thanks.' Steve squeezed his large frame into the front of the Fiat. There was a weird grating sound as the car sank a full two inches under his weight. *Goodbye, shock absorbers!*

'Thought I'd check on my girl. I'm on a coffee break.' Steve leaned over to kiss me, but I was a step ahead and looked away.

'What a piece of luck!' He went on, 'We almost missed each other.'

'But here we are,' I said.

'Telepathy.' Steve beamed. 'Olive said you'd already left. I know you sometimes park your car here.' He passed me the carnations. 'For you.'

'That's very sweet of you, thanks.'

'They're the flowers of love, doll,' said Steve. 'I wrapped the stems up in wet newspaper. They should be all right until you get them into a vase.'

'You didn't tell me you had a famous brother,' I said.

'You met Phil?' An agonized expression crossed Steve's face.

'He came to the *Gazette* this morning.'

Steve shook his head. 'No, Steve, don't ask her. Don't go there.'

'Don't go where?'

'I can't help it. I've got to know.' Steve looked at me with his tortured puppy-dog eyes and took a deep breath. 'We've got to be honest in this relationship. Tell me the truth, and I won't be upset.'

Had Steve been spying? Had he seen me open the shoebox? 'It's just work,' I said quickly.

'I knew it!' Steve cried with dismay. 'All the ladies fancy my brother. He asked you out, didn't he?'

'Oh. *That*. Don't be silly,' I said. 'I'm interviewing Phil for a day-in-the-life piece. I told you, I don't have time for relationships.'

'Phil's rich. A celebrity—'

'And you save lives,' I said firmly. 'That's far more important.'

Steve turned pink with pleasure. 'You're right. Steve saves lives.'

'Must you refer to yourself in the third person?'

'What?'

'Never mind,' I said. 'Any ID on the mystery woman yet?'

'She's gone, doll.'

'What do you mean, *gone*?'

'I heard they took her to Plymouth morgue this morning.'

'What's wrong with *our* morgue?' I was stunned and more than a little suspicious.

Steve raised his heavy shoulders. 'Stalk's orders.'

Stalk! It certainly explained why Pete was no longer bothered – but frankly, I was incensed. Not only had the woman died on Gipping territory, but she had died in very mysterious circumstances, and nobody seemed to care except for me.

'Come on, Steve,' I said flirtatiously. 'You're a smart and intelligent man. If it *were* just an accident, why would the police waste taxpayers' money moving the body to Plymouth? Are they doing another autopsy? Is Coroner Cripps losing his touch?'

'Search me, doll. I mean no disrespect but—' he hesitated. 'Don't get me wrong . . . She was only a gypsy. Know what I mean?'

'I'm surprised at you of all people, Steve,' I said hotly. 'Gypsy or not, the poor woman still deserves justice. And what about her family? Perhaps she has children? How would you feel—?'

'Don't panic! Keep your hair on, Vicky. Hang on a minute.' Steve frowned. 'There *was* something funny about her hair—'

'I thought she was wearing a wig.'

'She was, and it was obvious why. I got a good look at her in the morgue,' said Steve. 'There were a few small clumps and an unusual red rash on her scalp. Cripps thought it was a chemical burn and wanted to send off a sample to get tested, but we were told Plymouth would handle all that.'

Even more strange! 'Do you know anyone in Plymouth morgue?

'Why?'

'I wouldn't mind being kept in the loop,' I said with a smile. 'Something doesn't feel right.'

'Anything for you, doll,' said Steve. 'When can I see you?'

'How about after you've spoken to your friend in Plymouth again?'

Steve nodded. 'They'll get the results back tomorrow.'

'Tomorrow it is.'

As I drove away, a glance in my rearview mirror showed

Steve waving me out of sight. I felt a pang of guilt. Steve had proved to be a valuable informant in the past. Was I just leading him on? Using him as a source of information?

No more! I resolved to set the record straight – but not quite yet.

News that the body had been moved to Plymouth was certainly fishy.

Pete had told me to leave well enough alone, but I just couldn't. Christiane Amanpour would never allow herself to be deflected from finding out the truth.

Belcher Pike's arrival in Gipping-on-Plym couldn't have come at a more opportune time. Whittler had predicted there would be hundreds of gypsies arriving at The Grange. Surely someone would know who she was?

9

As I made my way to The Grange, I kept an eye out for a Land Rover with safari rack and overhead lighting, but only saw the common Keswick green variety.

Turning off the main road, I could just see the chimney tops peeping above the trees that screened the main house and wondered what chaos lay ahead.

Set in one hundred and seventy-five acres of parkland, there was plenty of space for the gypsies to call home.

Rumoured to have once run to over two thousand acres, the estate had shrunk considerably over the years, thanks to various gambling debts and a passion for snail racing.

There were three entrances to the estate – the main drive, a tradesman's back lane, and an overgrown access road that passed the abandoned cricket pavilion and cut through Trewallyn Woods.

Since Topaz was adamant that she'd never sell, The Grange was turning into a white elephant. She'd made a few half-hearted attempts at renting the stables out, but they had ended in disaster. No doubt the main house would gradually fall into disrepair, as did so many of these beautiful country homes dotted around

England, a vivid reminder of a time when Britain had an empire.

Good grief! I sounded just like my father, who complained that his target market – the upper classes – was steadily shrinking.

Dad was extremely fond of silver heirlooms, especially if there was a story behind them. He'd say, '*Mary Queen of Scots's lips touched this silver tankard the morning before she had her head cut off,*' and '*This candelabra was on Charles II's night table when he first seduced Nell Gwynne.*'

Thinking of my parents made me sad – especially the last memory of Mum, pushing me onto the train at Newcastle railway station, saying, '*Don't call us, we'll call you.*'

What was it like to live a normal life? Perhaps I had more in common with these gypsy folks than I realized. Hadn't my family been ostracized by society for Dad's lifestyle? Hadn't we been forced to move on from town to town?

A loud horn from behind interrupted my maudlin musings. A driver's cab filled my rearview mirror. Headlights flashed urgently. Startled, I accelerated, looking for somewhere to pull over, but the road was too narrow. The horn sounded again. The wretched lorry was on my bumper! In desperation, I yanked the steering wheel to the right and mounted the grass verge with a sickening thud.

A large truck from Gipping County Council – REFUSE WE CAN'T REFUSE – sailed on by without even so much as a thank-you! In the cab sat a grim-faced Ronnie Binns, Gipping's chief garbologist and recycling fanatic. On the flatbed was a selection of coloured wheelie bins tied down with rope. How unbelievably rude!

Slamming my foot on the accelerator, I bumped the Fiat off the grass verge and returned to the road with another nasty thud.

Rounding the corner, I saw Ronnie's lorry skid through the main gate to The Grange and barrel up the drive, hand hard down on the horn for good measure. What Olive saw in him was a mystery to me.

49

Arriving at the entrance, I stopped for a moment, unsure of what sort of reception lay ahead. Opening the glove box, I took out my makeshift PRESS placard and put it on the front dashboard. I'd heard that gypsies could get violent, and that their dogs were vicious and chased after cars. I read somewhere that a Molotov cocktail had been hurled at an innocent rambler who just happened to be walking by, minding her own business. Hopefully my press card might act as some kind of deterrent.

It looked as if trouble was already brewing. Flanked by abandoned Victorian gatehouses, the main gate had been lifted from its hinges and lay on the ground. A banner, stretching from roof to roof, said:

Morris Dance-a-thon!
Here! Saturday!
See Your Favourite Devon Sides
Dance Till They Drop!

The accompanying massive fluorescent-green billboard listing the other attractions – hedge-jumping and hedge-laying displays, a snail racing exhibition, and a bottled-jam boil-off, had been partially sprayed with graffiti.

The words SILENT AUCTION! TAKE HOME A PIECE OF CELEBRITY MORRIS MAN PHIL BURROWS had practically been obliterated.

Phil was not in as much demand as he thought.

A flash of blue caught my attention. My stomach turned over as I braced myself for a gypsy attack, but suddenly four figures in navy hoodies and jeans, aerosol cans in hand, burst from the undergrowth and scampered away. I recognized them immediately – Mickey, Malcolm, Ben and Brian Barker, aka the Swamp Dogs – Gipping's answer to a street gang. No doubt they were responsible for the graffiti.

I slipped my Fiat into four-wheel drive. Even though the last two weeks had been dry, we'd had a wet summer, and Ronnie's

50

heavy lorry had certainly deepened the ruts in the potholed surface. I dreaded to think what kind of damage would be done to the parkland. Add that to the hundreds of revellers expected on Saturday, and the place would be a quagmire.

As I drew closer to the main house, I wondered if there had been some mistake.

I counted just two painted wagons – the green-and-yellow one I'd seen earlier and a crimson one – two horses, and one 1960 orange-and-white VW camper van.

They were backed against a vicious blackthorn hedge that I knew had been earmarked for one of the hedge-laying displays on Saturday. Even I didn't need to have the gift of the Sight to predict trouble with hedge-layer Jack Webster.

But where was everybody? Where was the famous gypsy king, Belcher Pike? Was this *it*?

I was so preoccupied that I wasn't paying attention and narrowly avoided hitting a pedestrian with a limp.

Dressed in a red shawl and long dirndl skirt, the gypsy was still carrying her canvas bag filled with flyers. I did hope she wasn't planning on giving one to Topaz – or, rather, Lady Ethel, or was it Ms Ethel? Not moving in aristocratic circles, I wasn't sure how to address the niece of a dead aunt who had married a Duke.

I opened my window. 'Can I give you a lift?'

The woman turned and regarded me with suspicion. 'Why?'

'I'm going up to the main house,' I said cheerfully. I wasn't, but perhaps the gypsies had camped on the other side of the estate. 'Thought it might save you the walk.'

'I've seen you before.' The woman stepped up to my car and peered at the sign under my windshield. 'Are you a reporter?'

'Yes. I'm with the *Gipping Gazette*.' I gave her my best smile, anxious to prove Edward wrong and that, yes, she would love to talk to the newspaper.

'Just the person I want to see!' The woman slithered around to the passenger side and opened the door. Edward *was* wrong.

51

Planting her muddy, sensible shoes – I recognized them from Marks & Spencer – into my foot well, the woman slid into the front seat, clutching the bag to her chest. I caught a strong whiff of cheap perfume.

'I'm a reporter, too. Editor of *Romany Ramblings*,' she said. 'I go by my maiden name of Dora Pike, but just call me Dora.'

'Vicky Hill.' What a stroke of luck! A fellow reporter! I was thrilled. It had never occurred to me that the gypsies might have their own newspaper! Better still, if the dead woman *was* a gypsy, Dora Pike was bound to know who she was and demand justice.

'My newspaper is available online, in case you were wondering.'

I was. 'I'm impressed.'

'Don't look so surprised. It's no mystery,' said Dora. 'We use modern technology just like the rest of you. We have mobile phones and satellite TV.'

So much for a romantic life on the open road, free from twenty-first-century technology.

Dora rummaged around in her bag and pulled out a business card – MADAME DORA, EDITOR AND PSYCHIC JOURNALIST. *ROMANY RAMBLINGS*. 'Do you have one?'

I handed her the same cheap card Stalk had sneered at and braced myself for a derogatory remark.

Dora studied it with a frown, then smiled. 'Don't worry, your time will come, luv,' she said. 'I see big things for you.'

I could already tell that Dora and I would become the best of friends.

'Mind if I put this bag behind my seat?' she said.

Wedging the bag behind her, I noted that Dora looked at Barbara's parcel. Her eyes widened in surprise. My stomach flipped over. Did the gypsy woman's psychic powers sense there was something sinister about the contents? Or had she guessed that I'd opened something that wasn't addressed to me?

'I'm delivering it to a friend,' I said by way of explanation, wondering why I felt the need to do so.

Dora suddenly grasped my hand and turned it over. Her fingers traced my palm. Dad thought fortune-telling was a load of rubbish, but naturally Mum believed in the Sight. She said I'd inherited a sixth sense from her side of the family, and sometimes I was inclined to believe this was true. It had certainly helped me clinch three frontpage exclusives. Even so, as the saying goes, *the jury was still out.*

Finally, Dora looked up from her studies. 'I thought so,' she said with deep significance. 'A word of advice, luv. Be careful whom you pick for friends. Sometimes people are not as innocent as they seem.'

I didn't need a gypsy to tell me the obvious. I could think of at least ten people I could say that about.

'You are also not what you seem,' said Dora darkly.

I felt my face turn red and tried to snatch my hand away, but she held on tightly.

'Your eyes are the windows to your soul,' Dora said nodding. 'You have enemies. I see a woman. Is that true?'

'Possibly.' I recalled reading how fortune-tellers had a way of drawing information out of you. 'Actually, I'm more interested in my career.'

Dora dropped my hand, swivelled around, and pulled out a copy of the *Gipping Gazette* from her canvas shopping bag. It was folded open to the obituary pages on eleven and twelve, where my photograph – inappropriately smiling, I'd always thought – bore the caption: ON THE CEMETERY CIRCUIT WITH VICKY!

'Here you are now, but don't worry,' said Dora. 'You won't stay stuck in this dump forever. I'll be in the market tomorrow morning. Why don't you come, and I'll give you a proper reading.'

'No thanks. I can't really afford it at the moment,' I said. 'I already bought some lucky heather for five pounds. It was supposed to be three, but the girl didn't have change.'

'You can't go wrong buying heather from my daughter, Ruby,' Dora declared. Maybe not, I thought, but I was still overcharged.

I put the Fiat into gear and we began to bump up the drive.

'I wondered if you could tell me a little about Belcher Pike?' I ventured. 'I understand he's enjoying his final days here at The Grange?'

'He's my dad,' said Dora. 'Turned eighty-nine last month, but he won't last out the summer. He's bedridden now.'

'I am sorry,' I said. 'As you know, I write the obituary column for the *Gazette,* and I just wondered if I might be able to have a chat with him—'

'Chat? *A chat!'* Dora seemed appalled. I kept my eyes on the road ahead but could feel her fury. 'Do you want to send my father's soul straight to hell?'

'No, of course—'

'A terrible misfortune will fall upon gorgers who cross the threshold of a dying Romany!' *Idiot, Vicky!* Edward had mentioned something about gorgers not being allowed near dying gypsies.

'A vigil is kept around the clock,' Dora raged on. 'They must *never* be left alone. They must be *segregated* until death comes and finally releases them from the sufferings of this life. These are our customs, and they can never be broken.'

'Sorry,' I said, desperately trying to think of something to redeem myself. 'I suppose I'm nervous about his funeral – when he has one, if he has one,' I blundered on. 'It's just that I've heard that there will be hundreds of mourners, and I'm worried about leaving someone's name out.'

'Is that all?' said Dora. She patted my leg. 'Don't worry. I know the name of every family in England, luv. I'll help you when the time comes.'

'Thank you!' My relief turned to excitement. If the dead

54

woman was a gypsy, Dora would almost certainly know who she was – or, at least, know someone who might.

'When do you expect everyone to arrive?'

'In a week or so,' Dora said. 'We're the advance party, so to speak. Tell you what – why don't you come and have a cup of tea in my wagon? We'll talk about how we can help each other.'

'I'd love to.'

Ha! Edward wasn't right about everything.

As the main house came into sight, the drive split in front of a large oak tree.

'Take the right fork,' said Dora. 'I'm up behind the stables.'

My spirits lifted. I couldn't wait to see the inside of a traditional horse-drawn wagon and was positive that my new friend Dora's would be stuffed with horse brasses and Royal Crown Derby china galore.

'Just stop by the public footpath sign,' she said.

Cutting the engine, we both got out. I changed into my trusty Wellingtons and squelched my way after Dora along the muddy footpath that led around the back of the stable block and up a slope.

Moments later I stopped dead. There in front of me was a luxuriously sleek, silver Winnebago Sightseer. So much for a horse-drawn wagon.

I couldn't help but wonder if it was the same Winnebago that Florence Tossell's sister had seen in Brighton last month. Surely there couldn't be two?

'I had to drive in through the Ponsford Ridge gate,' said Dora, gesturing up the hill to a distant hedge, where a five-bar gate was just visible. 'She can't handle these small country lanes.'

'She's a beauty,' was all I could manage to say. Everyone knows that Winnebagos cost thousands and thousands of pounds, and this one looked practically new. There was obviously a great deal of money in telling fortunes! I was beginning to wonder if I was in the wrong business.

'I know what you're thinking,' Dora said cheerfully,

removing her muddy shoes and gesturing me to do likewise – fortunately, my socks were new. 'Times have changed. It's called *progress*.' She unlocked the door, and I followed her up three short steps into the RV. Donning a pair of sheepskin slippers, she added, 'There's nothing romantic about sleeping in a freezing-cold wagon. Even my Ruby prefers a VW camper.'

'And the man with the ponytail?' I felt my face redden and hoped Dora hadn't noticed.

'Noah?' Dora gave an indulgent chuckle. 'That's my nephew. Writes poetry. Plays the guitar. Now, he *is* a romantic.'

'So they're cousins?' I asked, realizing that I was glad that Ruby and my pirate look-alike were not an item.

'Oh, we're all related,' said Dora. 'And that's the way we like to keep it. Blood is thicker than water. That's just our way.'

It was also the Hill way. Dad's business activities were always kept within the family. He'd often say, *'If you can't trust family, then who can you trust?'*

As Dora boiled the kettle – she proudly pointed out a silent generator – I gave the Winnebago a once-over.

It was equipped with all the modern conveniences and reminded me of the celebrity trailers depicted on TV. Plush, wall-to-wall carpeting; sleek wooden fittings and fixtures; a state-of-the-art kitchen. There was even a flat-screen television, an expensive-looking camera, and a computer workstation complete with scanner. A glass display cabinet was stuffed with Royal Crown Derby china.

Although Dad only dealt in silver, he knew the value of everything on the black market. Royal Crown Derby was deceptively expensive. Some limited pieces ran into thousands of pounds.

Dora set down a tray containing an unopened packet of chocolate digestives, two china mugs, and a Brown Betty teapot.

Whilst the tea steeped in the pot, Dora handed me a copy of *Romany Ramblings*.

I had to admit it looked surprisingly professional. All eight pages were nicely laid out with full-colour photographs. 'I run off copies for those who don't have or can't afford the Internet. A couple of my boys take them around to other sites.'

I leafed through the newspaper, intrigued by the range of features, from gypsy campaigns to evade eviction to human-interest stories. One gypsy was even awarded an MBE from the Queen. There was a whole section dedicated to 'Young Ramblers', a column called 'Peep at the Past' chronicling a different gypsy way of life one hundred years ago, job opportunities, caravans for sale, and a helpline for victims of domestic violence.

To say I was impressed was putting it mildly.

Dora poured me a cuppa and gestured to the milk and sugar. 'I'm working on getting up a website with an audio stream. Get some of the old-timers to record their memories before our way of life is lost forever.'

Even the *Gazette* didn't have a website.

'But I want to reach a wider audience. Not just limit this to gypsies,' Dora went on. 'You gorgers are willing to believe the worst of us. We're not thieves. We don't destroy the countryside. It's our creed to live peacefully with nature. Live and let live is all we ask for.'

We sipped our tea in companionable silence. It was now or never. 'A woman drowned in Mudge Lane last night,' I said. 'It's been rumoured that she might have been a gypsy. I wondered if you'd heard anything?'

'Sorry,' said Dora. 'Not one of us, luv. I told you, I know everyone.'

'It happened only last night,' I pointed out.

'Vurma,' said Dora. 'Or you could call it a gypsy phone tree. There are fixed contact points throughout the country. Someone always knows someone. Believe me, if she was a gypsy, we'd know.'

'Are you quite sure?' I asked. 'The police don't seem to care.'

'Is that why you think she's one of us?' demanded Dora. 'Because the police don't care?'

'I didn't mean it quite like that,' I faltered.

'We've had centuries of discrimination,' Dora proclaimed. 'But not anymore. Times are changing. More tea?' I nodded. 'And I suggest you don't go asking questions. We don't like talking to reporters,' Dora went on. 'If you want to know something, ask me.'

'How long will you be staying at The Grange?' I asked, feeling quite flattered that I was obviously the exception to the rule.

A shadow crossed Dora's face. 'Who can say when God decides to take my father's soul?'

'Is it' – I hesitated – 'legal to stay here?'

'When I was a teenager, we'd camp at The Grange all summer,' said Dora. 'My folks picked apples and helped make scrumpy. Sir Hugh said we could come whenever we liked.'

'Sir Hugh died a while ago,' I said. 'I'm not sure how Lady Turberville-Spat – she inherited The Grange – would feel if it were too long.'

'The niece?' Dora gave a harsh laugh. 'She'll be in for a nasty surprise one day.'

My heart gave a jolt. 'What do you mean?'

'You'll see,' Dora said cryptically. 'We have a saying, 'In the hour of your greatest success are sown the seeds of your destruction.' But let's get down to business, shall we?'

Business? Dora got to her feet, limped over to the computer workstation, and hobbled back with a thick brown envelope.

'It's all in there. As a board member of the National Gypsy Council, I've written a detailed report about the disgraceful lack of legal stopping places for gypsies and the lack of sanitation and health care. We need the public to be aware that our kids are discriminated against in schools. I want this report on the front page of your newspaper, and believe me, Dora *always* gets her way.'

I was flabbergasted. 'The front page is not up to me.'

'And don't think I don't know the little tricks you gorgers try to pull, like framing us for fly-tipping and spreading rubbish about,' Dora declared. 'We follow the recycling rules, same as everybody else.'

'Actually, I believe Gipping County Council are dropping off recycling bins as we speak.'

'There is no way you can evict us, luv,' said Dora. 'We've got the law on our side these days. The Race Relations Act of 1976 recognizes Romanies and ethnic minorities deserving of sensitive treatment, and with my dad so close to death's door, you can't get more sensitive than that!'

'Right. Of course,' I said.

The door opened, and Ruby poked her head in. 'Whose Wellingtons are those outside? Oh.' She scowled on seeing me. 'I thought we were going to pick mushrooms.'

'Ruby, this is Vicky, who works for the newspaper,' said Dora. I resisted the temptation to ask for my two pounds change. 'She's going to publish my article on the front page this week.'

Blast! 'As I was saying, it's not really my—'

'And you believe her?' Ruby snorted. 'What did you go and talk to a bloody gorger for? And a reporter, too?'

Dora opened her mouth to answer and shut it again. The two women glowered at each other. Clearly this kind of discussion would not continue in front of the likes of me.

'Actually, I just write the obituaries,' I said. 'We were talking about your grandfather, Belcher Pike.'

'He's not dead yet,' snapped Ruby.

With Wellingtons on once more, I bid my goodbyes and left the luxury of the Winnebago. I reflected that things had gone rather well.

My fear that the names of hundreds of mourners would elude me were groundless. As for the gypsy woman's inflammatory report – let Pete deal with her. The front page was out of my hands.

Yet there was one thing that bothered me. Dora didn't seem remotely curious about the dead woman in Mudge Lane. Call it my own Romany instincts but Dora Pike was hiding something, and I was determined to find out what it was.

10

As I took the footpath back to my car, I had to stop to admire the view. It was magnificent. Born in the industrial city of Newcastle, it had taken me a while to appreciate the beauty and adjust to the silence of the countryside. Surprisingly, I'd grown to love it.

Grey clouds gave way to a watery sun. Below, stretching to the horizon was a patchwork of rolling green meadows divided by hedgerows, peppered with grazing sheep. Down to my right, screened by towering oak and beech trees, stood The Grange.

I could just make out the redbrick chimneys and dormer windows set into the slate roof – servants' quarters from another century.

To my left stood a forest of pine trees known as Trewallyn Woods. The tradesmen's entrance wound its way past Sir Hugh's Folly, a cylindrical tower built in Victorian times – for no reason whatsoever – to the rear of the main house.

I had to look hard to locate the two wagons and VW camper. Even the Winnebago was shielded from the road by a belt of trees and thick hedge.

From my vantage point, I tried to find Belcher Pike's

'segregated' wagon but to no avail. It was as if the gypsies weren't here at all, although I rather doubted this would be of any consolation to Topaz.

The Morris Dance-a-thon was to be held in an enormous field on the south side of the house. The original building had been Tudor. Then, as the years passed and fashions came and went, bits were added on here and there – Queen Anne sash windows with multipaned glass, gothic gables with hideous gargoyles peering down from bargeboards – and now, the front door was reached by taking a wide flight of stone steps leading up to a Palladian portico supported by grand Corinthian pillars.

A natural sloping bank descended from the upper garden – now a wilderness – providing the perfect spot for spectators to sit, picnic, and watch the proceedings below.

There were many preparations to make. An arena with a hard floor had to be laid out, tents erected, Port-a-loos brought in, and parking for hundreds of cars marked off.

There was plenty of space for everyone, and frankly, as long as Belcher Pike didn't die before Saturday, there was no reason why the Morris Dance-a-thon couldn't go ahead as planned.

Continuing down the footpath, I came to a T-Junction. One way took me past the Victorian walled kitchen garden, which I knew led directly to the rear of the house; the other, up to Ponsford Ridge. In front of me was the entrance to a bridleway flanked by an archway of trees that looked as if they'd definitely been disturbed. Branches were broken, and the ground was full of muddy footprints and tyre tracks.

Curious, I set off, promising myself that I'd walk for only ten minutes – I couldn't afford to get lost – but just when I was about to retrace my steps, I heard the faint chords of a guitar.

Drawing closer, I came upon a grassy clearing. Less than twenty feet away stood an elaborately carved bow-top wagon in a dull khaki green. There was no decorative scrollwork picked out in gold leaf, colourful shutters, or painted wheels.

Fierce-looking barbed wire encompassed the small camp.

There was even a sign reading GORGERS KEEP OUT. Dora certainly wasn't taking any chances with Belcher Pike's soul.

Noah was sitting on a tree stump quietly playing his guitar. A shaft of sunlight broke through the trees and shone down on him like a spotlight from heaven. My stomach turned over. I was utterly spellbound.

The song finished. Noah looked up sharply and saw me standing on the edge of the woods. I gave a shy wave, but he didn't wave back.

Hurrying over, he gestured to the sign, whispering urgently, 'You can't come here. You must leave.'

'Sorry. I heard you playing—'

'You don't understand.' Noah's eyes bored into mine as he grabbed my hand and led me away from the clearing. 'No one must see you here.'

'It's okay.' Frankly, I thought he was overreacting. 'Your aunt told me all about the gypsy customs. I just had tea with her.'

'Tea?' Noah frowned. 'Why?'

'I work for the *Gipping Gazette*.' Really, he had to be the sexiest man alive. 'I'll be writing Belcher Pike's obituary and usually visit the family at home.'

'Well you can't,' he said flatly, then tensed. 'Someone is coming! Go and hide behind the wagon. Quickly.'

His anxiety was contagious. I ran and squatted behind the rear of the wagon next to a small tarpaulin-covered box. A quick peek underneath revealed a shiny red, portable Honda generator, model number EU30i. I bet Belcher Pike had a television in his wagon, too. I also noted a tow-hitch receiver and a mass of crisscrossing tyre tracks that continued into another belt of trees and most likely up to Ponsford Ridge.

Voices came closer. Dora and Ruby were walking toward the wagon. Ruby was carrying a bulging gunnysack.

My heart gave a lurch! Why hadn't I guessed the obvious? The gypsies had been poaching. Nighttime rabbit shooting, which I thoroughly abhorred, was a common sight in the countryside. Land Rovers were the vehicle of choice, particularly one with the advantage of a safari roof rack and overhead lighting! I wouldn't be surprised if it were the same vehicle that had been used to tow this wagon to this very spot. Next time I saw Dora, I'd confront her.

The two women entered the wagon, but before I had a chance to eavesdrop, Noah appeared by my side. 'Quickly,' he whispered, pointing to a barely visible animal track behind me through the undergrowth. 'Follow that path. It will take you back to The Grange.'

He took my hand. Our eyes met again, and he smiled. 'You've got the most beautiful sapphire-blue eyes.'

'Thanks,' I said coyly. 'Believe it or not, they're my own.'

'Now – go!'

I darted into the undergrowth. It was thick with brambles and quite exhausting to fight my way through. Noah was right. About ten minutes later I found myself standing in the weed-riddled cobbled courtyard.

The Grange was even more rundown than I remembered. A row of ramshackle outbuildings revealed an old tractor with no wheels and an assortment of rusted farmyard machinery. There was no sign of the new wheelies or Ronnie Binns.

Annabel's extremely muddy silver BMW was parked next to Topaz's equally dirty red Ford Capri. Since Annabel had been assigned to interview her ladyship, there was no reason why I should be there, too. Yet, in a funny way, I felt a bit jealous.

Topaz may be as mad as a hatter but she was still *my* friend. Besides, I was curious to meet Topaz as her real self – if there was such a thing. Would Annabel see through her disguise?

As always, the back door was unlocked. I pushed it open and stepped inside.

There was only one way to find out.

64

11

The scullery was just as I remembered it – dark and soulless. A long slate-lined sink ran the length of a window that was covered in dirt and cobwebs. Bare stone counters lined the other three walls.

The kitchen was equally depressing. As far as I knew, the place hadn't been lived in for months, following a disastrous attempt at renting out The Grange to strangers.

I shivered. Despite it being August, the place was freezing. The room had a high-gabled roof, a flagstone floor, and a large inglenook fireplace. Tacked to the wooden mantle clung an old sheet – apparently an ineffectual attempt at stopping the draught howling down the chimney.

The kitchen was divided into two by a wooden counter. On one side were countertops, a kitchen sink, an unlit Aga, an old fridge, and a microwave.

Propped under the tall sash window on the far side of the immense room stood two camp beds. Tattered sleeping bags had been rolled up and deposited in a corner – no doubt providing a very nice home for rats. An ancient Chesterfield sofa was piled with open boxes, presumably containing the former tenants' meagre possessions.

The place smelled damp and musty and could do with a good airing.

I went through to the large inner hall. The floor was of black and white marble and resembled a chessboard. An enormous crystal chandelier hung from a domed atrium overhead. On my right, two suitcases stood at the base of the grand oak staircase. A soft woof came from above.

Looking up, I saw Topaz's old Labrador peering down through the bannisters from the landing. Slipper was exactly the kind of dog I liked – arthritic, practically deaf, and almost blind. Normally, I was afraid of dogs, but I had to admit that Slipper was a sweetheart.

I recalled Topaz mentioning that when her aunt and uncle were alive, they used a suite of rooms on the first floor. Presumably she intended to do likewise. Even though I wasn't afraid of Slipper, I couldn't quite bring myself to have to pass her on the staircase but fortunately, the sound of muffled voices coming from farther down the hall suggested that Topaz and Annabel were close by. I went to join them.

Suddenly there was the tinkle of familiar laughter followed by an unattractive snort. It seemed to be coming from inside the room with the daffodil painted on the porcelain door handle. A room I knew all too well.

'Oh, your ladyship, you are funny!' I heard Annabel say. I couldn't quite catch Topaz's response because I was in shock.

Topaz was showing Annabel her family heirlooms.

Always under lock and key – though neither would deter any seasoned burglar – Topaz had always claimed that she couldn't risk showing the 'priceless Spat silver' and the 'extremely valuable Trewallyn paintings' to anyone. I'd only seen them myself because she'd asked me to do an inventory one night.

I gently pushed open the door, unnoticed by the two women who were huddled over a table in the far right-hand corner.

The shutters on the tall sash windows were folded open. Light spilled into the usually kept dark room that afforded a view of Trewallyn Woods. Light also twinkled from the crystal chandelier above, catching the sheen of mountains of silver piled on top of the antique oak refectory table.

It reminded me of Dad's old lockup at Newcastle railway station, which I was allowed to visit as a treat when most kids were taken out for a strawberry milkshake.

Having taken Topaz's inventory before, I knew there should be a total of thirty-seven pieces – silver tea sets, compote services, candlesticks, candelabras, goblets, and a pair of silver swan centrepieces. But when Annabel stepped aside, I couldn't believe what Topaz held cradled under each arm – a pair of matching Georgian tea urns.

Of all the silver that came and went in the Hill household, Georgian tea urns were Dad's passion. He collected them and was famous for it.

I recognized the designer immediately. With the urns' simple, neoclassical style and beaded borders, they were almost certainly made by Hester Bateman in the late 1700s.

As one of the first well-recognized female silversmiths in England, I had always had a particular interest in Hester Bateman's work. Being a woman in a male-dominated workplace isn't easy these days, let alone two hundred-odd years ago.

'I just want one more photograph of the underside.' Annabel took a step back, holding her iPhone aloft.

'They're frightfully heavy,' grumbled Topaz.

I would never have recognized Topaz as the waitress from The Copper Kettle. For a start, she was wearing a 1960s black Jackie O-styled wig, horn-rimmed spectacles, and a pair of tight-fitting stretch jodhpurs that she'd filled with lumpy padding. A cream polo-neck sweater under a green tweed jacket topped off her lady-of-the-manner attire.

Topaz caught sight of me hovering in the doorway and gave a cry of alarm. 'Who are you? Get out! You're trespassing!'

Annabel spun round. 'What are *you* doing here?'

'I recognized your car outside, Annabel, and thought I should introduce myself to her . . . ladyship.'

'Out! Out!' shrieked Topaz, slamming both tea urns down on the table, seemingly not caring if she damaged either.

Flapping her hands in my direction, she yelled, 'Shoo! Shoo!' before grabbing a very startled Annabel and bundling us out of the room. *Honestly!* How typical of Topaz to go over the top.

'Now see what you've done,' hissed Annabel as Topaz pulled the door closed with a bang.

Pulling a key out of her tweed coat pocket, she made a meal of locking the door. 'I'm sorry, but there are *priceless* heirlooms in there. The viewing was for your eyes only, Ms Lake!' she trilled.

'I'm sorry—'

Wagging her forefinger at Annabel, Topaz raged on, 'You naughty girl! How *dare* you tell your friends!'

'I can assure you I did nothing of the sort,' said Annabel, throwing me a look of pure hatred.

'I'm afraid I might not want to do the interview, after all,' Topaz said with a haughty sniff. 'I don't think you can be trusted. Telling your friends—'

'She's not my friend, and I didn't tell her anything,' said Annabel hotly. 'Right, Vicky?'

'It's true. We just work together.' I found the whole thing amusing. Annabel had always been scathing about the waitress from The Copper Kettle, so the fact that she didn't recognize her now, and seemed intimidated in the bargain, was actually hilarious.

'Even so,' said Topaz, ignoring both of us. 'I'm not sure *television* is really my thing. It's so common.'

Annabel turned pale. 'But you agreed. Westward TV is excited. They're sending over a camera crew and everything.'

Topaz gave a heavy sigh. 'I'll think about it, but what if the sight of cameras starts a riot?'

'I don't think there is any danger of that,' I said mildly. 'There are three wagons, a VW camper, and a Winnebago. You'd hardly notice the gypsies are here at all.'

'*Hardly*?' scoffed Annabel. 'Pete said there would be hundreds turning up for that old man's funeral.'

'He's not dead yet,' I said.

'They're already a menace to society with all their rubbish,' said Annabel. 'You should see what's behind the pigsty! Her ladyship showed me earlier. An old mattress, a fridge, sheets of corrugated iron—'

'It's frightful,' said Topaz.

'All that stuff has been there for ages,' I said. 'Have the recycling bins arrived yet?'

'*Recycling!*' said Annabel with scorn. 'You expect people like that to *recycle*?'

I shrugged. 'They insist they're environmentally friendly.'

Annabel turned to Topaz. '*And* we've got the Morris Dance-a-thon to think about, your ladyship.'

'I am perfectly aware of the Morris Dance-a-thon,' said Topaz. 'That's why the eviction service is coming first thing Friday morning.'

I'd heard of eviction crews in the past. They arrived with their bulldozers and were basically thugs-for-hire. 'But Friday is when all the tents for the Morris Dance-a-thon will be going up. It'll be chaos.'

'My mind is made up,' Topaz declared.

'I'm sorry, but I think that's a really bad idea,' I said.

Annabel's eyes bugged out as if I'd answered back to the Queen of England. 'Surely her ladyship is entitled to do what she wants on her land.'

'You can't evict a dying man and his grieving relatives,' I said, although, frankly, I hadn't seen that much evidence of grief. 'It's a race relations and human rights issue.'

69

'I don't care,' said Topaz stubbornly. 'I want them off.'

'I spoke with a member of the gypsy council—'

'Is that the frightful woman in the Winnebago?' said Topaz with a sneer. 'If she can afford one of those, she can afford to live like a normal person in a proper house.'

'I agree,' Annabel chimed in.

'Apparently, Sir Hugh Trewallyn said they could camp here whenever they wanted,' I said. 'There is a public right-of-way from Ponsford Ridge and—'

'I don't care about the public right-of-way,' Topaz snapped. 'This is my land now, and I'll do what I like.'

'There are laws and—'

'Never underestimate a Turberville-Spat.' Topaz's voice was icy. 'I *will* get them off my land, and that's final. Now, if you'll excuse me, I have some unpacking to do. You may both leave.'

'But you'll still do the interview, your ladyship, won't you?'

'Come on, Annabel,' I said, shepherding her in the direction of the kitchen.

'Ms Lake? Wait!' commanded Topaz.

Annabel shook off my arm and stopped in her tracks. 'Yes?'

'Is it true that you live in Mrs Evans's sewing room?'

'How did you know that?' Annabel seemed taken aback. Of course, it was me who had told Topaz. 'And it's not Mrs Evans's sewing room anymore. I moved all her stuff out.'

'Whatever.' Topaz gave a dismissive wave of her hand. 'I trust she still runs her charlady business?'

'Yes. Why?'

'Do you have her telephone number? I need to hire her services immediately.' Topaz gestured expansively to her surroundings. 'I'd forgotten how enormous my ancestral home is.'

'Won't you be returning to *London*?' I asked pointedly.

'I must stay on the premises until this rabble have been evicted. There could be stragglers, and I can't risk anything being stolen.'

70

'Aren't you insured?' I said.

'Insurance is not the point,' said Topaz. 'These family heirlooms are irreplaceable – but I don't expect either of you to understand that. Some of the silver pieces were personal gifts from George III.'

'Like the Georgian tea urns,' said Annabel, turning to me with a bright smile. 'Which was why I suggested a few additional photographs just in case there were any problems.'

There was something in Annabel's expression that made me uneasy. Knowing that she had made a thorough study of all of Dad's foibles, she was bound to have discovered his penchant for a handsome tea urn with a nicely turned spigot.

'I thought gypsies only collected Royal Crown Derby china,' I said lightly. 'Antique silver is too distinctive and complicated to move on the black market without the right contacts.'

'And you should know,' Annabel said slyly.

Careful, Vicky! Annabel continued to try to catch me out.

'How fascinating.' Topaz turned to me. 'Ms Hill, I'd like a quick word with you. Alone.'

'Why? She's just the obituary writer.'

'How dare you question me!' Topaz pointed her finger at the kitchen door. 'Go and wait in the scullery, otherwise, there will be no television interview.'

Annabel opened her mouth and shut it again. Without a word, she slunk off and disappeared into the kitchen.

Topaz started to bray with laughter. 'What an absolute hoot!'

'Keep your voice down,' I said. 'She's bound to be listening.'

'Fancy her not recognizing me,' said Topaz.

'Why did you show her the silver?'

Topaz shrugged. 'I told her that all gypsies were thieves, and she asked if I had anything valuable in the house, and one thing led to another. Why? Did you think I'd lured her into the daffodil room for a naughty reason? Were you jealous?'

'No,' I said firmly. 'Just surprised. You never mentioned you had any Georgian tea urns.'

'You didn't ask,' said Topaz.

'And she did?'

'Who cares!' Topaz laughed again. 'I say, does this outfit make me look fat?'

'Yes. Very. I'd better go,' I said. 'Annabel is bound to be eavesdropping.'

But Annabel wasn't. She was outside in the courtyard, scrutinizing the grimy scullery window.

'What are you doing?' I said.

'I told her ladyship she ought to have a burglar alarm installed.' Annabel rapped the glass with her knuckles. 'With all that silver, it would be easy to break in. And she should have a surveillance system, too.' Annabel cocked her head, adding thoughtfully, 'Especially if it becomes common knowledge that there is a treasure trove of *silver* inside.'

'Why should it become common knowledge?' I said. 'I'm not going to spread the word around.'

'Aren't you?' Annabel smiled sweetly.

My skin began to prickle – perhaps that trace of Romany instincts in my blood was kicking in. Annabel was up to something, and I didn't like it one bit.

Fortunately, all further comments were forgotten as the sound of angry voices drifted toward us. They seemed to be coming from behind a row of outbuildings.

'I told you the gypsies would cause trouble,' said Annabel with ill-disguised glee.

It would seem that this time, she could be right.

12

Rounding the corner, we discovered Ronnie Binns and Dora embroiled in a heated argument. Dressed in his regulation gabardine overalls and thigh-high waders, Ronnie stood next to a neat row of coloured wheelies – blue, brown, grey and a dirty white – quivering with rage.

The courtyard may well have been a mess, but the situation behind the pigsty was a hundred times worse.

Behind the pyramid of garbage, a muddy bank sloped down to a fast-running stream. It, too, was filled with debris – I counted five large wooden pallets and an ancient refrigerator. Black and blue plastic bags were snagged on branches along the riverbank. The whole place was filthy.

'Ah! Vicky. Thank heavens! Dora's face was bright red. 'Tell this disgusting, *smelly* man that all this . . . this' – her arms encompassed the surrounding detritus of rusting bedsprings, tattered bags and empty paint tins – 'is nothing to do with us. Any idiot can tell it's been here for years!'

Ronnie thrust out his jaw. 'She would say that, wouldn't she?'

'This is fly-tipping. No doubt about it,' said Annabel,

73

snapping away with her iPhone. 'Did you know you could be facing fines of up to twenty thousand pounds?'

'What's the point of fining them?' seethed Ronnie. 'They'll only vanish in the middle of the night. Tow-bar getaways. That's what they're called.'

'This rubbish *has* been here for a long time,' I said, pointing to a stack of rusted corrugated iron sheets. 'The Romanies got here only yesterday.'

'I told you so,' said Dora triumphantly. 'Thank you, Vicky.'

'So?' said Ronnie. 'Now you people will see this as an excuse to dump your rubbish here, too.'

'Whoever owns this house didn't follow the rules,' Dora fumed. 'Rules for them who have it all and rules for us who have nothing. That's what's wrong with this country today, isn't that right, Vicky?'

'A lot of people say that,' I said warily. Although I tended to agree, I didn't want to get drawn into a political discussion.

'And what's more,' said Dora, 'why put the bins here? We want a set of recycling bins outside every caravan just like normal householders. We're entitled to it!'

'Entitled! *Entitled!*' Ronnie sputtered with rage. 'Over my dead body.'

Annabel started to giggle.

Dora turned on her. 'And what's so funny?'

'Nothing,' she squeaked, shoulders heaving with silent laughter. She caught my eye, and I had to look sharply away as laughter began to bubble inside me, too. The scene was just too ridiculous.

'Who are you?' demanded Dora.

'Annabel Lake,' she said, struggling to pull herself together. 'I'm an investigative reporter with—'

'Get off my land or I'll fire!' Topaz shrieked, storming into view. She was brandishing a twelve-bore shotgun.

'Oh Lawd! It's her ladyship!' cried Ronnie.

'She's not joking,' I said quickly. 'You'd better do as she says.'

Dora spun around to face Topaz, arms akimbo.

'Go ahead. Fire. I'm not afraid of you.'

Annabel grabbed my arm. 'Do something—!'

Topaz fired both barrels, and the recoil from the force of the blast sent her falling back into a pile of rusting paint cans.

Annabel screamed. Ronnie ran off, Dora stood her ground.

A strange smile spread across Dora's face. Quick as lightning, she snatched the gun out of Topaz's grasp.

Topaz was trembling violently. 'Golly. I didn't know it was loaded.' Hampered by all that padding, she was finding it difficult to sit up. 'My finger slipped. Frightfully sorry about that.'

'You'll be sorry all right,' said Dora in a low menacing voice. 'Threatening a gypsy with a gun! Firing a gun without a licence.'

'I might have a licence,' said Topaz faintly. 'I'm positive Uncle Hugh had one.'

'Your uncle Hugh said we could camp here for as long as we like,' Dora declared.

Topaz rolled from side to side like an upended sheep until Annabel gamely stepped forward and pulled her to her feet. 'My uncle is dead,' said Topaz with dignity, readjusting her clothes. 'The Grange now belongs to me.'

'You really think so?' Dora gave a harsh laugh. 'The Grange isn't yours, dearie. I can prove it.'

Colour drained from Topaz's face. 'What are you talking about?'

Dora smirked. 'Not so hoity-toity now, are you? Your *ladyship*.'

'You liar!' screamed Topaz, pushing Annabel roughly aside, but Annabel hung on tightly. 'Get off my land!'

Dora started to laugh.

'Let's go inside, your ladyship,' said Annabel. 'Have a nice cup of tea.' Thankfully, Topaz allowed Annabel to lead her away, leaving Dora and I alone.

'Is it true about The Grange?' I said.

Dora's expression was hard. 'Put it this way, Sir Hugh liked to exercise his rights as lord of the manor.'

Of course, I'd read all about droit du seigneur in my pirate novels, but the thought of old Sir Hugh – who I'd never met – seducing the virgins of Gipping-on-Plym was utterly repulsive.

'With one of your people?' I said stunned.

'Never!' said Dora. 'You'll see. You'll find out soon enough. And I'm warning you, be careful of that Annabel. She's no friend of yours.'

This was not news to me.

And with that, Dora limped away.

I retrieved my Fiat but had only gotten halfway down the drive when one of the Swamp Dogs flagged me down. The four youths descended on my car, hammering on my bonnet and windscreen.

I opened the window. 'What's happened, Malcolm?'

'It's Mickey.' I could never tell the two sets of identical twins apart. 'Over there. Quickly!'

Across the field, a Land Rover was parked next to a crimson gypsy wagon. Two figures seemed to be engaged in some kind of heated exchange given the amount of arm flailing by one of them.

'It's Jack Webster,' cried Mickey. 'He's got a machete! He's going to kill one of those gyppos.'

My heart gave a lurch. Who needed the battlefields of Afghanistan when there was Gipping-on-Plym?

'Stay here,' I shouted, and jumped out of my car. It wasn't easy climbing over a post and rail fence in Wellingtons, but I managed it and set off across the muddy field.

I could tell it was going to be one of those days.

13

The moment I saw the location of the crimson painted wagon, I knew the reason for Jack Webster's ire. It was parked against a hedge that had been earmarked for Saturday's hedge-cutting display. With a stab of disappointment, I realized his Land Rover did not have a safari roof rack, although obviously, it could have been removed.

A man in his early seventies sat on the steps of his wagon, seemingly unconcerned by Jack's foul-mouthed diatribe. If anything, he seemed amused.

Dressed in a red-checked shirt and jeans, the gypsy wore his long, grey hair in a single braid threaded with ribbon. A large gold-hoop earring dangled from one ear.

'Good afternoon, gents,' I said. 'What seems to be the problem?'

Jack Webster swung around to face me. I sprang back, startled. Mickey wasn't exaggerating about the machete – although in hedge-cutting circles, the instrument was called a billhook and was used for slicing through thick branches. Made of carbon steel and with a blade measuring a good nine inches, the knife could be lethal in the wrong hands – which it was today.

Never one of my favourite people, Jack bore the telltale signs of the heavy drinker – the bloodshot eyes, the purple nose, and the flushed complexion. 'Bugger off and mind your own business, you silly cow.'

'It will be my business if you land up on the front page.'

'That's no way to talk to a lady,' said the gypsy mildly.

'And you can shut up.' Jack jabbed his billhook at the gypsy and turned back to me. I caught a whiff of alcohol on Jack's breath. 'This bloody gyppo can't stay here!'

'Ma'am,' he said, touching his forelock. 'Name's Jimmy Kitchen. It looks like this gentleman is a little the worse for wear.'

'Vicky Hill,' I said. 'I work for the newspaper.'

'We don't want any trouble,' he said, 'but Sir Hugh Trewallyn used to let us camp here years ago. This is my spot.'

'And this is my hedge,' Jack Webster fumed. 'See? It's all been pegged out for Saturday.'

To the uninitiated, the hedge looked a mess of brambles, bracken, and unruly branches. But on closer inspection, small strips of white material divided it into sections of roughly ten yards apiece.

'We're having a Morris Dance-a-thon here on Saturday,' I said by way of explanation. 'This is part of a hedge-cutting exhibition.'

'Wait a moment,' said Jimmy Kitchen, giving an expansive smile. 'You mean you want me to move my wagon? The gentleman only had to ask.'

'Why – you bloody . . . !' Jack stepped forward, billhook raised.

'Jack, no!' I shrieked and tried to grab his weapon.

Jack lashed out with his other hand, accidentally catching the side of my face. It hurt.

Jimmy Kitchen leapt up with astonishing speed and grabbed

78

Jack's weapon, pushing him away, hard. Jack sprawled backward and landed flat on his back in a puddle of muddy water, where he lay still and in complete shock.

'Not in front of a lady,' said Jimmy grimly. 'If you want to fight with me, we'll go elsewhere.'

Shocked, I looked at the older, wiry man, who seemed to be bursting with vitality, versus Jack, who, quite frankly, was a corpulent slob.

'Gentlemen, please,' I said quickly. 'Let's be civilized and sort this out. I don't want to call the police.'

I was quite sure that Jimmy Kitchen wouldn't want the cops around, and Jack had clearly been drinking. Given that he'd been listed as MOTORIST MENACE OF THE WEEK on two occasions, it was a miracle he still kept his licence.

'She's right.' Jimmy extended his hand to Jack. 'No reason to call the cops.' After what seemed like eons, Jack reluctantly took it and was helped to his feet. The billhook was returned to its rightful owner.

All the wind had gone out of Jack's sails as he stood in his muddy clothes.

Jimmy Kitchen gestured to a glossy-coated piebald pony hobbled some yards away. 'Bess and I have been on the road these past weeks, and she's gone lame. I'd thank you kindly if I could move tomorrow – having taken her out of harness and all.'

At hearing her name, Bess raised her head and whickered. She limped toward us.

'What's wrong with the mare?' said Jack. 'She's favouring her off hind.' I remembered that Amelia often complained that Jack cared more about their farm animals than he did about her.

'Must have picked up a stone. She's bruised her sole badly,' said the gypsy. 'We came all the way from Brighton once we heard about Belcher Pike being taken poorly.'

'You should put a poultice on it,' Jack said gruffly. 'Rest her up a bit.'

'Thank you kindly, sir,' said the gypsy, giving me a wink.

Another Land Rover – minus a safari roof rack – bumped across the field toward us. Emblazoned on the door panel was the slogan LET'S GO OLYMPICS! JUMP 2012! My heart sank.

As Devon's champion hedge-jumper, Dave Randall and Jack Webster were sworn enemies. Since both hedge-jumping and hedge-cutting displays were two of the main attractions this Saturday, there had already been some territorial wrangling over a highly desirable stretch of blackthorn that had ended in a fistfight and both guilty parties spending a night in the slammer. The magistrate ruled that the hedge in question was off-limits and ordered that both events be held at opposing ends of the field.

I felt one of my rare headaches coming on. Honestly, what with Dora and Topaz, Jack and Jimmy, and now Dave – today had been utterly *exhausting*.

Dave Randall pulled up alongside us and wound down the window. Dressed in a black T-shirt, his muscular arms were bare and browned by what little sun we had managed to have this summer.

With a curt nod at me and another at Jack, he said, 'The Dogs told me Jack was in trouble.'

'It's all sorted now, thanks, Dave,' said Jack.

I was relieved, though not surprised, to see two sworn enemies become instant friends in the face of a hostile force. I'd seen it happen with Dad when the cops were involved. Once – rumour had it – Dad even sided with the Mafia.

Dave got out of his Land Rover and made a show of cricking his neck and rolling his shoulders. 'Isn't this your patch?'

'It's handled, Dave,' said Jack, mirroring Dave's neck crick and shoulder roll. 'This gent said he'd move this wagon on tomorrow. Horse is lame.'

'We can't afford for anything to go wrong on Saturday, Jack,' said Dave. 'A couple of my guys are on the radar for Olympic selection this weekend.'

'You already told me, *Dave*, and we've got some scouts for

the British national team coming down from Norfolk.'

'So you said a hundred times, *Jack*.' A vein began to pulse on Dave's forehead.

I sensed that the unconscious truce could soon be forgotten. 'Good. That's settled,' I said brightly. 'Is it true that the Nag and Bucket has all-day drinking?'

'Is that right?' said Jack Webster brightening. 'Fancy a snifter, Dave?'

'Yeah. Why not?' With a last nod at me and a scowl at Jimmy Kitchen, Dave clambered back into his Land Rover.

Jack followed suit, and the two men drove off in convoy.

'Fancy a cup of tea?' Jimmy said, breaking into a grin. 'I think I owe you one for saving my life.'

How could I possibly refuse? At last I would see the inside of a gypsy wagon.

14

It was just as I had imagined the inside of a gypsy wagon to be. 'What a wonderful home you have!'

I was seated on a buttercup-yellow three-legged stool. Jimmy was sitting on another that was painted a dark green. In front of him, an old kettle boiled merrily atop what I gathered was called a 'queenie' stove.

The upper half of the wagon door was wide open, affording a spectacular view of open fields and woodland. I could hear the cry of birds and the rustle of the wind through the trees and, frankly, couldn't think of anything more romantic than living life in one of these beauties.

'It's all so neat and compact,' I enthused. 'Where do you sleep?'

Jimmy pointed to the rear of the wagon. Beneath a casement window and atop a bow-fronted glass cabinet was a neat bed reminding me of a berth at sea.

It was definitely *cosy*. The actual living area couldn't be larger than a prison cell – but thanks to an abundance of cut-glass bevelled mirrors on all three sides, it didn't feel remotely claustrophobic.

I caught sight of my reflection, feeling decidedly out of place with my shoulder-length hair, jeans and light sweater. A long flowing gypsy skirt, peasant top and shawl, with my hair tumbling to my waist, seemed far more fitting.

Every surface was painted in two-tone greens and yellows with delicate grape and apple motifs except for the bowed ceiling, which depicted a pastoral river scene. There were masses of scrollwork covered in gold leaf.

A display cabinet was filled with Royal Crown Derby china.

There were a few photographs framed in silver plate. I gestured to one. A young couple smiled at the camera, arm in arm. The man was unmistakably a younger Jimmy with his ribbon-threaded braid. 'Is that you?'

'That's right.'

'She's very beautiful. Was that your wife?'

'Yes, but she wasn't the love of my life.' Jimmy pulled a tattered photograph of a woman from his shirt pocket and passed it to me. 'She was.'

The 'she' couldn't have been more than sixteen and was sitting on the step of what looked like this very wagon. The woman was stunning and reminded me of Bizet's Carmen from a poster the Gipping Bards bought on eBay to promote one of their more ambitious productions.

'What happened to her?'

'Gypsies and gorgers can't be together,' Jimmy said sadly. 'Ever.'

'That's ridiculous in this day and age,' I said. 'Do you know where she is? Can you find her?'

'I'm not sure she'd want that. It's too late.'

'Rubbish!' I cried. 'You should follow your heart.'

Jimmy raised an eyebrow. He seemed amused. 'You are young. What do you know about love?'

'Not much,' I admitted. 'But enough to know that outdated customs and traditions would never hold me back from someone I truly loved.'

83

'Some of our customs can only be broken by death,' Jimmy said quietly, but before I could press him further, there was a shrill whistle as the kettle came to a boil.

Jimmy took a tin tea caddy down from a rack of shelves set into the wall above the stove. He added three heaped spoonfuls – one per person and one for the pot – of *real* tea leaves into a Brown Betty teapot and poured on the boiling water. Given the amount and different brands of tea I consumed every day on my travels, I considered myself a tea connoisseur and had high hopes for this cuppa.

I was glad to see a packet of my favourite chocolate digestives join two mugs and a bowl of sugar on the pull-out table between us. These days I seemed to survive on a diet of tea, biscuits and cake.

Jimmy leaned over to his right and opened a small fridge to retrieve a pint of milk. 'These wagons are collector's items nowadays.' Clearly our conversation about love and longing was over, but not for me. The thought of being reunited with the love of one's life in later years was something I felt sure my mourner readers would go for. Perhaps I could have my own column? I made a mental note to mention it to Pete.

Jimmy poured the tea and gestured for me to help myself to a biscuit. 'This wagon is over one hundred years old. It used to belong to my grandfather.'

'Was he part of the Pike clan?' I said.

'We're all related. "Our caravan is our family, and the world is our family", a gypsy proverb,' said Jimmy.

'Why would anyone want to swap a beautiful wagon like this for a hideous camper?'

'Most of the youngsters these days prefer the modern conveniences,' Jimmy said. 'Electricity, running water, mobile phones and those ugly satellite dishes!' He shook his head. 'There's a growing divide between traditionalists and those who want us to be something we're not. We are what we are. Nothing more and nothing less.'

Dad would have agreed with him. I could still see the expression of acute disappointment when I announced I wouldn't be joining the family business. *'Going to work for the papers? Collaborating with the cops? You're no daughter of mine.'*

'You all right, luv?' Jimmy asked, squeezing my shoulder. 'You look a bit down in the mouth.'

'I just think it very sad that horse-drawn wagons are becoming a thing of the past,' I said quickly, realizing it was a perfect lead into a perfectly reasonable question. 'When you've set up camp, how do you get around? Other than the VW camper and Dora's enormous Winnebago, is there another vehicle? A Land Rover, perhaps?'

'We use bicycles,' said Jimmy. 'Why?'

'No reason.' I took a sip of tea. 'You've been on the road a long time and must know everyone . . .'

'Seventy years,' said Jimmy. 'I just turned seventy last month, and yes, I do.'

'I wondered if you'd heard about that poor gypsy woman who died last night in Mudge Lane.'

'She wasn't a gypsy,' said Jimmy firmly.

Funny that Dora claimed to know nothing about it but Jimmy did. 'Don't you think it disgraceful? The police don't even seem to care who this woman was?'

'Is that so?' Jimmy shrugged. 'That's the police for you. More tea?'

'She was dressed like a gypsy,' I persisted. 'Riding a bicycle, too. The wig was a bit weird, though. I nearly fell over because it got all tangled up in my legs.'

'You were *there*?' said Jimmy sharply.

'I found the body,' I said, trying to keep my tone casual. 'My car was hit by a Land Rover leaving the scene.'

'As I said, she wasn't one of ours.'

'What about all the mourners coming for Belcher Pike's funeral – I mean, to pay their respects?' I said. 'Perhaps one of them might know something?'

85

'Maybe,' said Jimmy slowly. 'Tell you what, why don't I ask around? Gypsies don't like to talk to gorgers. You won't get very far on your own.' Which is exactly what Dora had said, too.

'Thank you – but . . .' *Blast* – Topaz! I'd almost forgotten. 'I think it's only fair to tell you that the owner of The Grange has hired a professional eviction service to come here on Friday.'

'Eviction!' Jimmy's jaw dropped. 'They can't do that. We're allowed to camp here.'

'Sir Hugh passed away,' I said. 'His niece owns the estate now.'

'That can't happen. It mustn't,' Jimmy cried. 'If Belcher Pike is uprooted in his final days, his soul will go straight to hell.'

'Jimmy, we've got a problem.' Noah's face loomed large through the open half door. 'Some idiot reporter is—'

'Noah, lad!' said Jimmy with false joviality. 'Come on in for a cuppa and meet my guest.'

Jimmy's pathetic attempt at warning Noah of my presence was not lost on me. *Idiot reporter!* My face burned with indignation – and to think I'd been attracted to him and his wretched guitar.

'I was just leaving,' I said coldly. But, of course, I had to wait for Jimmy to move the tea service, push the table in, and pick up his chair so that I could squeeze past him.

I was rapidly going off wagon life. It was far too cramped.

'We'll be in touch,' said Jimmy, all smiles once more. He opened the lower door and took in a breath of fresh air. 'Now, that's what real life smells like. Off you go back to your stuffy office.'

Jimmy stepped aside to let me pass. I swept by Noah without giving him a second glance and tramped back to my car.

Idiot reporter? Noah's words stung. I might be an idiot for finding him attractive, but I certainly wasn't an idiot when it came to sleuthing. Dora and Jimmy were lying about the dead woman in Mudge Lane, and maybe they were poaching, too.

I kept circling back to the same questions. If the woman *was* a gypsy, why would they pretend she wasn't? If the woman *wasn't* a gypsy, why did the police say it was an accident but move her body to Plymouth?

It was only when I was halfway back to Middle Gipping and had reached Plym Bridge that I realized that I'd forgotten to post Whittler's cheque *and* drop off Barbara's mysterious package.

Fortunately I remembered there was a pillar box opposite Barbara's house. Barbara had been born in Gipping-on-Plym and given the scandal that she had supposedly created all those years ago, might be able to shed some light on the new residents at The Grange.

I turned the car around and headed back to The Marshes. Jimmy Kitchen's cup of tea had been very good, but I could always do with another.

15

Fifteen minutes later I arrived at The Marshes and pulled up outside Barbara's end-terraced house. Built on a ridge, Barbara's two-up, two-down overlooked a horseshoe of unattractive 1950s redbrick bungalows with metal-framed windows and corrugated iron roofing.

In the centre of the horseshoe was a patch of grass that always seemed to be waterlogged whatever the weather. Rumour had it that the bungalows had been built on a landfill and were steadily sinking – hence the local nickname 'Little Venice'.

Bill Trenfold's post van was parked next to the old-fashioned cylindrical red pillar box. I checked my watch. It wasn't even three thirty, and I knew the last collection of the day was supposed to be 5.30 p.m. Bill was picking up early.

I opened my window and shouted, 'Bill! Wait!'

But he didn't seem to have heard me. I'd no sooner gotten out of my Fiat when Bill simply drove off! It was little wonder that there were so many complaints about the postal service if the postmen had decided to enforce their own schedules.

Blast! I had given Whittler my word, and now it looked as if

I'd have to drive all the way back to Gipping to post his letter after all.

Turning to the main reason for visiting poor Barbara, I went to get the shoebox. It wasn't there.

Puzzled, I opened the rear doors and looked under the driver and front passenger seats, thinking it must have slid forward. With growing dismay, it dawned on me that the wretched shoebox must have been stolen, and I knew exactly by whom.

Blast the Swamp Dogs! No doubt they nabbed it when I was dealing with Jack Webster's shenanigans. Of course I'd confront them, but it was annoying. Besides, what use would an old shoe and a bicycle bell have for them anyway? Come to think of it, what use would either have for Barbara?

As Mum would say, '*What you haven't had you won't miss!*' The sender hadn't left a note or return address. If it were that important, I was quite sure we'd hear about it, but until we did, I had other things to think about.

I was tempted to leave, but experience had shown that Barbara had eyes like a hawk and ears like a bat. She was bound to have recognized my car and heard me shout out to the postman. I also noticed the curtains upstairs were open, suggesting Barbara was no longer lying stricken in a darkened room with a migraine.

I'd just pop in for five minutes.

On the front doorstep was a glass jam jar filled with wildflowers – forget-me-knots, ox-eyed daisies and some purple flowers that I didn't know the name of.

How romantic! Who would have thought Wilf had it in him!

I knocked on Barbara's front door and must have stood there for a good five minutes until I realized she wasn't going to answer.

I knelt down and opened the letterbox. 'Barbara?' I shouted. 'It's Vicky.'

There was no reply. Dad said empty houses had a particular feel to them, and I had to admit to getting that feeling.

I took the narrow path around the side of the house. A latch gate opened into a small, back garden surrounded by a high wooden fence. There was a neat lawn – no bigger than eight feet square – and a flagstone patio lined with tubs of geraniums and begonias. A white circular plastic table and matching plastic chairs stood under a blue umbrella emblazoned with the word *Campari!*

Peering shamelessly through the ground-floor windows, I saw a spotlessly clean kitchen with no telltale signs of a teatime cuppa left on the draining board.

Rapping smartly on the back door, I shouted again, 'Barbara!' But there was still no reply.

I tried to ring her home phone from my mobile but with no luck. I also tried her mobile and again drew a blank.

What if she'd fallen down the stairs – Barbara was getting up there in years despite her boasts of 'sixty being the new forty'.

I was in a dilemma. Should I break in?

A quick look at Barbara's window latches assured me of an easy access – but first, I had one more place to check.

Barbara did not own a car. Instead she went everywhere on her beloved circa 1940 pink bicycle. Convinced it was a collector's item and liable to be stolen for parts, Barbara stored it under lock and key.

At the end of the garden stood a wooden shed. As I drew closer, I noted the old padlock shackle dangling from the hasp. I opened the door, and among shelves filled with empty pots and gardening paraphernalia stacked neatly on the floor sat an empty bicycle stand.

Barbara's bicycle was gone, which meant she was out.

I returned to my car feeling distinctly uneasy. This was most unusual. Barbara *lived* for her job. Her life revolved around the bustle of reception, and she was often known to go into the office on her days off, 'just in case there is an emergency'.

A doctor's visit was out of the question. Following the shameful exit of Annabel's former beau, Dr Frost, from

Gipping-on-Plym, there was currently no GP. The doctors of choice were the sadistic Dr 'Jab-It' Jolly, the podiatrist, or Dr Bodger, who was a ten-mile drive away in Newton Abbot.

Consoling myself that I had at least *tried* to deliver a package that I didn't actually have, I could at least try to keep my promise to Whittler.

I knew my route back to Factory Terrace would take me past three red pillar boxes – Tripp Lane, Swing-Swang Road and Bexmoor Way – but first a quick check of the collection plate.

I was right. The last pickup of the day was 5.30 p.m.! There it was in black-and-white – MON–FRI: 9 A.M.–5.30 P.M. SAT: 9 A.M.–12 NOON.

It was then that I noticed that the cast-iron pillar box door was not set flush against the cylindrical wall. Bill can't have locked it properly.

I slammed the door shut.

Back on the road again, my thoughts turned to the evening ahead at 21 Factory Terrace.

Mrs Evans loved a good gossip. Since it was she who had told Reverend Whittler about last night's drowning in Mudge Lane, she was bound to have some information to share.

16

Annabel's silver BMW was already in the drive behind Mr Evans's green Austin Rover Metro.

As someone who had lived at Chez Evans for far longer than Annabel had, this particular privilege somewhat irked me. We were both supposed to park our cars on the street.

Annabel's 'temporary' stay in Mrs Evans's sewing room had surprisingly turned into a two full months.

Located in Lower Gipping, Factory Terrace was a row of dreary Victorian houses formally built for the workers at the six-storey wool and textile factory – another Trewallyn white elephant – that stood opposite. The factory had closed down years ago and now stood derelict and vandalized – hardly the kind of neighbourhood that Annabel claimed she was accustomed to. But with no man paying her expenses at the moment, presumably beggars couldn't be choosers.

One thing I loved about living with Mrs Evans was having my own key – unlike my previous landlady. I let myself in and was greeted by a delicious smell of baking pastry. Apart from Thursday night's disgusting liver and onions, Mrs E. was a decent cook, and at least there were always second helpings.

After hanging up my safari jacket on the hall coat stand, I noticed a pile of mixed objects left in an unceremonious heap at the bottom of the stairs – a pair of leopard-print ankle boots, a copy of bestseller relationship guru Fenella Fox's *How to Be Irresistible!,* a pink satin robe, a hairbrush and a bottle of red nail polish.

A note, written in Mrs Evans's bold handwriting, was tucked into the top of an ankle boot. It simply said ANNABEL. Obviously, Mrs E. was getting fed up with Annabel's possessions seeping into every corner of the house.

I found my landlady standing at the kitchen sink gazing out of the window. Her hair had the tight-curled look of the just-permed, and for once she had switched her usual floral housecoat for a bright yellow apron over a cream cotton blouse and skirt.

On her right was a countertop full of an array of colourful mini recycling containers for which purpose I knew off by heart. *Brown,* for food waste, garden waste and cardboard; *blue,* for paper, coloured cardboard – not wet; *white,* for plastic bottles, cans and tins – not polystyrene; and *grey,* for everything else. The same set that Ronnie had left at The Grange – only smaller.

Mrs Evans suddenly started to jerk her left arm about, crying, 'Bother! Drat!'

'What's wrong?'

She spun around. Two spoons were stuck to a metal band on her wrist. Mrs E. flicked it violently left and right in a futile effort to dislodge the cutlery. 'It's this wretched magnetic bracelet.'

'Why are you wearing it?' I laughed but Mrs E. scowled, clearly not thinking it funny at all.

'It's for my arthritis. My Sadie bought it for me when we had our girl's lunch in Plymouth last week.'

I was glad to hear there was a grain of generosity in Mrs Evans's wayward daughter's heart. Sadie Evans earned a ton of money pole-dancing at the Banana Club on Plymouth Hoe but was always on the scrounge.

'As long as I stay away from anything metal, it's fine.'

'Damn and blast!' I cried, remembering Whittler's envelope. 'I completely forgot to post a very important letter.'

'Why bother?' said Mrs Evans, clicking her ill-fitting dentures. 'The post is all over the place. Mrs Pierce swore she sent me a cheque a fortnight ago – it was a lot of money, too – and that Olive Larch *insists* her cheque cleared through her bank.'

I knew that Mr and Mrs Evans struggled to make ends meet. As a road worker for Gipping County Council, Mr Evans's salary was dictated by weather conditions and very unpredictable. Mrs Evans said snail breeding was expensive, too, and that Mr E. was always adding to his collection of terrariums.

Mrs Evans opened the cutlery drawer. A knife, spoon and fork catapulted onto her bracelet with a series of chinks. 'Oh, sod it!'

I helped her remove them. 'Why don't I lay the table?'

'Use the best linen. Middle drawer.'

I did as I was told and took out a white damask tablecloth with matching napkins.

We usually used a plastic tablecloth and paper napkins, so when Mrs Evans placed a cut-glass vase of roses picked from the garden in the centre of the table, I had to ask, 'Are we expecting visitors?'

'No.' Strain was etched across Mrs Evans's face.

'Is everything all right?'

'I'm trying to make an effort,' Mrs Evans said miserably, nodding toward the open kitchen window. 'Can't you hear them?'

I paused to listen. The familiar sound of Annabel's tinkling laugh drifted along the evening breeze. 'They're in the shed,' Mrs Evans went on. 'She's taken an interest in Lenny's snails.'

Honestly, Annabel was the limit! For the past couple of weeks, she had been blatantly flirting with Mrs E.'s husband, who was an enthusiastic snail breeder and took the sport very seriously.

As one of Gipping's most popular summer pastimes, I had tried to get excited about the various celebrity snails that either were raced every weekend or appeared as 'attractions' – Seabiscuit, Rambo, Bullet – but found the whole idea just too silly. I knew Annabel did, too. It was one of the few things we laughed about together.

'Ignore it, Mrs E. She's just insecure.'

'Why should I?' said Mrs Evans defiantly. 'I don't like to see her making a fool of my man.'

At the beginning, Mrs Evans told me she found Annabel's behaviour toward 'my Lenny' a joke, claiming she couldn't believe that anyone would find him attractive.

Without intending to sound unkind, I had to agree. I still suffered from nightmares following the time I accidentally walked in on the two of them fooling around. The sight of 'my Lenny' wearing nothing but a pair of bottle-green socks was firmly printed on my brain for all eternity.

But recently I noticed Mrs Evans make the occasional barbed remark at Annabel's mode of dress, the smaller portions she deliberately slopped onto her plate at dinner, and the circled classified advertisements for flats or cottages to rent left at her place setting at the kitchen table.

Needless to say, Annabel either was oblivious or didn't care.

A sudden burst of laughter sent Mrs Evans scurrying back to the kitchen sink to peer out of the window. 'Here they come!'

She took off her apron, darted to the counter, pulled out a drawer, retrieved a small compact mirror, and applied a layer of lipstick.

Moments later, Annabel and Mr Evans strolled through the back door arm in arm. The smell of Polo Sport aftershave filled the kitchen.

'Yum, yum,' said Annabel. 'I'm starving.'

'What's cooking, Millie?' grinned Mr Evans, his eyes sparkling. Having always seen Mr Evans in corduroys and an old threadbare sweater, I did a double take. Tonight he was dressed in jeans and a pressed short-sleeved shirt. He'd even shaved.

'Egg and bacon flan.'

'Don't you mean quiche Lorraine?' said Annabel. 'That's the right way to pronounce it. It's French, you know. And we love all things *French*, don't we, Lenny.'

Mr Evans blew Annabel a kiss. The meaning was plain.

'We call it flan in this house,' snapped Mrs E.

'Lovely,' I said. 'I love flan, and you're so good at making pastry.'

'Lenny's good at *everything*, aren't you, sweetie?' said Annabel, batting her eyelashes. Mr Evans turned pink with ill-disguised pleasure.

Mrs Evans's dentures clicked into overdrive. 'Not everything. The hinges on the wardrobe upstairs still need repairing.'

'Nag, nag, nag,' he said. 'That's all she ever does.'

'Wardrobe!' Annabel pretended to sound shocked. 'Have you been jumping off wardrobes? Naughty Lenny.' She suddenly burst out laughing. 'Oh, Mrs E.! You've got something dangling—'

'What's on your arm, you silly woman.' Mr Evans began to laugh, too.

'It's for my arthritis,' said Mrs Evans stiffly. She tore off the bracelet and threw it into the sink with a crash of clanking metal.

'You're getting past it, old girl.' Mr Evans guffawed, giving Annabel a wink. He flexed his muscles. 'You won't see me getting arthritis.'

'It's hereditary,' I said quickly. 'I have it and I'm only twenty-three. It's the damp weather.'

Mrs Evans stomped over to the stove and returned with a saucepan. She put five potatoes on each plate except for Annabel's, on which she put only one – and a deformed one at that. Annabel also got a burnt slice of flan.

Mr Evans gestured to Annabel's plate with his fork. 'See what little Annie eats?' *Little Annie?* 'Next to nothing. You should try that. Lose some of that pot belly.'

'You can talk,' Mrs E. quipped. 'Why don't you do something about that fat gut of yours?'

'I think it's rather sweet,' said Annabel. 'He's nice and cuddly.'

I caught Annabel's eye and glowered at her. She just smirked and started cutting tiny pieces of food and popping them daintily into her mouth.

Mr Evans reached over and gently smoothed Annabel's hair away from her face. 'I love long hair,' he said softly.

Mrs Evans's expression was nothing short of murderous, which reminded me. 'There was nearly a murder committed at The Grange today,' I said, glad to change the subject.

'Really?' Mrs Evans perked up, as I knew she would. 'Probably some stupid old man lusting after a girl young enough to be his daughter.'

'*God.* What a nightmare,' said Annabel. 'Her ladyship nearly shot a gypsy.'

'She should have shot the lot of them,' declared Mr Evans, bringing his hand down hard onto the table. 'They're parasites, leeching off the government.'

'Nonsense; they pay their way,' said Mrs Evans. 'Mend the roads, fix the roof. Tell fortunes.'

'I'd love to go to a fortune-teller.' Annabel wriggled in her seat. 'I wonder if I've already met the man I'm going to marry?' She looked directly at Mr Evans.

Mr Evans leaned back in his seat with a smirk. 'If I come back on the market—'

'Oh, for heaven's sake,' muttered Mrs Evans, viciously stabbing a potato with her fork.

'You've got a short memory, Millie,' said Mr Evans. 'Remember all that trouble years back?'

'What trouble?' Annabel and I chorused.

'I'm not one to gossip.' Mrs Evans sank her dentures into the pastry crust and then wished she hadn't. She gestured for us to wait a moment whilst she finished her mouthful.

'Get on with it,' said Mr Evans, rolling his eyes.

'And besides, it's not right,' said Mrs E. finally. 'These two girls work with her.'

'Oh, please tell us,' Annabel and I chorused again.

'There isn't much to tell. We'd just started courting, hadn't we, Lenny?' said Mrs Evans. 'Your Barbara took up with one of them and ran off for a week or two. Caused a big scandal.'

So *that* was the scandal! How unbelievably romantic!

'Hardly a *scandal*,' said Annabel with a sneer. 'I bet Barbara was a bit of a tart in her day.'

It takes one to know one! 'Neither of them were married, so why shouldn't she fall in love with whomever she wanted,' I protested.

'She was a real looker,' said Mr Evans wistfully. 'Hair down to her waist. Everyone took a run at Barbara.'

'The police got involved,' Mrs E. said. 'And then there was all that bother with Mildred.'

A light snapped on in my head. Hadn't the newspaper clipping in the shoebox mentioned the name Mildred? 'Mildred who?'

'Veysey. Wilf's poor mother,' said Mrs Evans. 'She had an accident in Mudge Lane. It was all very mysterious.'

'I'd just started with the council and I remember putting up that 'Beware of Cyclists' warning sign,' said Mr Evans. 'It's dangerous down there if you're not paying attention.'

'Mildred was riding a bicycle, too, just like that poor lady last night,' Mrs Evans said. 'Vicky found the body, didn't you?'

'That's right.'

'The police say she drowned,' said Annabel.

'Kelvin – that's Betty's son – doesn't think so,' said Mrs Evans. 'And why else would that important redheaded copper be involved? Kelvin says they've been told to keep out of it.'

My heart began to race. I *knew* something was up! Just *knew* it!

'Both in Mudge Lane,' Annabel frowned. 'How very strange.'

'Not really. The two incidents are decades apart, isn't that right, Mrs E.?' I said. 'By the way, the flan was delicious.'

'Interesting . . .' Annabel turned her attention back to her plate and fell silent.

Mr Evans nudged her elbow. 'Penny for your thoughts.'

'Don't do that,' snapped Annabel. 'I'm thinking.'

I desperately wanted to change the subject. Whatever had happened in Mudge Lane belonged to me. 'What do you think about the gypsies claiming they can camp at The Grange, Mr Evans?'

'Bastards!' He slammed his hand down on the kitchen table again. 'We taxpayers are continually getting shafted while the do-gooders in government use our hard-earned cash to pay out to nonconformists and the terminally idle.'

Annabel whipped out her notebook. 'Great quote. Mind if I use it?'

'If me and the lads had anything to do with it, we'd set fire to the lot of them!'

'No need,' said Annabel. 'They're being evicted on Friday and it's being televised and – *guess what?* – I'm going to be on TV!'

'Evicted, eh?' said Mr Evans. 'Now you're talking. I can't wait to see that.'

'Yes, her ladyship wants them off,' Annabel said. 'Oh, Mrs E., I almost forgot. Your cleaning services are wanted at The Grange.'

'I've already spoken to her, thank you very much,' said Mrs Evans with a sniff. 'She telephoned.'

'What's for pudding?' I said.

'Spotted *dick*,' spat Mrs E.

'Not for us.' Mr Evans looked at his watch and stood up. 'We'll skip pudding and fill up on popcorn.'

'Where are you going?'

'The Gipping Film Club is showing *Basic Instinct* tonight,' said Mr Evans.

Mrs E. stood up, too. 'I'll be ready in five minutes.'

'Don't you have some Morris knee pads to sew for Saturday?'

Mrs Evans sat back down, a look of defeat on her face. 'You know I do.'

'Vicky?' said Annabel sweetly. 'Hardly your scene, but you are welcome to come with us.'

'No thanks,' I said. 'I thought I'd help with the sewing.'

The moment Mr Evans and Annabel disappeared, Mrs E. covered her face with her hands.

'It's not his fault,' she whispered. 'It's *her*.'

'He's just having a midlife crisis.' I'd grown fond of Mrs E. and couldn't bear to see her humiliated. 'It's just a phase, honestly,' I said. 'He'll come to his senses.' Although Dad never did – I knew for a fact that Pamela Dingles followed him to Spain. My mother caught them watching a bullfight together.

'Yes. Yes, of *course*!' Mrs Evans suddenly sat up straight. I noted a fierce gleam in her eye. 'When did you say the gypsies were being evicted?'

'Friday. Why?'

'No one tries to steal my husband from under my nose. No one.'

Mrs Evans obviously had some kind of plan and seemed to perk up considerably. Unfortunately, she wasn't in the mood to talk about Mildred Veysey, Barbara, or the dead woman in Mudge Lane, steering every question around to 'when Lenny and I first met.'

After sewing a total of thirty-four bells onto strips of coloured cloth, I was very glad to finally get to bed.

Just as I snapped off the light, my mobile phone rang. It was Steve.

'Just calling to wish my girl good night,' he said. 'You sound sexy. Are you in bed?'

'No. I was cutting my toenails.'

'I wish I could be there to hold your foot.'

'Very sweet of you, Steve,' I said. 'I'll save my nail clippings.'

'Would you?'

'Do you have any news from Plymouth?'

'A little. I thought we could meet tomorrow night.'

I sat bolt upright. 'You've heard something, haven't you?'

'You're tired. We can talk about this tomorrow.'

'At least give me a hint,' I said. 'I'll never sleep otherwise.'

'I don't sleep anyway.' Steve gave a heavy sigh. 'I just can't stop thinking about you.'

Stifling a groan, I said, 'Thanks. So what did your friend say?'

'You're killing me, doll,' said Steve. 'All right, I'll tell you.' He paused, presumably for dramatic effect. 'There's going to be an internal police inquiry.'

An *internal* inquiry! The only reason for an internal inquiry was when something was not quite kosher in the Devon and Cornwall Police Constabulary. 'Any idea who would want one?'

'Why don't you ask your *friend*, Probes,' said Steve bitterly.

'I just might.'

'No, don't do that,' Steve said. 'My man will be getting the toxicology results in the morning. Be interesting to see what comes back.'

'That would be great,' I enthused. 'What time do you want to meet?'

'Tomorrow night. I'll call you.'

It seemed a small price to pay for some potentially excellent information.

101

17

'There's been a break-in!' shrieked Topaz. 'I knew that would happen! I told you so!'

'There is no need to shout,' I said crossly. Being woken up by a hysterical woman on the other end of the phone was not my idea of fun. Squinting at the luminous dials on my alarm radio, I let out a groan. It wasn't even seven.

It had taken me hours to get to sleep last night, and when I did, I was haunted by a naked vision of Steve, dressed in Mr Evans's bottle-green socks, sitting on a three-legged stool in a gypsy wagon, drinking a cup of tea. 'Just calm down and tell me what's happened.'

'I *told* you they were thieves!' Topaz squealed.

I sat up in bed. 'For heaven's sake, *what's happened*?'

'There's been a *robbery*!' Topaz sounded triumphant. 'You'd better come quickly if you want the scoop.'

I scrambled out of bed, dragging off my pyjamas with my free hand and reaching for my clothes, which were always neatly folded on the floor next to my bed. Childhood habits of nighttime police raids die hard.

102

'I'm surprised you didn't ask your new best friend,' I said, pulling on my jeans with one hand.

'Why would I?' said Topaz. 'The church is your area of expertise, isn't it?'

I sank onto the edge of the bed. 'What are you talking about?'

'They've taken the silver from St Peter's the Martyr Church,' said Topaz cheerfully. 'Reverend Whittler is frightfully upset.'

'That's terrible.' And strange – why would gypsies steal from the church? 'I've got to get dressed,' I said. 'I'll meet you there in twenty minutes.'

'Are you mad?' said Topaz. 'I'm not leaving The Grange. The gypsies are bound to target me next.'

Racing out of my bedroom, I bumped into Annabel on the landing. She was wearing sky-blue pyjamas embroidered with pink kittens. 'Where are you off to?' she demanded. 'Is there a fire?'

'Emergency church business—' Which I thought a very clever answer because it was true.

'Church? Ugh.' Annabel pulled a face. 'Rather you than me. See you at work. Don't be late for our Page One update.'

It was only when I turned into Church Lane and pulled up behind a police panda car that I had a sudden thought. How on earth did Topaz know about the theft at such an early hour? Not only that, but she seemed almost gleeful.

Carefully locking my Fiat – this time I wasn't taking any chances – my Topaz musings were cut short by a rustling in the undergrowth.

DC Bond materialized from a large elderflower shrub. He was adjusting his uniform, and judging by the pink flush on his face, I suspected that the young copper had been answering a call of nature. 'Morning, Ms Hill.'

Naturally, my mind flew to DC Bond's comments on the woman in Mudge Lane. It might be prudent to make friends with this young copper, especially as I would need a mole for the internal police inquiry.

'It's Kelvin, isn't it?' I said with an indulgent smile. 'You probably know a very, *very* good friend of mine. Detective Sergeant Colin Probes?'

DC Bond's eyes narrowed. 'Don't you mean Detective *Inspector* Probes? He's been promoted.'

How could Probes have been promoted so quickly? *Again?* It just wasn't fair.

'I knew that,' I said. 'Freudian slip. Old Colin seems to get promoted a lot.'

DC Bond seemed to swell with the inflated authority of the newly anointed. 'I don't remember seeing you at his promotion party?'

'A journalist never stops working,' I said smoothly. 'Colin and I had our own private celebration. I thought I might just pop into the church to say hello to him.'

'He doesn't handle theft,' said DC Bond suspiciously. 'You're that reporter girl, aren't you?'

'That's right,' I said. 'Vicky Hill.'

'We've been told not to talk to the press,' Bond said. 'Run along now.'

Run along? I had to be *years* older than him! 'I want to talk to the vicar.' I tried to step round him, but he blocked my path. 'Please get out of my way.'

DC Bond gestured to the lych-gate a few yards farther on. The entrance to the churchyard had been transformed into a spider's web of yellow plastic CRIME SCENE DO NOT ENTER tape. 'You can't go in there without authority.'

'It looks like you can't get in there at all,' I said dryly. 'I got a phone call from Reverend Whittler to come here quickly.' Not strictly true. 'How else would I have heard about the robbery at this time of the morning?'

'Sorry. Orders are orders.'

'Oh, for heaven's sake . . .'

Without another thought, I sprinted toward the waist-high stone wall to the right of the lych-gate. Launching into the air, I executed a perfect straddle jump that would have made champion hedge-jumper Dave Randall proud.

'Oi!' shouted DC Bond. 'Come back!' but I didn't, and tore up the brick herringbone pathway toward the church porch.

Reverend Whittler was in the vestry nursing a balloon of brandy. Dressed in his usual black attire, he was slumped in an oak high-backed chair seated behind a scratched wooden table. The far wall was covered with black cassocks and white surplices dangling from wooden pegs. Scattered around the room were various odds and ends – a chipped headstone, a pair of broken papier-mâché angel wings from the Sunday School play, a stack of moth-eaten bibles, and four croquet mallets.

'I'm afraid my fears were justified, young Vicky,' said Whittler. 'The gypsies didn't waste any time.'

DI Stalk emerged from a walk-in storeroom with a flashlight. 'What the hell – pardon me, vicar – are you doing here?' I noted he hadn't shaved this morning and must have left home in a rush. 'I gave DC Bond strict instructions—'

'I'm not here in a professional capacity,' I said, 'but as a friend.'

'How kind, dear,' said Whittler. 'They've taken everything, Vicky.'

'No questions!' barked Stalk. 'This is a crime scene.'

'I'm not asking any,' I protested. 'But frankly, the more people who know about it, the better. We could offer a reward on this week's front page. How about PILFERING AT ST PETER'S: RECTOR OFFERS REWARD! as a headline?'

'Would you, Vicky?' Whittler took a large quaff of brandy. 'Don't you think that an excellent idea, Inspector?'

Stalk grunted an assent but looked cross. 'Forensics will be here shortly to dust for fingerprints.'

'All the altar artifacts have gone.' Whittler took another swig of brandy 'The ciborium, both cruets, a silver paten, and, of course, the Trewallyn chalice.'

'The Trewallyn chalice?'

'It was given to the church by Sir Hugh's great grandfather at the beginning of the nineteenth century. It's embedded with two large rubies and is of tremendous value.'

How odd that Topaz – supposedly so obsessed with her family heirlooms – hadn't mentioned it?

'Distinctive silver like the chalice is relatively easy to recover,' I said – reluctant to add, unless it was to be melted down. 'It's bound to appear on the black market eventually.'

'What do you know about black markets?' sneered Stalk.

'I'm a reporter and make it my business to know.' I'd also make it my business to contact Chuffy McSnatch – my godfather, go-between, and Dad's right-hand man. Chuffy knew everything and everyone on the black market.

With a start, I realized I couldn't do that anymore. Having refused to follow Dad's orders, Chuffy had made it clear that I'd been excommunicated from the family firm, and I was not to contact them ever again. He'd even changed his pager number. Mum had made an unexpected call from a pay phone in San Feliu to try to make me change my mind, but by then it was too late. The damage had been done.

For months and months I'd pretended to be an orphan, and now it was true. I was on my own.

To my dismay, I felt my eyes begin to prickle, and a solitary tear ran down my cheek.

'Don't cry, Vicky dear,' said Whittler kindly. 'Here, take a sip of brandy.'

I shook my head. 'Sorry.' I gulped. 'It's so sad. I hate thieves.'

'God is all seeing and all knowing.' Whittler downed the last of the amber liquid. 'The culprits will not go unpunished in the afterlife.'

'Those ruddy gypsies will steal anything not bolted down,' said Stalk grimly, echoing Whittler's words of only yesterday. 'I've already given orders to search their wagons this morning. But don't be surprised if they've already scarpered. They could be halfway to China by now.'

Hardly, I thought. The VW camper was ancient, and those horse-drawn wagons weren't exactly fleet of foot.

Perhaps I'd been wrong about gypsies and silver – but why rob from the church, especially since Topaz had ordered the eviction. Wouldn't the gypsies have stolen from her, since she lived so conveniently on their doorstep?

Stalk's phone rang and shattered the unhappy silence in the vestry.

'I'm sorry, Inspector,' said Whittler. 'There are no mobile phones allowed in the Lord's house.'

Stalk scowled and walked into the nave, but we could hear his voice ricocheting around the cathedral roof. 'What do you mean, they can't get through the lych-gate?' he boomed. *'Goddamit.* Do I have to do everything myself?'

Stalk reappeared in the doorway. 'Do you have any scissors, vicar?'

The moment the odious Stalk was out of earshot, I retrieved my reporter notepad and a pencil from my safari-jacket pocket. 'We've got a Page One meeting today,' I said. 'I'd like to take down some details. It was Topaz – I mean, her ladyship, who tipped me off this morning. Any idea how she could have known?'

Whittler poured the last dregs of brandy into the cut-glass balloon. 'Holy Communion is at six on Thursdays.'

'Excuse me?' I had to pinch the inside of my leg. 'Are you saying that her ladyship actually came to *church* this morning?'

'That's right. A lot of the farming folk drive to Taunton for the livestock market.'

'Her ladyship isn't a farmer,' I pointed out.

'Ah, but Lady Clarissa, her ladyship's aunt – a Turberville-Spat – was always a regular churchgoer. Of course, Sir Hugh Trewallyn never bothered when he was alive, but it's wonderful to have a Spat back in the congregation again.'

I had to hand it to Topaz. When she was assuming the role of a different character, she did her best to be authentic. *Wait!* What was I saying! Of course she was authentic. She was playing herself.

'Her ladyship called me the night before, offering to come early and help lay out the artifacts,' said Whittler. 'She arrived shortly after I discovered the cupboard was empty. Of course we had to cancel the service.' He groaned with despair, adding, 'How could I conduct Holy Communion without the sacred vessels?'

I walked over to the storage cupboard and inspected the door handle. 'It doesn't look like this was a forced entry.'

'There wouldn't be.' Whittler's voice sounded defiant. 'I trust my parishioners. They would *never* steal from the church.'

I looked inside. The cupboard smelled musty. Apart from one empty shelf – presumably where Whittler's 'sacred vessels' had been stored – the place was a chaotic mess of pamphlets, Parish newsletters, and candle stumps.

I spotted a metal cash box labelled TREWALLYN TRIO, tucked behind a framed picture of Saint Peter. 'What about money?'

'I keep very little here. Each week I pay the cash directly into the church bank account,' he said. 'Did you post the cheque to Windows of Wonder?'

I felt my face redden. The envelope was burning a hole in my pocket.

'You really should install a safe in that cupboard,' I muttered.

'You are a suspicious young lady.' I noted Whittler's eyes were beginning to glitter, and his usual sallow complexion had turned a little pink. 'Goodness. I'm beginning to feel a little light-headed. Shall we walk to the rectory and have a cup of tea?'

Despite being absolutely parched *and* starving, I had to turn Whittler's offer down. En route to the office, I posted Whittler's envelope in the first pillar box I found.

This morning's unusual robbery, the dead woman in Mudge Lane, the missing Land Rover, the stolen shoe-box, and

Barbara's uncharacteristic absence from work all suggested something was definitely up.

There was no way I could risk missing a minute of this morning's Page One update meeting.

18

'You can't do that! It's just not fair.' Annabel stamped her foot and continued to pace back and forth in front of Pete's desk.

The atmosphere in Pete's office sizzled with tension as what had started as a normal Page One update had dissolved into Annabel having an enormous wobbly.

'If you don't like it, take it up with Wilf,' snapped Pete.

'This is the second time I'll have cancelled the camera crew,' she cried. 'I'll never be taken seriously again!'

'Get over yourself.' Tony wore a huge grin on his face and was practically bouncing with glee on the tartan two-seater. He was clearly enjoying the show.

'Oh, shut up,' said Annabel.

Edward and I were also squashed onto the sofa, but whereas he calmly leafed through his reporter notepad, I was becoming increasingly nervous about the prospect of pushing Pete's temper over the top.

Tucked inside my safari-jacket inner pocket was Dora's report, which I was having second thoughts about giving to Pete in his current mood.

'Her ladyship will go ballistic when she finds out, won't she, Vicky?' Annabel raged on. 'You were there. You saw her fire that gun.'

'It was an accident,' I pointed out. 'But, yes, I don't think she'll be happy.' And boy, was I glad to not be the bearer of that bit of news.

'Her ladyship has already been informed by the police,' said Pete. 'The eviction is off, and that's final. Do you understand?'

'It just doesn't make sense,' Annabel persisted. 'Vicky? Come on. What do you think? Really.'

Although I was relieved that Annabel's debut as anchor-woman for Westward TV had been cancelled, I, too, was confused.

'Has it been called off because the gypsies are legally entitled to stay at The Grange,' I asked gingerly, 'or because they're suspects in the robbery at the church and have been told they can't leave town?'

'Who cares? Pete, *please* listen to me.' Annabel flicked her auburn Nice 'n Easy tresses and slithered onto the edge of his desk. As she leaned toward him, he got an eyeful of cleavage whereas we were rewarded with the rear view – the Y of a lilac-coloured thong peeping above the waistband of her low-rider jeans.

'Don't you understand that having a camera crew here with the police is good television?' Annabel pleaded. 'We could film them searching the caravans and everything.'

'There will be no searching of caravans,' Pete said coldly. 'Now get off my desk and go and sit down.'

Annabel childishly flung her pencil across the room and flounced back to the sofa.

'Conducting a search, a *televised* search, would throw up all sorts of legal issues,' said Edward.

'But they're thieves!' shrieked Annabel. 'If they didn't steal them, who did?'

111

'Gypsies are very superstitious,' said Edward. 'They'd never steal holy artifacts from a church, especially at night.'

'The Swamp Dogs?' I suggested, but even I knew their parents were atheists and would never set foot in a church.

'No,' said Annabel slowly, and turned to look straight at me. 'My instincts tell me this could be the work of a professional thief.'

'Don't start that The-Fog-is-in-Gipping nonsense again, Annabel,' warned Pete. 'I won't save your job next time.'

My heart began to pound in my chest. I *had* to steer the subject away from Dad.

'Take a look at this.' I handed Dora's envelope over to Pete. 'Dora is on the National Gypsy Council,' I said, 'and believe me, she knows her rights.'

'The woman with the Winnebago?' said Annabel with a sneer. 'Have you any idea how expensive those things are to buy? I bet she didn't get the money from telling fortunes!'

Pete pulled out the newsletter. *'Romany Ramblings?'*

'It's for gypsies and travellers,' I said. 'Dora has an office set up in her Winnebago with a printer and a scanner. She said a lot of the younger folk have computers and iPhones so can get it online.'

Annabel hurried around to Pete and snatched it out of his hands. 'God. Listen to this. It says here that the Queen awarded an MBE to a gypsy called Gloria Buckley. I quote, "We are part of the human race, a microcosm, and there is good and bad in our community as there is everywhere else." Blah-blah-blah. Apparently, they're organic conservationists—'

'Let me see that,' said Tony.

Annabel tossed the publication onto his lap. 'Be my guest.'

Tony skimmed the contents. 'I don't like them any more than you do, but last night I sneaked up to The Grange to take some photographs of all that rubbish behind the pigsty—'

'Don't tell me they're using the recycling bins?' scoffed Annabel.

'They sure are. Couldn't believe my eyes. The stuff that couldn't fit had been sorted into neat piles. Scrap metal. Paper. Even cardboard boxes had been broken down,' said Tony incredulously.

'I don't care about recycling or about Belcher Pike!' Pete slammed his hand down on his desk. 'Right now all I care about is Page One. We've got no bloody lead story!'

'How about a reward for the missing silver?' Annabel and I chorused, then looked at each other with distaste.

'I'm the one who has the relationship with Lady Ethel, and it was the Trewallyn chalice that was stolen,' said Annabel.

'And the artifacts,' I said. 'The church is my area of expertise.'

Pete drummed his fingers on his desk. 'What else have we got?'

'But that's a great lead!' said Annabel.

'How about a day-in-the-life of Phil Burrows?' I suggested. 'What's it like for him to be dancing with the Turpin Terrors instead of the Gipping Ranids?'

'You won't make yourself popular,' said Tony. 'No one will care.'

'What's going on with "Motorist Menace of the Week"?' said Pete. 'Any poor bugger been caught by Stalk for drunk driving?'

'I was,' I said. 'Almost.'

'Speaking about Mudge Lane,' said Edward. 'When I bumped into Coroner Cripps at the petrol station this morning, he told me they still had no ID on the woman who died and that she had been moved to Plymouth.'

'That's strange,' said Annabel.

My stomach clenched. Half of me didn't want anyone to know about this, but the other half wanted to see Pete's reaction.

'I already told you,' said Pete. 'It's not our problem.'

'Not our *problem*?' Edward rarely raised his voice.

We all looked at one another, stunned. Since when did Pete

not seize the chance to stir up trouble with his controversial front-page scoops? His cavalier attitude toward the stolen silver and his blatant indifference to a dead woman were seriously worrying. What was wrong with him?

'With all due respect,' Edward began, 'I feel—'

'If you've got any complaints, take it up with Wilf,' Pete snapped. 'And Vicky, Stalk has already called me this morning to complain about your behaviour at the church. Apparently you disobeyed a police officer.'

'Sorry,' I mumbled.

As we were dismissed, Edward asked Pete for a quiet word but was bundled out and had the door slammed in his face.

The four of us stood quietly shocked in the reporter room. 'He's losing it,' said Tony.

'Don't take any notice of him,' said Annabel. 'I think he's having problems at home.' Grabbing her favourite Mulberry bag off her desk, she looked directly at me. 'I'm off to The Grange to talk to her ladyship. I think she should know there could be an international thief in the area.'

'Good idea,' I said mildly.

Recalling that Dora was going to be in the market square this morning, I decided to take her up on her offer of telling my fortune after all. Perhaps she could enlighten me on Annabel's plans.

I'd also keep my eyes peeled for a Land Rover with a safari roof rack and overhead lighting. Thursdays at Gipping market often attracted a different kind of crowd.

Pete's insistence that the dead woman was not our problem had only made me determined to make it mine.

I had no intention of letting sleeping dogs lie.

114

19

I was relieved to find Barbara back at work. When I'd arrived earlier this morning, the office was still locked up and the front door blinds down. I'd had to let myself in via the side entrance and discovered everyone else had done so, too.

The shutters to Barbara's beloved street-side show window were wide open, and only her ample rear – clothed in a poppy-print skirt – strong calves and sturdy Birkenstocks protruded from the aperture.

'I'm so happy to see you,' I said, realizing this was true. 'You won't believe what's been going on. We've had a weird drowning in Mudge Lane, someone has stolen the church silver, and we've got gypsies at The Grange.'

Barbara edged backward out of the opening and stood up. Her face was pale. Large dark circles lay beneath her normally inquisitive eyes, which today seemed dull and listless. Her hair, although scraped back into its customary bun, looked dishevelled, with loose tendrils escaping from their pins.

'Are you feeling any better?'

'No, I'm not,' said Barbara. 'Just *look* what that wretched Olive has done to my window!'

I peered over Barbara's shoulder and gave a gasp of dismay.

Dead centre was a life-sized standee of Phil Burrows dressed as an action hero in white trousers, a black T-shirt and Terminator sunglasses. A slogan said I AM BACK!

On Phil's right stood Beryl – the creepy horse mascot with the highwayman mask. On his left was *another* life-sized standee of Phil Burrows dressed as a Turpin Terror in a red tatter three-quarter coat, black breeches, a white cravat, a tricorn hat, and a highwayman mask. Along the base of the window, various Turpin Terror souvenirs had been arranged in a neat row – tricorn hats, mugs, key rings and scarves.

Tucked in the rear left-hand corner stood the Gipping Ranids mascot – a bright-green man-sized frog, with huge webbed feet, bulbous eyes, and a goofy smile. The banner GIPPING RANIDS RULE! was lying on the ground and partially hidden by carefully placed musical instruments – an accordion, pipes, tabors, a concertina and two fiddles – in a symmetrical design. Olive was always one for straight lines.

'How could you let her do this?' Barbara's voice was heavy with accusation. '*No one* is allowed to touch my window displays!'

'I thought no one could,' I said. 'Don't you have the only key?'

'The padlock was snapped off with wire clippers,' Barbara said. 'And we know who always keeps a pair of those in his dustcart cab: Olive's ghastly boyfriend.'

'In fairness to Olive, she was put on the spot,' I protested. 'I was here when Phil Burrows came in yesterday, and he demanded she put all his things in the front of the window; otherwise, he'd pull out of Saturday's event. We tried to find you—'

'And what am I supposed to tell the Ranids?' said Barbara. 'Jack Webster will have a fit. He's the squire this year, and you know what his temper is like.'

'Can't we just change the mascots around?'

'You don't just *change* it around,' said Barbara with scorn.

116

'There is skill involved.' She marched over to the nook and drew back the star-spangled curtain to reveal a pile of Ranid-themed souvenirs, posters and flags. 'Where am I supposed to put all these?'

'There's space—'

'Oh, to hell with it,' said Barbara, throwing up her hands. 'I don't have time for all this.' She stormed over to the counter, yanked up the flap, and let it fall behind her with a deafening crash. 'Let Olive take the blame. I don't care.'

This was so unlike Barbara. I'd never seen her so upset. Clearly, she must be suffering from pre-wedding nerves, and yesterday's migraine was evidence of that. Mum often said that when something major was bothering Dad, it was the little things – overcooking the potatoes, losing a sock – that used to send him off the deep end.

'Where is Olive now?' I asked.

'God knows.' Barbara gestured to the neat stacks of paperwork and heaps of coloured ribbons along the counter. 'She was supposed to have sorted all this out. I'm not going to her hen party now. She can stuff it.'

'Don't be silly. Olive would be terribly hurt. She's been planning it for ages.'

Good grief. This was worse than being at school. I looked over to the front door. Speak of the devil. 'Here comes Olive now.'

'Good. I'll give her a piece of my mind.'

Olive nudged the door open with her shoulder and walked in cradling a small brown paper bag in her hands. Barbara and I immediately recoiled. There was the most terrible stench.

'You'll never guess who I've just seen,' enthused Olive, oblivious to Barbara covering her nose. 'A gypsy fortune-teller and healer. Her name is Madame Dora.'

'Was she any good?' I said.

Olive gently set the brown bag down on the counter and retrieved a small business card from her cream hand-knitted cardigan pocket. Today she wore a yellow butterfly barrette in her sleek bobbed hair. 'Barbara, this is for you. I thought she might be able to help your Wilf with his bad eye.'

Barbara pinched her nose and spoke. 'No, thank you,' she said in a nasal voice. 'It's not *bad*. He only *has* one eye.'

'What's in that bag?' I said.

'Whatever it is, stinks,' muttered Barbara.

'It's goose dung,' Olive said proudly. 'Collected by the light of a new moon.'

Barbara gave a snort. 'Oh *please!*'

'It's a cure for Ronnie's baldness. I have to keep the dung moist until midnight. Then, when the clock strikes twelve, I have to smear it over Ronnie's head.'

'Gosh,' was all I managed to say. I glanced at Barbara and was relieved to see the beginnings of a smile rapidly contort into suppressed mirth.

'Won't it get on the pillows?' I said, struggling not to laugh myself.

'No. He's got to wear a woollen cap for a whole cycle of the moon. Twenty-eight days,' Olive declared.

'How much did that *dung* set you back?' sniggered Barbara.

'Five pounds. You really should go.'

'Did she tell you to put Phil Burrows's equipment in my window without consulting me?' demanded Barbara.

Olive turned pink. 'Well. I— I—'

'You're right. I should see Madame Dora,' I said. 'Shall I get a love charm, Barbara? See who I am going to fall in love with?' The only way to distract Barbara was to talk about matters of the heart.

'Love brings more trouble than it's worth,' Barbara said bitterly.

Olive winked at me and whispered loudly, 'They must have had a row.'

'I heard that,' said Barbara.

It would certainly explain Barbara's unheard of absence from

118

work and the I'm-sorry-I-love-you flowers on her doorstep. I wondered what the row was about.

Did you get your present?' said Olive suddenly.

Barbara frowned. 'What present?'

'Someone delivered it here yesterday,' said Olive. 'I thought you were going to take it over to Barbara's, Vicky?'

Thank you, Olive. 'Silly me left it at home today, but I did try to see you yesterday. You must have gone out.'

'Out?' said Barbara sharply. 'I wasn't out. I was asleep. I had a migraine.'

I was about to argue with her but had a better idea. 'Have you checked on your pink bicycle recently?' *Nice one, Vicky.* 'With all the thieving around, I'd hate for you to lose it.'

'Unless it's been stolen in the last two hours,' said Barbara. 'How else could I get to work? Magic carpet?'

'The gypsies have already taken the church silver and the Trewallyn chalice,' said Olive. 'And they ride bicycles.'

'Why do they always get the blame?' Barbara glowered. 'Do you have any proof?'

Olive seemed to wither beneath Barbara's fury. We were both glad when the door to the inner hall opened and Wilf stepped into reception.

'I've just had a phone call from Jack Webster,' said Wilf. 'He told me that the Ranids mascot has been put at the back of the window. What's going on?'

'Ask Olive,' snapped Barbara. 'It was her idea.'

Olive froze as Wilf swung round and zeroed in with his good eye. 'Well?'

There was a horrible silence as we waited for Olive to speak. Her face began to turn blue from holding her breath.

'The flowers you gave Barbara were lovely, sir.' I couldn't think what else to say. Olive made a reassuring gasp.

'Flowers? What flowers?'

'The ones you left on Barbara's doorstep?' I faltered.

A tide of crimson raced up Barbara's neck. 'I don't know

what she's talking about,' she said quickly. 'Silly girl. You must have imagined it.'

'No. I didn't.' I was getting fed up with Barbara. But then, in a flash, it hit me. The flowers must have been from another admirer, possibly the anonymous shoebox, too. The only people who took time off during the middle of the day and weren't ill or going on holiday were those who were having affairs.

I looked at Barbara – was that *guilt* in her eyes?

'You're right,' I said. 'I was getting confused with your neighbour. Shall we change the window display together?'

'But what about Phil?' Olive whined.

'As a matter of fact, I'm interviewing Phil Burrows tonight for a day-in-the-life,' I said. 'I'll tell him. I'm sure he'll understand.'

'Hold up on that day-in-the-life,' said Wilf. 'There has been some bad feeling going around about Phil coming back to Gipping for this so-called guest appearance. Let's keep him low key.'

'Of course, sir.' *Low key?* I'd worked with local celebrities before, and they had massive egos. If Phil got wind of the fact that not only were his standees being pushed to the rear of the show window *but* he wasn't getting a mention in Saturday's newspaper, I was sure he'd pull out.

'I believe Phil's holding a silent auction,' I said. 'Should I just get a list of the items?'

'What's it in aid of?' said Wilf.

Blast! I had no idea. 'Let me find out.'

Barbara ultimately rejected my offer of help, insisting that since it was Olive's fault, she should be made to put things to rights.

I stepped outside into the High Street thoroughly perplexed. The world as I knew it seemed to be crumbling away, and it had all started with the arrival of Belcher Pike and his merry band of gypsies.

With that in mind, I set off for the market square.

20

Towards the top of the High Street, the traffic was at a standstill. Some motorists had their car doors open and were balancing on the sills to get a look at the holdup. One motorist hit his car horn, and suddenly everyone's car horns were blaring in a deafening chorus.

There was a buzz of excitement in the air. In a flash, I knew what was happening. The much-awaited gypsy invasion had begun.

I broke into a jog, cursing the fact I'd left my Canon Digital Rebel in my Fiat glove box. Rounding the corner, I came across a wall of onlookers.

A Garrett showman traction engine, circa 1913, was completely blocking the street. It seemed to have stalled. Steam belched from the black funnel that protruded through the bright red-and-green-striped canopy that stretched the length of the shiny green engine.

Along the sideboards THE GORDON was embellished in fancy scrolls and picked out in gold. Hanging from the rear was a rather worrying sign – COME AND RIDE THE GORDON! THE GRANGE! THIS SATURDAY! £1 A GO!

At the helm stood Mary Berry, a sixty-something do-it-yourself mechanic dressed in an orange boiler suit.

Following the death of her husband – champion hedge-cutter Gordon Berry – Mary had been determined to finish his lifelong labour of love, namely rebuilding this showman traction engine so that one day she could drive the hundred-plus miles to the Great Dorset Steam Fair.

Three times the iron monstrosity jolted forward several inches, then rolled back with a screech of brakes, sending a cry of alarm from the growing crowd of spectators. Pete had wanted a new front-page lead, but I wasn't sure if this was what he had in mind.

For a moment, I faltered. It's one thing to imagine the worst and quite another to bear witness to it. As another cry of fear erupted from the crowd, my knees turned to jelly. Did I really have what it took to be the next Christiane Amanpour?

Forcing myself to get a grip – after all, Christiane must have witnessed much worse in the trenches – I plunged into the fray and pushed my way through to the front amid cries of 'Those wheels will squash him flat' and 'Mary Berry's drunk.'

There was a sudden round of applause. It was all over. With a cheery wave and long peep on the whistle, the showman tractor lurched forward and slowly chugged up the hill.

Thanks to Simon Mears's quick thinking, tragedy had been averted. First Gipping Scout Group's Akela had saved the day by miraculously wedging a large cinder-block under each rear wheel. Where Simon found them was anyone's guess, but it certainly took the Boy Scout motto of 'Be Prepared' to a new level.

Traffic began to move and the crowd dispersed, chattering with excitement and comparing this near-death experience with alpine avalanches and other natural disasters.

Simon joined me, shaking his head with disbelief. Dressed in beige trousers and a beige-and-brown-patterned shirt, he reminded me of a giraffe with his long and intelligent pointed face. Even though Simon wasn't dressed in uniform this morning, he wore the distinctive scout trefoil badge on his winged collar.

'Mary's determined to give rides to the kiddies at this Saturday's event,' he said. 'With all this rain, foot traffic, and cars, the ground surface will be like an ice rink. It's just not safe.'

'I suppose I could have a word with her sister-in-law, Eunice Pratt.' Though the thought didn't thrill me.

'Please do. I believe she's in the market square this morning. I would have been happy to do so but the truth is—' he paused and looked a tad uncomfortable before plunging on, 'I don't really like Eunice, and she's become so militant with her petitions.'

This didn't surprise me. Eunice Pratt was hugely unpopular, and her endless petitions were legendary.

Simon lowered his voice and added, 'I think Mary Berry was drunk.' This didn't surprise me, either. I'd never seen Mary Berry sober.

'I don't really want to report her to DI Stalk,' Simon went on. 'Let's hope Eunice will intervene.'

The thought of talking to the odious Eunice Pratt brought back all sorts of memories. Not that long ago, and for all of forty-eight turbulent hours, I'd been obsessed with her handsome nephew, the gorgeous Lieutenant Robin Berry of Her Majesty's Royal Navy.

What a disappointment he had turned out to be – just like all the other men I'd had such high hopes for. As Barbara said, love only seemed to bring trouble.

Four alleys led into each corner of Gipping Pannier Market – to use its correct name. Built on the site of an original Roman encampment, the market still retained its original perimeter walls. In the centre was a large open-sided, glass-roofed building topped with a Victorian clock tower and weathervane.

Inside and centre were two rows of stalls that extended along the entire building, with a farther row lining the perimeter. The area outside the market was scattered with more stalls and exhibits, making this one-of Gipping's prime tourist attractions during the summer months.

The traditional market was always held on a Wednesday, with the sale of livestock, local produce, and crafts. Today was the general market, consisting of second hand furniture, household effects, and cheap clothing – and it was packed.

I entered the south alley flanked by high stone walls. At the end was the familiar sight of Eunice Pratt, clipboard in hand. There she stood in the perfect position to strong-arm anyone into lending his or her signature.

A couple in front of me did an abrupt U-turn, muttering, 'We'll have to take the west alley' and 'Can't stand that old battle-axe.'

Eunice stood in front of a three-panelled display board reading KEEP GIPPING TIDY! GYPSIES GO HOME! Photographs of rusting old fridges, mounds of rubbish, and filthy raw sewage were laid out in gory detail.

One look at Eunice's sour expression and I was already regretting my rash promise to Simon Mears.

Frankly, I was irritated. Why should I be made responsible for Mary Berry's behaviour? What if someone really *was* killed on Saturday; would it be my fault? Maybe I *should* talk to DI Stalk regardless?

Eunice's usual perm was a vibrant shade of violet. She wore a severe charcoal-grey long-sleeved dress and flat shoes. Mixed in with her usual aroma of mothballs was the pungent smell of hair chemicals, suggesting a recent visit to the hairdresser.

I mustered up a smile. 'Morning, Eunice! Lovely day, isn't it?'

'It would be if it wasn't for them.' Eunice pointed to a queue of women waiting outside a candy-striped tent. A pennant depicting a crystal ball fluttered atop in the summer breeze. Ruby – being ignored – was pacing back and forth with her basket of extortionately expensive lucky heather.

'Gypsies,' hissed Eunice. 'Always laws for them and laws

for us.'

Here we go. 'There are only a handful of them,' I said. 'I'm told they won't be here long.'

'They're camped at The Grange, you know' she fumed. 'Why don't I buy a caravan and go and plant it anywhere I like, throw my rubbish around the countryside and then clear off?'

'Not all of them are like that,' I protested. 'Some of them even recycle!'

'They're thieves, the lot of them! I suppose you heard about the church silver?'

'Nothing has been proved—'

'Nothing ever will,' she said. 'Her ladyship at The Grange had even booked an eviction service, but the police told her to cancel. It's New Labour with their rights-for-all, isn't it? What's wrong with this country?'

'One of the gypsy elders is fatally ill, and they can't—'

'Well, we're going to do something about them.' Eunice's eyes were slits of spite. 'Jack Webster has a plan. Do you know how many sides we've got coming from all over Devon?' I told her I knew I should, but I didn't. 'Including the Ranids and that silly Burrows chappy – *nine*!' she exclaimed. 'We won't allow these criminals to ruin the Morris this Saturday.'

'Speaking of mining things,' I said. 'I really need you to talk to Mary.'

Eunice scowled. 'What's she done now?'

'It's about The Gordon,' I said. 'She's not really going to give rides to the children, is she?'

'Mary is stubborn and pleases herself,' Eunice snapped. 'She won't listen to me,'

'What about Robin? Would he talk to her?' I said. 'Is he still at sea?'

At the name of her favourite and only nephew, Eunice's entire face transformed. Her eyes shone. She actually smiled. 'Darling Robin. He'll be home this weekend. I'll speak with him. If anyone can make Mary see reason, it's her son.'

125

I recalled my first date with Robin, during which he spent most of the evening texting his wretched aunt. I'd thought about that a lot since then, and frankly, it's not normal. Mum was right when she said, '*Sometimes being rejected means being saved.*'

Eunice thrust the clipboard under my nose. 'Sign here.' I noted there were dozens and dozens of signatures.

'As a journalist, I have to stay impartial,' I said, 'Sorry.'

'You don't have to write your real name. No one is going to check.'

Fortunately, I was saved by a sudden burst of applause coming from the direction of the Public Toilets just a few yards away, where a crowd of women stood clustered around the exit to the Gents.

Phil Burrows emerged and was instantly mobbed by a sea of female admirers. He was dressed exactly like his action hero standee – white trousers, black T-shirt, and Terminator sunglasses.

'Excuse me, Eunice,' I said, glad to make my escape. 'I need to talk to Phil Burrows. As you know, he's making a guest appearance.'

'I can't think what for,' she said. 'He's got some nerve showing up here after all the Ranids did for him.'

'The *Gazette* is doing a day-in-the-life,' I lied.

'No one will read it,' said Eunice. 'You should be writing about the Ranids. That's traditional Morris dancing for you. The Turpin Terrors are just young upstarts.'

'I'll bear that in mind.'

I caught up with Phil in the refreshment area on the opposite side of the square. The statuesque figure of sensible Gillian Briggs, a former cook in the Royal Navy, stood behind a long trestle table piled with freshly baked goods and a steel tea urn. I was ravenous.

Phil was seated at one of the many wrought-iron tables and chairs surrounded by his posse and, judging by the squeals of delight and photographs held aloft, signing autographs.

He waved me over. 'Enough ladies, enough!' he said beaming. 'Give me five minutes with Vicky.'

With groans of disappointment, the women moved away to reveal a table strewn with black-and-white head-shots. I took the empty chair and sat down.

'They exhaust me,' said Phil happily. 'Everyone wants a piece of Phil. You should see what's on offer for the silent auction. Two of the ladies almost fainted when I told them I was flogging the shirt I wore when I met the Hoff.'

Eunice was wrong. There were many people who would like to hear all about a day-in-the-life of Phil Burrows – especially his newfound friendship with David Hasselhoff, who was a *real* celebrity.

I brought out my notebook. 'What's the silent auction in aid of?'

'Me, of course,' said Phil. 'I'm raising money for my trip to Los Angeles. My agent says if you want to break into America, you've got to physically be there.'

'Good idea,' I said. 'Perhaps you could give me a list of the auction items for the newspaper?'

'I've left it at Gipping Manor,' said Phil. 'I've pencilled you in for six thirty tonight. We'll catch a quick bite. I've got to call my agent at seven thirty in LA, and then I've got a tanning session at eight. Hey! Danny-boy!'

I glanced over my shoulder and, to my surprise, saw Noah walking by carrying two take-out cups of tea.

Phil jumped excitedly to his feet. 'What are you doing here?' he cried. 'Come and join us! Come and meet Vicky.'

For a split second, Noah hesitated, then turned on his heel and walked off in the opposite direction.

'Well I never.' Phil's jaw dropped. He seemed bewildered. I thought it just plain rude.

Phil sat back down. 'Danny was as chatty as you please in Brighton two weeks ago.'

'Maybe you're mistaken?' I said. 'That's Noah Pike. He's one of the gypsies up at The Grange.'

'No,' said Phil firmly. 'I never forget a face or a name. I can't afford to in my profession. His name is definitely Danny. He plays the guitar – got a pretty good voice, too. We got to talking whilst waiting for the bank to open.'

Even if Phil had gotten Noah's name wrong, he certainly had the right man. The gypsies had been in Brighton, and Noah did play the guitar.

'He must be here for Saturday's event,' Phil went on. 'My fans come from all over the country. They can get intimidated. When we first met, Danny didn't know I was famous.'

More likely Noah was embarrassed about being a gypsy and didn't want to admit it. Who was I to judge? Didn't I lie about my parents? I still regretted inventing the story of their death-by-lions in Africa. Even to me it sounded far-fetched.

A flutter of admiring females descended upon us. Phil grinned and flexed his muscles.

'We're back,' gushed young Nicola Mears, First Gipping Brownie's Brown Owl and Simon Mears's wife. 'It's been exactly five minutes. We timed ourselves.'

I wondered if her husband knew she had a crush on Phil Burrows whilst he had been out there risking life and limb under the wheels of The Gordon?

Reassuring Phil that I'd meet him at Gipping Manor tonight, I headed straight for the refreshment table. If I didn't have a cuppa in the next three minutes, I'd collapse from malnutrition.

'That's Phil Burrows, isn't it?' said Gillian Briggs, handing me a cup. 'I remember him and his brother, Steve, when they were little. Phil was always the handsome one. Always stealing Steve's girlfriends. Oh! You're back—' she smiled.

I turned to find Noah and, to my annoyance, felt my face go hot. He really was handsome.

'I'll take two more rock cakes, Mrs Briggs.' Noah turned to

me. 'Can I have a quick word, Vicky? It's important. For a rockcake?'

Gillian Briggs raised her eyebrows and winked.

'Okay,' I mumbled. 'I'm listening.'

'No. In private. Follow me.'

With a cup of tea in one hand and a rock cake in the other, I hurried after him, wondering what on earth it could be about.

Moments later, Noah stopped at the mouth of the rarely used east alley, which led to the industrial estate. It was a well-known hideout for lovesick teenagers after dark. Being mid-morning, the place was deserted. I felt inexplicably jittery.

'I owe you an apology,' said Noah. 'I was rude yesterday. The thing is—' he took a deep breath. 'You make me nervous.'

I was stunned. 'But you don't even know me.'

'I feel as if we've met in another life,' said Noah, staring deep into my eyes.

My stomach turned over. Had he known me when I lived in Newcastle with Mum and Dad?

Gypsies got around a lot. It was certainly possible. 'I don't think so,' I said, adding wildly – and inexplicably, 'I'm an orphan.'

'An orphan? Me, too.' said Noah. 'Both my parents died of the flu when I was twelve. The doctors refused to treat gypsies in the hospital.'

'That's awful,' I said. 'Mine were on safari – actually, I can't talk about it.' Somehow I just couldn't bring myself to tell Noah the death-by-lions-in-Africa story.

'I live with Aunt Dora,' he said. 'You know we didn't steal that silver. It's always the same. We're always blamed for everything.'

'I know. I'm sorry.'

'You're different from the other gorgers, aren't you?' He brushed a strand of hair away from my face – just as Mr Evans had done to Annabel. A bolt of electricity passed between us.

'Am I?' I said, feeling even more jittery. Was this what he

had in mind when asking to see me in private? Things were moving very fast. *Good grief!* Was he going to kiss me in broad daylight?

'Is this why you've brought me here?' I said coyly. 'No. I didn't want to be overheard,' said Noah. 'I need to talk to you about the woman in Mudge Lane.'

All thoughts of love flew right out of my mind. 'You know who she is?' I gasped.

'You mean to say you don't?' Noah seemed surprised. 'I thought you reporters worked closely with the police?'

'They're not interested,' I said exasperated. 'I don't understand it.'

'Why?' said Noah. 'What did they say?'

There was a crash of breaking glass followed by another, as a wave of empty beer bottles sailed in our direction. A pack of schoolchildren added stones to their ammunition.

'Clear off you dirty pikeys!' they yelled.

'You'd better leave,' said Noah, as the kids drew closer. Some were armed with sticks. Frankly, I'd never seen such open racial hatred and was embarrassed for my kind.

'What was her name?' I cried, as he began to back away. 'Was she a gypsy?'

'Meet me by the gatehouse tonight at ten,' said Noah. 'I'll tell you everything.'

And with that, he tossed his empty cup aside and ran off down the alley with the kids in hot pursuit.

I stared after him, feeling incredibly excited. I had recruited a brand-new informant and a handsome one at that. But first, a quick word with his aunt, Madame Dora, was in order.

21

In the past hour or so, the queue of women waiting to see what the future held had grown considerably longer. Clearly, rumours that the gypsies were responsible for the theft of the missing church silver and priceless Trewallyn chalice had not affected Madame Dora's business a bit.

I felt a twinge of disgust. Only yesterday, most of these ladies were desperate for the 'pikeys' to be gone, but today they were lining Dora's pockets with pounds.

I felt a slight wave of anxiety. What if she sensed I'd planned to meet one of her kin tonight? What if she peered into her crystal ball and saw something – *romantic!* Hadn't Jimmy said that gypsies and gorgers could never be together?

The tent flap lifted, and Mrs Evans emerged clutching a brown paper bag. Ruth Reeves broke away from her friends, pawing at Mrs E.'s arm, saying urgently, 'Was it worth the money?'

Seeing as how Ruth had been married to hedge-cutter John Reeves for decades, I wondered why she would need to see Madame Dora at all. Mum says only unhappy people want to know the future.

'If it works, it's worth every penny,' said Mrs Evans grimly.

'That's not goose dung, is it?' I said, joining them.

'No it's most certainly not,' said Mrs Evans. 'It's a charm to put a stop to Lenny's wandering eye.'

'What's in it?'

'I'm not allowed to say.'

Dora poked her head out of the tent looking decidedly different from the last time we met.

Heavily made up with false eyelashes and crimson lipstick, a colourful bandana was wrapped around her head. Two large hoops dangled from her ear lobes, and her wrists jangled with an abundance of gold bracelets.

'I thought I heard your voice, Vicky,' she said. 'Come on in.'

Ignoring the grumblings and cries of 'She's jumped the queue' and 'What's so special about Vicky Hill?' I ducked inside.

Securing the flap behind us, Dora gestured for me to take the wooden stool whilst she settled into a high winged-back chair. A large crystal ball sat atop a round table that was covered with a gold-fringed, deep purple tablecloth. Behind Dora's chair was a three-panelled Chinese screen painted with mysterious symbols. In the corner stood a potted plant and a small painted wooden medicine chest with dozens of little drawers containing various herbs – if the labels were anything to go by.

This setup must have taken some time to put together to say nothing of transportation to and from The Grange. How did it get here?

'Ruby brought all this in her VW camper,' said Dora, as if reading my thoughts.

'I was just wondering,' I said.

'We didn't steal that silver,' Dora said bluntly. 'Someone is trying to frame us. Someone is throwing rubbish around the pigsty,' Dora raged on. 'Rubbish we spent a whole day clearing up and putting away into the correct recycling bins.'

'I'm not sure if what you saw in a crystal ball will hold up—'

'I'm not daft, luv. I've got it all on camera – and more besides!'

'*On film*?'

My suspicions as to Topaz's involvement were growing by the minute. 'I *am* sorry, Dora,' I said in my friendliest voice. 'I have a feeling I know who is doing this. Why don't I have a word with that person? I'm sure that person will apologize.'

'Don't bother,' said Dora. 'I already know who is doing it, and I'm going to make sure she goes to prison.'

Good grief! 'Aren't you being a bit hasty?'

Dora regarded me with utter contempt. 'Hasty? *Hasty?* There's a dying man just feet from her back door! She's shown no respect for our culture. It beggars belief.'

'At least let me talk to her first. I'm sure it was just playful high spirits.'

'Why? Friend of yours, is she?' said Dora with a sneer.

'Not exactly.' *Blast,* wretched Topaz and her ridiculous disguises.

'Good, you've got some sense, then.' Dora leaned back in her chair and cocked her head. 'You've had a rough life, luv,' she said gently. 'Be careful of these so-called friends. They'd think nothing of betraying you.' She leaned forward and took my hand, turning it palm side up once more. 'You're an outsider,' she said. 'Stick to your own kind. And, whilst we are on the subject, gorgers and gypsies should not be together. *Ever.*'

I felt my face redden. 'I don't understand what you mean.'

'You know who I'm talking about.'

The tent was becoming claustrophobic. I snatched back my hand. What a fool I'd been to come here. The gypsy could obviously 'see' me with Noah.

'That'll be five pounds,' said Dora. 'But since you've got my article on the front page, I'll do this for free.'

Front page? 'Thank you, but you do know that Page One is not up to me?' I said. 'I'd still like to talk to her ladyship about this so-called film.'

Dora gave a harsh laugh. 'Don't waste your breath. My mind is made up.'

I got to my feet thoroughly rattled, though I wasn't sure if it was because of Dora's stubborn determination to get Topaz incarcerated – though I'd often thought of doing that myself – or her uncanny knowledge of my rendezvous tonight with Noah. Either way, I wanted to get out of this tent. *Now*.

Outside, a chorus of 'Are you going to meet Mr Right?' and 'Will you win the lottery?' greeted me, but I had no desire to stand and chat.

It suddenly occurred to me that I had triple-booked myself tonight – an interview with Phil for a day-in-the-life, a rendezvous with the gorgeous Noah, and somehow, mixed in with all this, drinks with Steve.

An extremely trying evening loomed ahead.

22

Three times I tried to call The Grange to speak to Topaz about this so-called film, but the phone just rang and rang. Needless to say, she didn't have a mobile or an answering machine.

Finally, on the fourth attempt – journalism is all about persistence – I was taken aback by the sound of a familiar voice and, for a moment, thought I must have dialled the wrong number.

'Annabel, is that you?'

'What do you want, Vicky?'

'Are you at The Grange?'

'Well, duh?' said Annabel. 'Where else do you think I'd be? The moon?'

'What are you doing there?' I said. 'I thought the eviction was off.'

'It may be off for *now*,' she said, 'but actually her ladyship is in a dreadful state.'

'Why? What's happened?' Topaz had seemed very cheerful on the phone this morning.

There was an exasperated sigh. 'Because of the Trewallyn

135

chalice. It was stolen, remember? Fortunately, I was able to tell her ladyship that the *Gazette* would be offering a reward of fifty pounds for any information leading to its recovery.'

Frankly, I thought fifty pounds a bit cheap. 'It was my idea.'

'It was *our* idea,' said Annabel briskly. 'However, since it's me who has the relationship with the Lady Ethel, it's all my idea now.'

Blast Annabel and *blast* Topaz! 'Can I talk to her, please? It's important.'

'She's resting, and anyway, all her calls go through me now,' said Annabel. 'What would it be regarding?'

I hesitated. Even if Dora was bluffing, I didn't want Annabel to jump on this bandwagon, too. 'Tell her, tell her... it's about Belcher Pike's funeral arrangements.'

As I ended the call, I wondered why I was bothering to talk to Topaz at all. With Annabel as her new best friend, she'd probably repeat our conversation.

I felt strangely depressed and a tiny bit jealous. *Get a grip, Vicky!* I had far too much on my plate to give way to maudlin musings.

Outside the *Gazette,* a handful of people were clustered around the show window, chattering animatedly. I caught snatches of conversation: 'Burrows shouldn't even be in there!' 'Long live the Ranids!' 'Burrows put Gipping on the map!' 'It's a disgrace!'

Before I got dragged into God-knows-what – I'd had more than my fair share of drama today – I darted across the street to get a better view of what was causing so much excitement.

It would seem there were two opposing camps stationed on either side of the show window. In the middle, Barbara and Olive were reorganizing the display to cries of dismay or yelps of delight from the onlookers.

Out went Phil Burrows's horse mascot. *In* came the Ranids's bright green frog. *Out* went Phil Burrow's Turpin Terror standee. *In* came a life-sized mannequin of a Gipping Ranids

Morris man in full-on costume, bells et al. Olive seemed to get tangled up in his baldricks, and the two of them toppled over to the glee of the pro-Burrows clan. Barbara threw up her hands in frustration.

This was one of the rare times when I did not want to be part of the action. My stomach rumbled again – the rock cake had not been that filling.

Realizing it was the day that Mrs Evans 'did' for Margaret Pierce, I decided to go straight home and raid the pantry. I'd also had an idea.

There was still the mystery of the missing shoebox. Since it was the summer holidays, the Swamp Dogs were bound to be festering in their lair at the abandoned wool and textile factory opposite my home. I might grill them on the church silver. Who knows – maybe they might have seen a green Land Rover with a safari roof rack and overhead lighting.

I went to get my car and set off for Factory Terrace.

Rounding a corner, I saw Bill Trenfold's post van driving away from the pillar box on the corner of Tripp Lane. I looked at my watch with astonishment!

This time it wasn't even 3.30 p.m.! Bill's collection time was getting earlier and earlier – no doubt he was sneaking off home and pretending to put in a full day's work.

On a whim, I stopped by the pillar box and found that, once again, he'd forgotten to close the door properly. This was unacceptable.

I sped after Bill and managed to catch him at his next port of call – the pillar box at the entrance to Bexmoor Way.

Making sure to cut off his escape with a PIT manoeuvre – precision immobilization technique that I'd seen on an American show on the telly – I leapt out of my Fiat and strolled over, giving a playful rap on the bonnet of his car.

Bill wound the window down and scowled.

'Hi, Bill,' I said. 'Nice day.'

Bill regarded me with his rheumy eyes. 'Forecast says we'll

have scattered showers on Saturday, but what do they know?'

I noted he hadn't shaved. Grey whiskers peppered his chin and sprouted from his nostrils in tufts.

Reminding myself that despite the rumours that brother and sister loathed each other, Bill had still lost his only living relative. Suppressed grief could do funny things to people and might explain why he was becoming so forgetful.

'How are you coping?' I said. 'Are you eating properly? Feeling light-headed?'

Bill looked wary. 'Why?'

'You might want to double-check those pillar boxes in Tripp Lane and The Marshes. Both doors weren't closed properly.'

All the colour drained from Bill's already pale face. He opened his mouth and shut it several times but no sound came out. Finally, he managed to croak, 'I've got a lot on my mind.'

'Don't worry. No harm done.' I gave him my most reassuring smile, but deep down I was worried. I pointed to the collection plate. 'Are you coming back again at five thirty?'

'Eh?' Bill scratched his head under his polished peaked cap.

'It's just turned three thirty,' I said helpfully.

Bill stared at me again, then blurted out, 'New times,' he said. 'It's not my fault It's head office. They keep cutting down my hours.'

Of course, everyone in the entire country knew about the enforced closure of hundreds of village post offices. Many postal workers were being laid off as the government slashed postal budgets, and countless petitions had been signed by customers worried about saying goodbye to yet another landmark of British country living.

'You mean, you're only picking up post once a day?' I said.

'What?'

'Is there a new time?' Really, this was quite maddening. 'Because if there is, these collection plates need to be updated.'

Bill's bottom lip began to quiver. 'You won't tell anyone, will you?' he said. 'I don't want to get the sack.'

138

'Of course not.' Poor man. If Reverend Whittler was right, Bill already had enough money problems; 'I just don't want you to get into trouble.'

Bill got out of his post van. He pulled out a large fob of keys from his pocket and made a meal out of slamming and locking the door shut. 'Happy now?'

Leaving him to it, I set off once more.

Tripp Lane was narrow with a series of blind corners. A cyclist coming in the opposite direction was upon me before I could brake, but fortunately, he pressed himself against the hedge. As I sailed on by, I caught a glimpse of a bright yellow shirt and long ribbon-threaded braid. An empty gunny sack was slung across the handlebars. I was *positive* it was Jimmy the gypsy. I was also positive that he was poaching rabbits. And in broad daylight, too!

Thinking of food, my thoughts turned to Mrs Evans's homemade blackcurrant jam, but it would seem that my afternoon snack was destined not to be.

Jack Webster's Land Rover was parked outside Chez Evans. It was unusual to see Jack in these parts. I hadn't realized he and Mr Evans were close friends and only hoped he wasn't planning on leading my landlady's husband astray.

Since I didn't want to bump into Jack Webster, I drove my car on past and stopped outside the factory's main gate.

No sooner had I cut the engine then I heard the distinctive grating sound of metal scraping on concrete. The main gate edged open, and to my astonishment, Jack Webster emerged. Immediately, I ducked out of sight.

Through the side mirror, I watched Jack pull the peak of his flat tweed cap down over his eyes and saunter back toward his Land Rover.

What on earth could Jack Webster want with the Swamp Dogs? Having been instrumental in getting the lads prosecuted for theft on at least three occasions, it didn't make sense.

Jack surprised me again. Instead of driving off, he marched

up the front path of number twenty-one and rapped on my front door. Moments later, Mr Evans appeared and gestured for him to step inside.

To say I was intrigued was putting it mildly. One of my favourite after-dinner games in the Hill household was called Whistle Blower! When it came to playing the interrogator, I'd never once been beaten.

The Swamp Dogs had better watch out.

23

I found the four Barker brothers – or Swamp Dogs, as they preferred to be called – standing in the far corner of the cracked concrete forecourt.

Mickey was drawing in the dirt with a long stick. I heard, 'No, that won't work,' 'It's in the wrong place,' and 'We won't know until Saturday.'

I gave a loud cough. 'Hello boys!' All four spun around, guilt etched across their features.

'What the hell do you want?' snarled Mickey.

The boys shuffled closer together, forming a human wall and conveniently hiding Mickey's handiwork on the ground behind them.

Malcolm pointed a finger at me. 'You're trespassing.'

'Yeah. Clear off,' squeaked Ben, whose voice hadn't broken yet. Seeing all four stand side by side with their matching outfits, light-brown hair, and blue eyes, the only way to tell them apart was by height and acne damage.

'I was just hoping that Jack Webster wasn't giving you any trouble,' I said.

'You must be blind,' said Mickey quickly. 'He wasn't here. And if you know what's good for you, you'll stay blind.'

'Yeah, if you know what's good for you,' the others chorused, slamming fists into palms, trying to look tough.

Their hostile demeanor did not intimidate me. Having been surrounded by real crime families who used to join us for Sunday lunch at home in Newcastle, dealing with these kids was a piece of cake.

'Nice try, boys, but I saw Jack Webster leave just a minute or so ago, and since he's never been a fan of yours, I wondered what he was up to.'

'None of your business,' said Mickey sullenly. 'And, anyway, why should you care?'

'Firstly, it was *you*, Mickey, who told me that Jack was threatening the gypsies with his billhook,' I pointed out. 'Why the change of heart?'

'I made a mistake,' said Mickey defiantly. 'We don't want the gyppos here, destroying the countryside with their litter.'

'Sleeping with our women,' cried Malcolm.

'Stealing from the mouths of babes,' squeaked Ben.

'Blaspheming in the Lord's house,' declared Brian.

Clearly, Jack had got to them already. 'You don't want to get mixed up with Jack Webster.'

'Why not?' Mickey said.

'I would have thought it obvious.' I gave a benevolent smile. 'Jack has called the cops on you boys enough times. Why would he ask for your help now?'

'We're not helping,' piped up Ben. 'We're being hired.'

'Shut up,' said Mickey. 'Idiot!'

'To do what? Burn down their caravans?' I didn't exactly like the Barker boys, but I would hate to see them get locked up in prison permanently just to satisfy Jack Webster's agenda.

'Who says it's about gypsies?' Ben squeaked and was promptly given a swift kick to his ankle. 'Ouch. What was that for?'

142

'I'm sure your parents would like to know about this,' I said. Mickey scowled. 'You wouldn't *dare.*'

'Please don't, Ms.' Ben started to snivel. 'Dad will kill us.'

'We're not doing anything, okay?' said Mickey. 'And you can't prove anything. I know my rights.'

'It's just a friendly warning,' I said. 'But since we're on the subject of theft. I'd like that package back that you stole out of my car yesterday.'

'I don't know what you mean,' said Mickey.

'Oh, *please.* Not that old line. You were seen by her lady-ship,' I lied. 'And I *will* tell your parents about that, and then whatever Jack Webster has hired you to do won't matter really, will it?'

Mickey cursed under his breath and gave a curt nod to Ben, who broke ranks and scampered off into the derelict building.

His exit allowed me a quick glimpse to what lay on the ground, but all I could make out were tiny heaps of stones set around a circular piece of rubber hosing.

We waited in silence for Ben to reappear, shoebox in hand.

I removed the lid, relieved to find the white shoe and bicycle bell still inside.

'Where is the brown outer wrapping? And the newspaper clipping?'

'Dunno.' Ben shrugged. 'Its just rubbish. We burnt it.'

'Why did *you* have it anyway?' said Malcolm suspiciously. 'It was addressed to Barbara Meadows.'

'She left it behind at the office, and that's none of *your* business.'

'So, we're all cool?' Mickey said.

Handing Mickey one of my cheap business cards, I told him to be careful of Jack Webster and to call me if he ever needed any help. My offer was met with scorn.

By the time I returned to number twenty-one, I was relieved to see that Jack's Land Rover had gone and Mr Evans was back in his shed, tending his snail champions.

As I polished off three pieces of toast and homemade black-currant jam, my phone rang. It was Steve. 'The most terrible thing has happened, doll.'

'The woman was murdered?' I said hopefully.

'They're short-staffed in Totnes.' Steve groaned. 'I've got to work tonight, but I'm hoping it won't be for long.'

'Don't give it another thought.' *Excellent!* I had been worried about how to keep my rendezvous with Noah a secret from Steve, and now I didn't have to. 'We can do it another time.'

'I should be finished around ten. I'll come over.'

'No, don't do that,' I said quickly. 'I'm working, too.'

There was a long pause, then he said, 'What's going on?'

'Nothing.'

'Oh God.' He groaned again. 'She's lying to you, Steve.'

'I'm not lying,' I said hotly. 'I *am* working. I'm interviewing your brother at six thirty.' This part was true.

'My brother!' Steve uttered a cry of anguish. 'I knew it. I knew he'd do this to me. Oh God.'

'For heaven's sake, stop being so dramatic. I'm doing a day-in-the-life feature on Phil, and to get it into this Saturday's paper, it has to be finished by tomorrow lunch-time.' This wasn't true.

There was another long pause. 'I'm not happy about this. Where are you meeting Phil?'

'Gipping Manor.'

'You're going to his *hotel*?'

'No. We'll be in the bar,' I said.

This time the pause lasted a full minute. 'All right. Well, I suppose my news will have to wait.'

'What do you mean?'

'My man came through for me at Plymouth morgue,' said Steve. 'I've got a name, but it doesn't matter. We can talk some time next week.'

My heart gave a leap. 'What is it?'

'I can't remember.'

Blast Steve! Of course he remembered. 'Look,' I said smoothly. 'What time do you go on duty?'

'Eight.'

'Why don't you sit in on my interview with Phil at six thirty? That way you can be sure that nothing weird is going on. Phil told me he had an appointment at seven thirty, so we'll be able to have a little bit of time together.'

'All right. Sorry, doll.' Steve gave a heavy sigh. 'It's just that Phil always steals my girls. He can't help himself.'

'I promise that he hasn't a chance with me.'

Steve made a strange gurgling sound. Was he *crying?* 'Thanks, doll. I really needed to hear that.'

Somehow, I had a feeling that this evening was going to get complicated.

24

When I broke the news that I wouldn't be eating Mrs
Evans's liver and onions tonight, my landlady said,
'Good. It'll be just Lenny and I, like old times.'

'What about Annabel?'

'Dining with her ladyship,' said Mrs E. 'She's gone all la-di-dah.'

Since Topaz's culinary skills left much to be desired – her
Copper Kettle fare usually consisted of stale buns and Tesco
produce well past their expiry dates – I thought, rather you than
me. Even so, Annabel's presence certainly put the kibosh on my
idea of having a quiet word with Topaz about the recycling
situation before my meeting with Noah.

'What time will Annabel be back?'

'She didn't say.' Mrs Evans grinned. 'You see! That charm
I bought from the gypsy is working already.'

I went upstairs to change. What should I wear? Of course,
I'd put on my usual jeans, clean shirt, and safari jacket, but
maybe, just tonight, I'd don my worn-only-once Wild Nights
Millennium lingerie from Marks & Spencer. Not that I intended
to get fresh with Phil, Steve, or Noah, but – as the Boy Scout

motto of 'Be Prepared' had certainly proved true in the High Street today, it was better to be safe than sorry.

I had a quick shower in the bathroom I shared with Annabel. On the old marble washstand was a small package gift-wrapped in pink flowery paper and tied with a pink ribbon. The tag read, 'To Annie with love.'

Poor Mrs Evans. So much for Madame Dora's love charm.

Half an hour later I pulled into Gipping Manor car park. An hour later, I was sitting in the themed 1920s hotel bar, thoroughly bored with listening to Phil Burrows droning on about David Hasselhoff this and David Hasselhoff that. Phil also claimed to have enjoyed a one-night stand with sixties icon Cilla Black, but of course, there was no way of proving it.

But what was really annoying was the fact that Phil was on a diet. Our 'catch a quick bite' was one shared iceberg lettuce with blue cheese dressing because he 'only wanted a nibble.' At least with Steve I could always count on at least three courses.

One of Jack Webster's cronies, John Reeves, strolled into the bar and made a beeline for our table.

'Here comes another fan,' said Phil, smoothing back his hair. But I wasn't so sure. John Reeves was wearing a dark green sweatshirt with RANIDS RULE! emblazoned across the chest. His formidable handlebar moustache was fairly bristling with indignation.

Phil instantly whipped out his pen and magically produced a headshot seemingly from thin air. 'I get just as many men as ladies, you know,' he boasted.

John Reeves towered over Phil. 'You're not wanted in Gipping,' he said bluntly. 'If you ever want to dance again, you'll pack up your bags and leave. Do you understand?

'Loud and clear,' Phil replied with a smirk, seeming completely unfazed.

'Good.' John Reeves turned on his heel and stalked over to the bar.

147

'Loser,' said Phil with a nasty laugh.

'Wow. You were amazing.' I was impressed at Phil's sangfroid but far more excited about a potential real story – TURPIN TERROR TERRORIZED: A VICKY HILL EXCLUSIVE!

'I get threats like that all the time,' boasted Phil. 'Goes with the territory. It's jealousy. I broke out of Gipping. Did something different. It was a big risk joining the Turpin Terrors.' He gestured to my open notepad on the table. 'I hope you got all that down.'

'Yes,' I said. 'Word for word.'

Phil leaned over and kissed me lightly on the cheek. 'You're cute.'

'What the hell's going on?' Steve pushed his way between us.

'Phil's just had a death threat,' I said quickly. Why was I feeling guilty?

'And he's about to have another one.' Steve jabbed his finger into Phil's shoulder, hard. 'Leave my girl alone.'

Phil laughed. 'Don't worry, baby brother. She's just not my type.'

Thanks! Even though I didn't want to be Phil's type, it still wasn't nice to be rejected in such a dismissive manner.

Phil pulled out his iPhone. 'I'm going to text my agent. What was that old bloke's name again?'

'John Reeves,' I said.

Steve dragged up a chair. I caught the familiar scent of Old Spice and antiseptic. He was already wearing his white medical coat.

'What's that?' said Steve, pointing to the half-nibbled iceberg lettuce on Phil's plate that had been divided into two. 'You must be starving.'

'I am a bit hungry,' I said.

'Cheryl?' Steve gestured to a passing waitress in a black-and-white parlour-maid outfit and white frilly cap. 'Burger and chips for Vicky,' he said. 'And the same for me.'

Looking at the two brothers with their startling blue eyes and cherub-shaped faces – despite Phil's distinctly orange pallor – they couldn't have been more different.

'You should get your cholesterol checked,' chided Phil. 'You're a walking heart attack.'

'Women like something to hold on to,' said Steve defensively. 'Isn't that right, doll?'

'It sure is,' I said, wondering if I should have ordered extra chips.

Phil's *Flashdance* ring tone erupted from his man-bag. 'That will be LA. I sent my agent an email, and he's freaking out about that death threat.' Giving me a wolfish grin, he added, 'You remember my room number for later, don't you, Vicky?'

'She's not going to your room,' snapped Steve.

'It's five-oh-nine,' said Phil with a wink. 'I'll keep the champagne on ice.'

'Why you—' Steve rose to his feet, taking the tablecloth with him as usual. There was a tinkle of cutlery as it scattered across the stone floor. I made a quick save for the wine glasses.

'You're so easy to wind up,' chortled Phil.

Steve and I watched him weave his way through the tables to the exit, acknowledging admiring fans and enemies alike.

'Don't take any notice,' I said.

'I don't trust him with you, doll. Everyone wants to go out with Vicky Hill.'

They do?

'Hell-lo—' Steve's expression hardened. 'Speak of the devil. What's he doing here?'

I glanced over my shoulder to see Detective Inspector Probes stroll into the bar. He paused to scan the room, clearly looking for someone. Our eyes met. A shadow of distaste crossed his features.

Suddenly, Steve fastened his lips onto mine and kissed me hard. I felt dizzy. Delicious tingles ran through my body. I tried to keep my lips clamped together, but Steve was relentless. I just couldn't help but kiss him back. Why, oh why, did this have to be *Steve*?

'Would you both like ketchup?'

Steve stopped kissing me immediately. 'Yes. And pickles.'

Cheryl set two plates of burgers and chips in front of us without batting an eyelid despite shouts from other customers – 'Get a room!' and 'Go for it, Steve!'

I was mortified and looked around for Probes, but he had vanished.

Steve tucked a paper napkin into the top of his white uniform and plunged a fork into a pile of chips. 'Eat up, doll.'

The skin on my face began to prickle. *Damn and blast!* I'd completely forgotten. Steve may be a good kisser, but on the two occasions we had accidentally made out, he'd always given me a skin rash.

The food was delicious, and after a few minutes of eating in silence – except for loud appreciative groans from Steve – I turned my notebook to a fresh page. Now that Steve had kissed me, I felt I'd earned the right to ask him a few questions.

'You mentioned your friend had some news from Plymouth morgue?'

Steve swallowed an enormous mouthful, washed it down with half a glass of water. 'Got a name for you,' he said. 'Carol Pryce.'

The name meant nothing to me. 'Pryce, spelled with a y?'

He nodded. I jotted it down. 'How about an address?'

'Nope.'

'What about her bicycle?' I said. 'Was there any damage from the Land Rover?'

Steve shook his head. 'Clean as a whistle. Poor lady definitely drowned. But the toxicology report came back with something really weird.' Steve speared another five chips onto his fork.

I waited impatiently for Steve to finish his mouthful.

'A sample of her hair contained sodium hydroxide –

otherwise known as lye or caustic soda. Probably explains the chemical burns on her scalp.'

'Could that have killed her?'

'I doubt it,' said Steve. 'Maybe it was a form of torture?'

I shuddered. 'And why she wore a wig.'

'All they know is that she was unconscious when she hit the water.'

'What about the internal police inquiry?'

'He said he'd keep me posted.' Steve wiped his mouth on his napkin and pushed back his plate. 'Got to go. I'll escort you to your car.'

We headed for the exit, passing a corner booth in the dimly lit bar. I recognized the back of Probes's curly red hair but could not see who his companion was. For a horrible moment I wondered if it was Annabel.

Outside in the fresh air, Probes's Smart car was parked in a spot reserved for motorcycles. Steve gallantly opened my door, and I slid in quickly, narrowly avoiding another full-on kiss.

Promising to call Steve later, I set off for The Grange feeling very pleased with myself. Who was this mysterious Carol Pryce, and why was her death surrounded in secrecy?

I had high hopes that Noah had the answer.

25

I didn't want to risk bumping into Annabel so decided to leave my Fiat along Ponsford Ridge and continue down to The Grange on foot.

It was still early and wouldn't get dark for another hour or so. I loved summer evenings, the smell of freshly cut hay and the sounds of birds singing at the end of their day.

My trek to The Grange took me past the bridleway entrance to Belcher Pike's wagon. I had plenty of time before I met with Noah and decided to take a quick detour. Call me curious, but I just wondered if the 'never leave a dying gypsy alone' palaver was true or just for tourists.

As I drew closer to the clearing, I was startled to hear someone sobbing his or her heart out, and I just *had* to investigate. It was just as well I was wearing my khaki-coloured safari jacket – I'd be difficult to spot.

Slowly, I crackled my way through the undergrowth until I had a good view of Belcher Pike's wagon. Dropping to a crouch, I headed toward a handy elderberry bush and crawled underneath its branches.

There, just a few yards away, tough-nosed Ruby sat on a fallen tree trunk shedding copious tears.

The wagon door opened and Jimmy appeared with a china mug in his hand.

'Drink this,' he said, sitting down by her side – presumably this was tea, the only thing to drink in a crisis.

'Don't cry, luv,' said Jimmy, putting his arm around Ruby's shoulders. He tried to pull her toward him but she sat there, rigid, just staring ahead.

Perhaps Belcher Pike had died. A lump came into my throat. Ruby's grief was so tangible that it tugged at my heartstrings. Quite unexpectedly, I was consumed by a wave of acute homesickness.

Suddenly, Ruby pushed Jimmy away and stood up. 'This is all your fault, Dad!'

Dad?

I was confused. Did this mean Jimmy Kitchen and Dora Pike were man and wife? I remembered Dora saying she went by her maiden name but had never thought to ask why. Maybe she was a feminist? I'd been to Jimmy's wagon, and there had been no sign of a woman's touch, and the same could be said of Dora's Winnebago lacking that manly vibe. In fact, Jimmy had led me to believe he was a widower! Perhaps they were estranged? Could gypsies.get divorced? I wasn't sure.

'You don't know what you're talking—'

'I know what you did!' Ruby flung the mug to the ground, spilling liquid everywhere.

'Ruby, luv,' Jimmy pleaded. 'It's not what you think—'

'Don't! You *always* say that.' Ruby ran to the wagon and jumped up the steps, slamming into Dora as she poked her head out of the door. 'What's going on?' she demanded.

Ruby pointed an accusing finger at her father, who was still seated. 'Why don't you ask *him*? He's doing it again! Don't you have any self-respect?'

'Keep your voice down.' Dora shot Jimmy a filthy look.

'I want to leave this place!' Ruby cried. 'Why do we have to stay?'

Jimmy had his back to me, so I couldn't see his expression. 'We'll leave when we're ready, and that's final,' he said coldly, all warmth from his voice gone. 'Get on with your work.'

I only moved a fraction of an inch, but it was enough to startle a brace of pheasants that took flight with their distinctive cry.

Jimmy spun around. I drew back into the elderberry bush as far as I could and closed my eyes tightly.

'Noah? Is that you?' shouted Jimmy.

I sat as quiet as a mouse, trying to make sense of what I'd just heard. Was Belcher Pike a week away from being snapped up by the Grim Reaper? What exactly had Jimmy done to make Ruby so upset? What exactly was he 'doing again'?

Without another word, the two women disappeared into Belcher's wagon. Jimmy stayed put. Several times he looked over in my direction. Time passed. All was quiet. Finally, dusk fell, and I was able to make my retreat.

I had quite a lot of questions for Noah, and the Mudge Lane mystery was just the beginning.

26

I took the animal track that led back to the rear of The Grange. It was dark by the time I reached the courtyard, but a quarter-moon shone brightly in the night sky.

A solitary light shone down from an upstairs window. New signs had been erected – BEWARE OF THE DOG, BEWARE OF THE OWNER, and YOU ARE ON CAMERA – though I saw no sign of all three.

To my dismay, Annabel's car was still parked next to Topaz's red Capri. With just under an hour to kill, I had toyed with the idea of scrounging a cup of tea before casually mentioning that her attempts to sabotage the gypsies recycling efforts had been caught on film.

Annabel's presence had certainly put the kibosh on *that*.

What could they be doing? Watching television? Playing Scrabble? Sharing a bottle of wine? Would Annabel tell her new best friend that she suspected I was the daughter of The Fog? Wait! I *was* the daughter of The Fog!

I wandered aimlessly around, repeatedly checking my watch. The minutes seemed to crawl by. Perhaps I should check the recycling bins? Tony had seemed impressed at their neatness, and at least it would give me something to do.

It was even darker behind the pigsty. I took out my Mini Maglite.

Banked against the wall stood Ronnie's recycling bins. Tony was right. Someone had been tidying up. Each coloured bin was filled to overflowing with the correct contents. Whatever couldn't fit in lay on the ground in an orderly pile. Even the rusted iron pylons and scraps of indecipherable metal had been neatly stacked to one side.

Suddenly, a hand was clapped over my mouth; my right arm was yanked up behind me and my face thrust against the rough stone wall. Instinctively I lashed out. My foot connected with a leg, and there was a yelp of pain.

Breaking free, I whipped out my handy-sized Mace Screecher and spun around. 'I've got Mace,' I shouted. 'And I'll use it!'

'Vicky?'

'Noah!' I gasped, catching his startled expression in the beam of my flashlight.

'What the hell are you doing here?' he demanded. 'I thought you were on our side. Aunt Dora said we were being framed, but I never thought it would be you.'

'Of course it's not me.' I lowered my Mini Maglite, feeling a tad shaken. 'I was just having a look around.'

'Since when have you been interested in recycling?'

'This is Devon. We're all interested in recycling. When Tony told me you had tidied up the courtyard, I wanted to see for myself. You've done a good job.'

'Am I supposed to take that as a compliment?' Noah seemed to relax a little. 'Where's your car?'

'I left it at Ponsford Ridge. My colleague Annabel is a friend of the owner of The Grange. I didn't want her to see it and get the wrong idea.'

'And what idea would that be?'

I paused, not quite sure how to answer. 'That I was spying on her.'

'And here I was thinking it had something to do with me,' he said softly.

I gave a nervous laugh, acutely aware of a sudden frisson between us.

'You've got quite a kick,' he said. 'My leg hurts.'

'So does my arm.'

'I have just the cure for that, but you'll have to come to my wagon.'

'My arm doesn't hurt that much.'

'I thought you wanted to talk about the woman in Mudge Lane?' said Noah.

'Can't we talk about her here?'

'Come and have a drink,' he teased. 'I don't bite.'

'All right.'

Noah took my flashlight and switched it off. 'I prefer walking by moonlight.' He held out his hand. 'Come on.'

I refused it, but I did follow him through fields filled with the fragrant smells of a summer night.

I started to get nervous. It wasn't that I thought anything bad would happen – I was not one of those stupid women in horror movies who were too dumb to live – I just hadn't felt so violently attracted to anyone before. But as long as I kept my wits about me, remembered to actually talk about poor dead Carol Pryce, and, most of all, refused all offers of alcohol, I was sure all would be well.

We passed Ruby's battered VW camper and Jimmy's crimson wagon. Noah's green-and-yellow wagon was parked at the far corner of the field. Both horses whickered a greeting and ambled toward us.

Noah stopped, delving into his pocket, and gave each pony a handful of green pellets. I kept my distance.

'Don't you like horses?' he said stroking their velvet muzzles.

157

'I'm a bit afraid of them,' I said. 'I was brought up in the city. The only horse I rode was at the fairground.'

'Hold out your hand.' He didn't wait for a reply, just took it. 'Hold it flat, like this.' He put a few pellets in the middle and gently held it under the skewbald pony's muzzle. 'This is Ellie.'

Elbe's lips tickled on my skin and made me squirm but Noah held my hand steady. 'What's a city girl like you doing in Devon?'

'It's a long story.'

'I like long stories.'

We continued onto the wagon. Noah paused at the bottom of the steps, gallantly saying, 'After you.'

It was dark inside until Noah flipped a switch and several hurricane lamps simultaneously burst into rich golden glows. The interior was gloriously decorated in deep crimson and yellow, with horse-head motifs painted in gold leaf.

I felt cheated. 'Is that *electricity*?'

Noah laughed. 'It's a portable generator.'

'I don't hear anything.'

'You won't. Honda makes a silent one,' he said. 'The EU30i. I can even run my laptop.'

'Laptop?' I said with dismay.

'Sorry to disappoint you, but I've even got Garage-Band installed in my computer.' He gestured to his guitar, propped in the corner. 'I'm working on a CD of songs. I love gypsy life, but I want to do something more. Break away from—' He stopped. 'Never mind.'

But I understood more than he could possibly understand.

There was the traditional queenie stove and a ton of fitted mirrors, but whereas a built-in bow-shaped cabinet spanned the width of Jimmy's wagon, a heavy curtain on a brass rail stretched across the rear of Noah's.

'What's behind the curtain?'

In three quick strides, Noah drew it back with a flourish. 'My bed.'

158

I felt my face redden. Noah's bed seemed designed for lust-filled encounters. It looked very much like a berth aboard a sleeper train – only bigger. How could I have ever considered hedge-jumper Dave Randall or tight-fisted Robin Berry suitable candidates for such a monumental occasion in my life? Of course, I wasn't intending to do anything right *now*, but I couldn't think of a more romantic location to make me a woman.

'Go ahead. Take off your shoes,' said Noah. 'Make yourself comfortable.'

'That's okay,' I said quickly. 'I'm happy standing.'

'Wait! I almost forgot,' said Noah, heading for the door. 'Don't go anywhere. I'll be right back.'

The moment he left I gave his wagon the usual onceover. I was pleased to see a copy of the *Gipping Gazette* atop a pile of newspapers on the counter, opened to the Gipping Roundup page – a summary of local societies, upcoming events, and various fund-raisers. The newspaper was dated three weeks ago. I took a quick look at the others in the stack, surprised that they were all from north Cornwall – the *Padstow Packet,* the *Tintagel Times* and the *Camelford Chronicle.*

'These are for you.'

I gave a guilty jump. 'Sorry. Oh!'

Noah thrust a posy of violets and wood anemones into my hands.

Stunned, I said, 'They're beautiful.'

'Like you.'

'Gosh. I don't know what to say.' I was never good at receiving, a compliment and desperately wanted to change the subject. 'Are you going to Cornwall?'

'Yes,' said Noah. 'In a week or two.'

'What about your grandfather, Belcher Pike?' I said. 'I thought he couldn't be moved?'

'That's right, he can't—' Noah stammered. 'It's really up to Uncle Jimmy. Aunt Dora, too.'

'Do you always get the local newspapers before you visit a town?'

'Why?' Noah said sharply.

'How do you get hold of them?'

'What do you mean?'

'If you don't live in the area, it's practically impossible unless you can find them online,' I said. 'A lot of the smaller newspapers don't even have websites. The *Gazette* doesn't.'

Noah shrugged. 'I don't know. Aunt Dora has connections everywhere—'

'But—'

'I don't want to talk about newspapers or my aunt,' said Noah. 'I want to talk about you.'

Noah took the posy and put it on the counter. He steered me toward the bed. 'Sit down. I promise, I'm a gentleman.'

Feeling only slightly reassured, I perched on the edge. But I was *not* going to take off my shoes!

Noah reached into a small built-in cupboard and pulled out a bottle of wine. 'My cousin Ruby makes the best elderberry wine,' he said, and poured us each a glass.

'I can't have too much,' I protested. 'I'm driving.'

'It's just fruit,' said Noah. 'Hardly any alcohol at all.'

Two *very* small glasses later, I was sprawled on the bed listening to Noah playing a Willie Nelson country-and-western song on his guitar. 'Mama don't let your boys grow up to be' – he paused – '*gypsies.*'

Just as Noah had promised, he *was* the perfect gentleman, and now I found myself longing for him to make a move. Instead he regaled me with wonderful stories of life on the open road, but they were also tinged with sadness.

He told me of evictions that resulted in wagons, handed down from generation to generation, being burned to the ground; of being bullied in the few schools he had attended; and of the elderly Romanies who had died before their time because of lack of crucial hospital care.

'I owe my aunt and uncle everything,' said Noah. 'But sometimes I want to be my own man. What about you?'

'Excuse me?'

'Who brought you up?'

'Bit like you . . .' I hesitated. 'Just an aunt and uncle. Marie and Derek.' They were my code names for Mum and Dad.

'Where? You're not from the south.'

'No, I'm not.' I was beginning to get uncomfortable. This was exactly why I could not afford to get involved with anyone. I felt a sudden flash of anger against my parents. Would I ever lead a normal life? Find love? Would I always be looking over my shoulder?

'Why are you *really* in Gipping-on-Plym, Vicky?' said Noah. 'Come on, you can tell me.'

'Work,' I said. 'And speaking of which, you said you had something to tell me about Carol Pryce.'

'Carol Pryce?' Noah said. 'You mean the woman in Mudge Lane?'

'I thought you knew who she was!'

'She *could* be an Irish traveller,' said Noah slowly. 'What do the cops think?'

'I told you, they don't seem to care,' I said. 'But I do.'

'Why bother?' Noah edged toward me. 'We true Romanies don't like the Irish travellers, and vice versa. They're scum.'

'I have to bother! I write the obituaries!' Really, this elderberry wine had quite a buzz to it. 'I found her body!'

'You're very cute.' Noah took my wine glass and set it down. He leaned toward me. 'Can I kiss you?'

I didn't have time to say no as our lips touched. I braced myself for the inevitable descent into dizziness, but to my disappointment, I remained perfectly aware. It was as if I were a spectator in my own love scene. I opened my eyes, and met Noah's staring right back into mine. It was so unnerving that I closed them again.

True, Noah's kisses were pleasant enough, but they had none

161

of Steve's passion. I also didn't care for his moustache. It really tickled.

Suddenly, my phone rang. The mood was ruined. I jumped like a scalded cat.

A glance at my caller ID confirmed my worst fears. *Blast!* It was Steve. 'Sorry. I have to take this,' I said. 'It's work.'

I wriggled off the bed and walked to the far end of the wagon in the vague hope I would be out of earshot.

'Hello?' I gave a big yawn and hoped I sounded as if I were half-asleep. *Good grief!* Was it really half past eleven? 'Who is this?'

'You know who it is, doll. It's Steve.'

'I was almost asleep.'

There was a pause. 'Where's your car?'

A peculiar feeling came over me. 'Where are you?'

'Outside your house. Mrs Evans said you hadn't come back yet.' There was a muffled, anguished cry. 'Oh God. You're with Phil, aren't you?'

'I'm at Barbara's,' I said, very much aware that Noah had untied the ribbon from his ponytail. His hair fell to his shoulders. Now he really did look like a pirate. 'You must be tired, Steve. Why don't you go home? We can talk tomorrow.'

'I'll come to Barbara's place.'

'No, don't do that,' I said quickly. 'I'm already in the car on my way.' *Blast! Blast! Blast!* I ended the call and spun right into Noah's arms.

'Problems?'

'Sorry, I have to go. It's a work emergency.' I ducked past him and went to retrieve my shoes.

I set off at a jog to get my car from Ponsford Ridge.

Perhaps it was a blessing that Steve had called. Things had been moving quicker than I expected in the romance department.

Up the track to Ponsford Ridge I went and was so consumed with what I was going to tell Steve that I failed to see the object laying across the path in the semi-darkness. I fell to the ground, hard.

Some idiot had left a bicycle just lying in the mud. Cursing, I picked myself up and realized with a start that it was a distinctive pink bicycle, circa 1940, with a large wicker basket.

It was Barbara's.

I stared at it for a full minute until I heard the murmur of voices coming from a small copse to my left.

Tiptoeing through the undergrowth, I paused at the edge of a grassy clearing just as the moon peeped out from behind a cloud.

There, in a passionate embrace, stood Barbara and Jimmy! They weren't doing anything disgusting like kissing – and luckily, were fully dressed – but just stared into each other's eyes as if they were the only two people on the planet.

Frankly, the pair of them resembled a book cover from a Harlequin romance, with Barbara's grey hair cascading down her back to match Jimmy's unbraided tresses.

I was repulsed but fascinated as both began to slowly dance, hands touching hands, in perfect symmetry.

It was incredibly intimate and unbelievably romantic. It was also clear that Barbara and Jimmy were no strangers to each other.

And then it came to me in a flash.

How could I have been so stupid! I thought back to Ruby's grief that now seemed as if it had nothing to do with Belcher Pike at all. Her Dad was having an affair, and Ruby knew it.

For as long as I'd known Barbara, she'd talked about Jimmy Kitchen – the 'man who got away' and the 'love of her life.'

I withdrew, knowing I'd witnessed something I shouldn't have. It had never occurred to me that Jimmy Kitchen was a *gypsy*! No wonder they couldn't be together! What's more, I was almost positive that this was the scandal that Whittler and most of Gipping had alluded to.

Poor Barbara. What rotten luck. Engaged to one man but in love with another. What was she going to do?

Yet Barbara's predicament paled into insignificance when measured against mine.

Steve was waiting.

27

I turned into Factory Terrace and had to drag myself away from Barbara's predicament to focus on mine.

It was just as I feared. Steve was pacing back and forth across the road smoking a cigarette. This did not bode well. For a start, I had never even seen him smoke.

I pulled up behind his VW Jetta 2.0 TDI outside number twenty-one, switched off the engine, and cut the lights. A glow from the upstairs bedroom window revealed a crack in the curtains and Mrs Evans's face pressed against the glass.

God. I hated scenes, and I wasn't about to have one in the middle of the street for all the neighbours to hear. I leaned over and pushed the passenger door open. Steve trudged toward me and peered inside. In the gloom of the interior light, his eyes looked all red and swollen.

'You're being really silly.' *Attack is the best form of defence!* 'I told you I was going to see Barbara tonight.'

'Oh, really?' Steve took an exaggerated drag on his cigarette. 'When?'

'If you want to talk about it, get in the car,' I said. 'And please get rid of that cigarette.'

Steve tossed it into the gutter and lowered himself onto the front seat. He slammed the door, hard.

'Just tell me the truth, Vicky,' he said. 'That's all I'm asking. Don't lie to me, doll. It will kill me.'

'I'm not lying. I did see Barbara.' This was absolutely true. 'Why don't you ask her if you don't believe me?' Given Barbara's new circumstances, I was quite sure I could count on her giving me an alibi if push came to shove.

'I will and I don't.' Steve turned to me. His face was etched with such pain that I felt guilty. I never intended to hurt Steve and still couldn't quite work out how I had gotten myself into this situation.

'Why didn't you call earlier?' I said.

'I did.'

'You can't have done. The phone didn't ring.' This was worrying. I might have to change my service provider. I had to be accessible 24-7. 'Maybe there wasn't a signal? Did it go straight to voice mail?'

'I don't like leaving messages. *Then* I called Phil.' Steve's voice broke. 'He didn't answer, either.'

'Phil had told me he had a tanning session booked.'

'Yeah. Right. *Tanning.*' Steve gave a heavy sigh. 'It's no good. I've got to do this, doll. I've got to look.'

Before I could blink, Steve reached up and snapped on the interior light and grabbed my chin, forcing me to look at him. 'It's true,' he cried. 'Oh God. Your face!'

'What?' I nipped down the visor. Not only was my chin covered in blotches, my lips were puffy, too. *Blast!* So I wasn't *just* allergic to Steve. Or perhaps it was Noah's moustache? Maybe I was allergic to every man who kissed me?

'I know you, Vicky,' Steve wailed. 'You always get that flushed look after kissing.'

'I'm not *flushed,*' I snapped. 'I'm allergic to your aftershave.'

'I don't believe you,' said Steve. 'Oh God. I want to die.'

This was ridiculous! I was beginning to tire of Steve and his

166

wretched insecurities. I thought longingly of Barbara, wild and free, being held by the love of her life in the moonlight. Steve wasn't for me, and I was being incredibly unkind by keeping him hanging on, even if he was a good informant.

'You're right. This isn't working,' I said. 'I think we should cut our losses and stay good friends.'

Steve's jaw dropped. 'Are you breaking up with me?'

'Yes, I'm afraid I am.' I don't know why I hadn't ever thought of breaking up with Steve before – probably because as far as I was concerned, we weren't having a relationship.

Steve shook his head with disbelief. His eyes welled up with tears. 'After all we've gone through,' he whimpered. 'I don't believe it. This isn't happening to me. It can't be.'

Don't cave, Vicky. Be strong. 'Sorry,' I said firmly. 'But I think this is for the best.'

Slowly, Steve opened the door and got out of the car, dramatically pausing to whisper in a voice filled with pain, 'You've broken my heart, doll.'

Steve started his car and began revving the engine, pedal flat to the floor. He made so much noise that lights popped on, up and down Factory Terrace. I was mortified.

Suddenly, Steve thrust his Jetta into gear with a crunch, slammed his foot down on the accelerator, and took off like a bullet – in the direction where the cul-de-sac ended in the high factory wall!

Good grief. Surely he wasn't intending to *kill* himself? There was a squeal of brakes, then – thankfully – the car headlights came back into view. Steve tore past me, hands gripping the steering wheel, eyes straight ahead.

I let myself in the front door feeling utterly wretched. Fortunately, Mrs Evans wasn't waiting up for me as I had feared, and I managed to get into my room without any interruptions.

The first thing I saw was Barbara's shoebox, which I planned to give her tomorrow. Even though the newspaper clipping was missing, I knew it was significant and intended to steer the conversation around to Mildred Veysey – after all, she would have been Barbara's future mother-in-law had she still been alive.

Tonight had been as traumatic as I had predicted, but something told me that tomorrow could be worse.

28

Annabel did not come home that night. I slept badly, haunted by dreams of Steve walking in on me having sex with Probes in Noah's wagon.

The next morning, my face still bore traces of my allergy to Steve – or Noah – but even though I caught Mrs Evans watching me closely at breakfast, she just asked how 'Sexpot Steve' was taking the news.

When I remarked, 'badly', she nodded agreement but said that Steve had taken his breakup with her daughter, Sadie Evans, 'far, far worse', and that at one point they thought he could be 'suicidal'.

Of course, I knew that Sadie and Steve had been an item well before I moved into Chez Evans, but if Mrs E. had thought this news would make me feel better, it didn't.

True, I had never aspired to be Steve's girlfriend, but there is nothing more sobering after such a traumatic breakup than to discover you weren't the love of someone's life after all.

'Don't feel sorry for him,' Mrs Evans went on. 'He was only using you as a transitory object. He never really got over my Sadie.'

'Thanks, Mrs E.,' I said, but felt her remark was more of an insult than a comfort. But having half expected Steve to be bombarding me with phone calls begging for another chance, I had to assume she was right. My phone had not rung once.

I arrived at the *Gazette* just after nine and noted that the show window had been drastically altered.

Positioned front and centre, two mannequins dressed as Gipping Ranids flanked the man-sized frog mascot. Wearing Panama hats decorated with badges, each mannequin sported a green-and-white-spotted neckerchief, a white shirt, and bottle-green breeches with bell pads decorated in green and white ribbons. Crossed baldricks passing diagonally across the chest and also covered in small bells and white rosettes completed the outfit.

On the far right was an assortment of banners and various percussion instruments. Tucked way in the back was one standee of Phil in Turpin Terror costume alongside his mascot, Beryl. A small flyer had been tacked in the bottom left-hand corner of the window simply saying PHIL BURROWS. GRANGE. SATURDAY.

Tucking the newly wrapped shoebox inside my safari jacket, I entered reception.

Barbara was behind the counter. She looked tired. Her eyes were ringed with heavy dark circles. Even her sunshine yellow summer polka-dot frock seemed drab. She certainly did not bear the radiant telltale signs of a woman in love or the haunted look of guilt.

'The new window looks great,' I enthused.

'No thanks to Olive,' Barbara grumbled. 'She's getting too big for her own boots these days.'

'Where *is* Olive?'

'God knows. She's always late.' Barbara gestured to the pile of papers and ribbons on the counter. 'She still hasn't done these! They've been sitting up there for a whole month, and the event's *only* tomorrow!'

I, however, was glad that Olive was late. She might be slow, but she didn't miss much, and my efforts at rewrapping the shoebox had left much to be desired. For starters, the only paper I could find at Chez Evans was the pink, floral variety that Mr Evans had used to wrap up that mystery gift for his 'Annie'.

I set the shoebox on the counter. 'This is for you. Sorry. I kept forgetting to bring it in.'

Barbara pulled a face. 'Not another wedding present.'

'Aren't you excited?'

'I don't know,' she said with a heavy sigh. 'I'm not sure if I can be bothered.'

'But you're getting married to the man of your dreams,' I said, adding slyly, 'Having second thoughts is perfectly natural.'

Barbara merely grunted. She grabbed a pair of scissors from the countertop and stabbed at the paper. Lifting up the lid, she savagely ripped through the pink tissue paper – also stolen from Mrs Evans's kitchen drawer.

Barbara froze. All the colour drained from her face as she lifted out the shoe and then the bicycle bell.

'What is it?' I asked, all innocence. 'Is that a shoe?'

'No!' she gasped. 'No! It can't be!'

She grasped at the edge of the counter and suddenly keeled over, hitting the floor with a sickening crash.

'Barbara!' I shrieked and crawled under the flap to find her lying motionless on the ground. Since her eyes were staring at the ceiling, she was either conscious – or dead. I picked up her wrist and, to my relief, felt a pulse.

'I'll call for an ambulance,' I said, hoping that Steve was off-duty and I'd get Tom.

'No, don't do that.' Barbara grabbed my hand. 'Help me sit up. Hide them,' she whispered urgently. 'Don't let Olive see, please Vicky.'

I got to my feet and swiftly stuffed the shoe back into the box and under my safari jacket just as Olive walked through the front door.

Wearing a cream trouser suit with a gold barrette in her sleek grey bob, Olive seemed excited. 'Good, Barbara's not here yet,' she said, beaming from ear to ear. 'I've got *two* surprises for her at my party tonight.'

'I am here,' shouted a voice. Barbara popped up from behind the counter, her hair all dishevelled. I gestured to the bulge under my safari jacket and gave her the thumbs-up. 'And I told you I hate surprises.'

'Are you feeling all right? You look awful.' Olive frowned. 'Don't you think it's time to have all that hair cut off?'

'You're right, Olive,' Barbara declared. 'I just might.'

'I *knew* something was wrong!' cried Olive. Barbara always maintained that men loved long hair. 'You're not thinking of cancelling tonight, are you?'

'No, she's coming,' I said, and pointed to the mounds of paper on the counter. 'But only if all this work is sorted out first. Barbara, I need something in the archive room.'

'Why?' Barbara guarded her meticulously organized archive room just as she did the show window – under lock and key.

'I'm trying to find some background on Gladys Trenfold for her obituary,' I lied, but discreetly tapped the bulging shoebox under my safari jacket. 'Didn't she do some shoplifting?'

Olive gave a nervous titter. 'You can't put *that* on page eleven!'

'I just might,' I said, giving Olive a wink.

'Oh wait,' said Olive. 'Did you give that package to Barbara, Vicky? Was it a wedding present?'

'No,' Barbara said coldly. 'They were bulbs for the garden.'

Olive frowned. 'I do wish I could remember who had delivered it. Was it from a catalogue?'

'Remember what I said about Barbara coming tonight?' I said.

Olive plunged into the papers whilst I followed Barbara into the archive room.

'Close the door,' I said. 'We need to talk.'

172

29

It had been quite some time since I'd been allowed into Barbara's closely guarded kingdom.

Floor-to-ceiling wooden shelves stood on three sides, packed with dozens of labelled cardboard boxes sorted by subject and year. Funerals took up one entire wall, weddings and births, the second. The third was shared equally among social events, including the Women's Institute, Flower Shows, Jumble Sales, Police Reports, and Court Transcripts. I noted a new box marked TREWALLYN TRIO WINDOW APPEAL.

A TO FILE tray filled with various-sized newspaper clippings and sheets of paper stood on the narrow wooden table in the centre of the small storeroom.

I set the shoebox down. 'Do you want to tell me about Jimmy Kitchen?'

Barbara paled. 'I don't know what you are talking about.'

'It's no use denying it,' I said. 'I saw you together last night in Trewallyn Woods.'

'That wasn't me.'

'Barbara, it's okay. Everyone is entitled to be happy.' Although when Dad said that to Mum during his affair

173

with Pamela Dingles, she punched him. 'What's going on?'

To my dismay, Barbara burst into tears.

I pulled out the low stool cum stepladder from under the table and sat her down, perching on a portable shredder myself. 'I'm sorry. I didn't mean to upset you.'

Barbara pulled out a cotton handkerchief from her yellow hand-knitted cardigan and blew her nose furiously.

'Surely it can't be as bad as all that?' I said, trotting out one of Mum's favourite – and rather irritating – phrases. 'The gypsies will be gone soon.'

This prompted another wail of anguish. 'It's all so unfair.'

I put my arm around her shoulders. 'You've talked about Jimmy Kitchen for as long as I've known you. I just didn't realize exactly who he was. Not that it matters.'

'It mattered back then in those days,' said Barbara. 'Gorgers and gypsies could never be together. My dad had a fit, and his folks were furious.' Dabbing at her eyes with her handkerchief she added wistfully, 'We were like Romeo and Juliet.'

'Things are different now,' I said, thinking of my own tryst with Noah last night. 'It's obvious you still love each other. I think you should follow your heart.'

'Follow my heart?' Barbara gave a bitter laugh. 'I tried that once.'

'It's just so romantic. The love of your life comes back after all these years—'

'You don't understand,' Barbara said. 'Jimmy lied to me. *Again.*'

'About being married?'

'They're *estranged* – or so he claims.' She gestured to the shoebox. 'I don't know what to believe now.'

'The shoe?'

Angrily, Barbara wiped away her tears and got to her feet. She marched over to one of the shelves, pulled down a box marked POLICE REPORTS 1960-1965, and withdrew a press clipping. She thrust it into my hand. 'Read that.'

174

I immediately recognized the headline from the torn clipping that the Swamp Dogs had so inconveniently tossed away.

Mildred Mourned by Millions!

Authorities are seeking witnesses to a hit-and-run accident Monday evening that left our beloved Mildred Veysey dead at age forty-one. It was Mildred's endearing habit of being late for everything that ended her life as she took a shortcut to attend the Gipping Women's Institute's Bottled Jam competition at Gipping Manor.

A white convertible with a red top was spotted entering Mudge Lane – a well-known spot for lovers – moments after Mildred's bicycle. Mr & Ms X – whose names are being withheld for obvious reasons – discovered Mildred's lifeless body later that evening.

Widowed during World War II, Mildred leaves behind her only son Wilfred, who currently writes the obituary column for this very newspaper.

Good grief! Was it possible that Barbara was the mysterious Ms X?

'It was a blind corner.' Barbara's voice was barely a whisper. 'It happened so fast. It was such a blur, and it would have been our word against theirs.'

'Wait a minute—' I wasn't sure if I had understood properly. 'I thought you *found* the body.'

'We did.' Barbara twisted the handkerchief in her hands. 'Jimmy owned a white Hillman Super Minx convertible. He loved that car,' she said quietly. 'We had to get rid of it afterward. Drove it to Larcombe Quarry, shoved a brick on the accelerator, and sent it over the edge. It's probably still there.'

With a sheer drop of at least two hundred feet, the former slate quarry had been flooded decades ago.

'I don't quite follow. Oh!' *Idiot Vicky.* The clipping said a

175

white convertible with a red hood. 'Jimmy Kitchen was driving—'

Barbara shook her head. 'She was just lying there in the road. We'd had a few glasses of scrumpy – there were no drunk-driving laws then – fooling around.'

'*You* were driving!' I said stunned. 'I thought you couldn't drive.'

'I've never driven since.' Barbara turned to me with a haunted expression. 'I swear Mrs Veysey was already on the ground. I've never seen so much jam. There was broken glass everywhere.'

'Why didn't you stop? Or at least come forward? People would have understood.'

'Of course they wouldn't have understood,' Barbara said bitterly. 'They hated the gypsies. Jimmy was already in trouble with the police for spray-painting the Gipping War Memorial. But there was something else . . .' Barbara struggled to compose herself. 'Wilf and I were courting . . .'

'You mean you were *dating* Wilf?'

'He was besotted with me – of course I had a lot of admirers back then. Wilf was nice and dependable – boring, in fact – but it was always Jimmy who had my heart,' – she paused – 'and always will.'

'Oh.' I was so shocked, I didn't know what else to say.

'We tried to elope,' Barbara said. 'I was underage. Sweet sixteen. The police came and got me, dragged me home.'

No wonder the town had talked! 'What happened next?'

'I didn't hear from Jimmy again until he found me on Facebook.'

'*Facebook?*' This was exactly why I refused to have anything to do with Facebook. It was too easy to track people down on the Internet. Dad always said the invention of caller ID was bad enough, but in his profession, Facebook was the curse of the twenty-first century.

'I thought you hated modern technology.' In fact, Barbara

176

had kicked up quite a fuss when Pete insisted she have a computer in reception. Barbara only learned to use it after Olive bought a MacBook Pro and started boasting about how often she tweeted on Twitter.

'Jimmy just turned seventy,' said Barbara. 'Milestone birthdays do that to us. You're young. You have all the time left in the world, but we don't.' Barbara gave a harsh laugh. 'Just when I finally convince Wilf to marry me, Jimmy walks back into my life.'

'When did all this start up?'

'Tuesday evening. After the Graying Tigers shindig,' said Barbara. 'Jimmy knew I was having a party – thanks to Olive and her silly Twittering – so he waited for everyone to leave and just knocked on my front door. Bold as brass.'

The same night Carol Pryce died in Mudge Lane, not five minutes away from Barbara's house. Could history repeat itself?

'Does Jimmy drive a Land Rover?' I said suddenly.

'No he does not. He rode his bicycle,' snapped Barbara. 'And I know what you're trying to imply.'

'It just seems a bit of a coincidence that a second cyclist died in Mudge Lane, that's all,' I said. 'It must have been weird seeing him again after all these years.'

'Nothing had changed between us. We've always had passion,' said Barbara. 'I tingle all over when Jimmy touches me. His kisses make me dizzy.' She gave a big sigh. 'I can't expect you to understand. You're far too young.'

But I did, only by some cruel trick of nature it was with the wrong man: Steve.

'If you don't love Wilf, you can't marry him!' I said firmly.

'I don't want to let Wilf go,' Barbara declared. 'It would devastate him.'

'He'll get over it and meet someone else.' Wasn't Sadie Evans the love of Steve Burrows's life before I came along? 'Believe me, there are plenty of eager widows in Gipping.'

'Jimmy and I are finished.'

'But I thought—?'

My head was beginning to spin with all of Barbara's drama. One moment she hated Jimmy, the next she didn't. Frankly, I wasn't sure why she was telling me all this, but one thing I did know was that I would never end up like Barbara. What a mess! Surely at her age she should have worked all this love stuff out by now?

'Not now. Not after this.' Barbara gestured to the shoe. 'That shoe is mine.'

'And the bicycle bell?'

'He took it as a – souvenir – don't ask me why. We were young and stupid,' Barbara cried. 'Oh Vicky! There was so much blood!' She gave a violent shudder at the memory. 'When Mrs Veysey came off her bike, she fell onto the broken jam bottles. A glass shard had gone into her neck. Right here.' Barbara pointed to her carotid artery. 'It was horrible. Horrible.'

With a sickening jolt, I realized that the stain on Barbara's white shoe was not terracotta clay at all but blood and strawberry jam.

'I hate to ask you this, but what part of Mrs Veysey did you actually run over?'

'I think it was her . . . her . . . legs.'

'You didn't see her fall *off* her bicycle?'

'No. Why?'

'What about the coroner report?' I said suddenly. *Forensic Detectives* was my favourite television show, especially when old cases were solved and convicted people proven to be innocent after all. 'Maybe Mrs Veysey had a seizure or a heart attack? You said yourself she was already lying in the road.'

'Do you think so? That would make me feel so much better,' Barbara said, brightening, but then she slumped over and her face crumpled. 'Jimmy took my shoes and promised he would throw them away,' she moaned. 'He broke his promise.'

'That doesn't make sense,' I said. 'What is the point of sending the shoebox to you at all? Why not just give it to you in person?' Naturally, I didn't mention the missing press cutting. 'And why mark the box *confidential*?'

'Confidential?' Barbara frowned and picked up the floral wrapping paper. 'It's not marked "confidential".'

'I must have been thinking of something else,' I mumbled. 'And where's the other shoe? Why send only one?'

'Oh.' Barbara frowned. 'You're right. It doesn't make sense.'

I suddenly thought of Ruby and Dora. 'How do you know that it was Jimmy who sent the shoe at all?' I said adding slyly, 'Was there a note?'

'No,' said Barbara, brightening up once more, only to plunge back into gloom a second later. 'But if he didn't, then he must have told his wife.' She grabbed my arm. 'What if she black-mails me? Threatens to tell Wilf ?'

This was distinctly possible. Barbara had really gotten herself into a mess.

There was a loud knock on the door. Barbara swept the shoe, box, and wrappings off and under the table.

Olive peeked in, her face flushed with excitement. 'The gypsies have done it again!' she cried. 'This time they've robbed The Grange!'

179

30

Annabel was in reception fairly bouncing with glee. 'Her ladyship is distraught,' she said. 'The police are at The Grange right this second!'

'What happened?'

'Last night someone smashed the window in the heirloom room and stole a ton of silver,' gushed Annabel. 'Of course, I couldn't hear anything because I was sleeping in the attic.'

'Those would be the servants' quarters,' chimed in Olive. 'I'm surprised her ladyship put you up there. Doesn't The Grange have twelve bedrooms?'

Annabel grunted. 'That explains the lumpy bed. Really. The *servants'* quarters?'

'I wonder how the burglars got past her ladyship's high-tech security system,' I said dryly, but the sarcasm seemed to be lost on Annabel.

'They were professionals, obviously.'

'The gypsies did it, didn't they?' Olive declared. 'They'll *have* to be evicted now.'

'That's right,' shouted Barbara from behind the counter. 'Blame them for everything, why don't you!'

It didn't take a brain surgeon to work out that Topaz was up to her tricks again, and she'd managed to fool Annabel into the bargain. The whole thing was a joke, and if Topaz didn't watch out, she would find herself in serious hot water for wasting police time.

'I hope there will still be a reward,' said Olive. 'Ronnie has already started searching on his rounds, looking in all the dustbins for clues.'

'The silver would hardly be bidden in a *dustbin*.' said Annabel with scorn.

'You'd be surprised what people throw away,' Olive sniffed. 'Ronnie is always bringing home bits and pieces.'

'I'll be going to Plymouth today, of course.' Annabel flapped a piece of paper in my direction. 'This is a detailed list of the missing silver items. I need to make sure they appear on the front page.'

'You're going to Plymouth?' Normally I would be envious of Annabel going to the printers in Plymouth with Wilf and Pete, but not today. Annabel's absence would give me the perfect opportunity to grill Topaz alone.

'I almost forgot, Vicky – Pete needs the Trenfold obit pronto. Excuse me, I have a *ton* of stuff to do.' Annabel headed for the door that led to upstairs, muttering, 'It's *so* exciting being me.'

Ten minutes later, Pete and Annabel were ensconced behind closed doors in his office, and I was tackling Gladys Trenfold's obituary.

Now that I realized that Wilf, too, had written the obituaries – and risen through the ranks to become the editor – my feelings toward my job had changed.

I was proud of ON THE CEMETERY CIRCUIT WITH VICKY! and even got fan letters. I always liked to treat my subjects with respect and made sure their lives sounded interesting and meaningful. I wanted to make sure each life counted for something. After all, what I wrote was recorded for all time.

I made a few phone calls to various Gipping townsfolk, who

seemed to enjoy telling me how much money Gladys lost on snail racing and about her obsession with the QVC shopping channel on TV. Apparently she'd even worked for the post office for a short time before getting fired.

I was surprised to learn that twenty years ago, Bill had been charged with receiving stolen goods after two of Gladys's sprees in Debenhams department store in Plymouth. As Dad says, *'once a thief, always a thief.'*

Before I could dwell further on Bill Trenfold's poor character, Pete's door flew open, and Annabel emerged looking flushed and happy.

'Thank God there is justice in this world,' she declared. 'Pete's given the okay for the camera crew tomorrow to come to The Grange.'

I was shocked. 'The eviction is going ahead? What about the Morris Dance-a-thon?'

'My people aren't coming about the eviction, silly,' said Annabel. 'They're interested in the stolen silver.'

'Why?'

'Several of the items were priceless,' Annabel said. 'Those Georgian tea urns for example. Her ladyship said they were given to one of her ancestors by King George III when he was passing through Gipping.'

Annabel adds, 'They were real beauties, weren't they?'

'Were they?' I said. 'I didn't notice.'

'Luckily, I took a photograph of the urns with my iPhone,' said Annabel. 'Pete said he's going to put it on the front page. It'll get a lot of international attention.'

'You think the urns have gone overseas already?' I scoffed. 'How?'

'Everything's global these days,' said Annabel. 'I've already uploaded the photographs on my Facebook page and tweeted three times this morning.'

'But if you claim the gypsies stole it, why all the bother with the Facebook-Twitter thing?'

182

'Oh, it's not a bother.' Annabel smiled. It was one of her calculating smiles that I had come to know so well. She was up to something and I had a sneaking suspicion it might have something to do with me. 'I'm afraid I can't say much at this present time.'

'Is that you, Vicky!' yelled Pete through his open door. 'Where's the Trenfold piece?'

'Coming!' I quickly printed off the document and walked into his office, closing the door behind me.

Pete looked up sharply. 'I don't like my door closed.'

'I just wanted to express my concern that Annabel might be on a wild-goose chase with this silver theft nonsense,' I said, adding with an indulgent chuckle, 'We don't want a repetition of what happened the last time.'

'I'm perfectly aware of the balls-up that Annabel made last time,' said Pete. 'But she's got some pretty firm evidence. Why don't you just concentrate on your job and let me decide. I'm the chief reporter.'

'I'm glad you brought my job up,' I said jovially, 'because I've got a name for the woman who drowned in Mudge Lane.'

A flicker of alarm crossed Pete's face before he focused on loading papers into his leather briefcase. 'Not our turf anymore. Not our problem.'

Not our problem? 'It was Carol Pryce,' I plunged on. 'Spelled with a y. One of the gypsies said he'd help make some discreet inquiries.'

'Goddamit, Vicky,' shouted Pete. 'Didn't you hear what I said? Stay out of this!'

'Don't you care if the *Bugle* gets the scoop?' If there was one newspaper that Pete hated in the entire world, it was the trashy *Plymouth Bugle*.

'There is no *scoop*.'

'With all due respect, as the official funeral reporter, I can't stay out of it. Carol Pryce died within our reader circulation area and I found the body!' I had a sudden thought. 'In fact, I'm

183

happy to talk to Wilf about this. I know he'll understand how I feel since he once did my job.'

'Keep Wilf out of it.' Pete locked his briefcase with a snap and headed for the door.

'Did you know that his mother died in Mudge Lane, too?' I said. 'That road is a death trap for cyclists. The public should be warned!'

Pete's eyes met mine. I braced myself for another torrent of abuse, but Pete just gave a heavy sigh. 'You're a good reporter, Vicky,' he said quietly. 'But I'm asking you, just this once, to let this one go. Now get out of my way.'

I stepped aside and let Pete pass.

I'd never received a compliment from Pete before, but far from letting things go, I was determined to dig deeper. After all, isn't that what good reporters do?

I wasn't remotely bothered about the missing silver and Topaz's silly game. If Annabel had fallen for it, she deserved to have egg on her face. But I was bothered by Pete's reaction. It just wasn't like him at all. But wait! Pete was a notorious womanizer, and Mudge Lane was just the kind of place he'd pick for a rendezvous. Perhaps he'd borrowed the Land Rover from a friend?

Exasperated, I knew that wasn't it. And then I had an epiphany.

Although the two hit-and-run accidents were decades apart, they had one common denominator.

31

At The Grange, preparations for tomorrow's Morris Dance-a-thon were already underway.

As I drove up the drive, the parkland on my left was bustling with activity. Tents of all shapes and sizes were going up; an arena was pegged out and strung with coloured bunting. 'Testing, testing, one two, three' erupted from Barry Fir's public address system, accompanied by the usual ear-splitting screeches and feedback.

Bleachers, in the form of rows of rectangular bales of straw, were placed in tiers up the grassy bank that rose to a majestic stone balustrade, spanning the width of the main house.

I pulled over to let a large tractor-trailer full of Boy Scouts go by and gave Simon Mears a cheerful wave. This was followed by his wife Nicola's minivan jammed with Brownies all eager to lend a hand.

The sky was blue. The sun shone. Perhaps God would smile on tomorrow's big event, and all would be well.

Jimmy Kitchen cycled toward me with an empty gunnysack slung around his shoulders. I made a mental note to tell Barbara to remind her boyfriend that poaching was illegal and that this particular landowner would not hesitate using her twelve-bore shotgun.

For some reason I felt awkward, wondering how close knit the 'tribe' was and if Noah might have mentioned our own little tryst from the night before.

I waited for him to draw alongside, anxious to hear his thoughts on the recent silver scandal, noting that, unlike Barbara, he didn't look the worse for wear. I couldn't help wondering what happened after I left them to it.

'Did you hear about the robbery last night?'

'They're trying to pin that one on us, too,' snorted Jimmy with disbelief. 'I insisted the cops search our wagons.'

'That was a good idea,' I said. 'Are the cops still there now?' I did not want to bump into Stalk.

'No. They've gone,' said Jimmy. 'We'll be moving on next week.'

'What about Belcher Pike's soul?'

'It's his decision, not ours.' Jimmy gestured to the shouting and banging going on around us. 'This place is like a three-ringed circus. We're accused of theft and fly-tipping. It's no place for a dying man.' Jimmy touched his forelock. 'Best get on.'

News of their departure filled me with mixed feelings. Apart from the obvious fact that I would not have to deal with Belcher Pike's funeral, I realized this meant Noah would be moving on, too, and I wasn't sure how I felt about that.

Thoughts of Noah were soon forgotten when I pulled into the rear of The Grange. Jimmy had been mistaken about the police being gone – DI Probes's ridiculously small Smart car was dwarfed next to Topaz's Ford Capri.

As Topaz's very distant cousin, it stood to reason that she'd have involved Probes in recovering the family heirlooms. Of course, he and I were the only two people who knew of Topaz's double life.

I found the back door unlocked and ajar – defeating the purpose of all Topaz's new warning signs.

Presumably, Topaz was in her 'suite of rooms'. I took the stairs up to the first floor, pausing to admire the stained glass window depicting the family motto – HOMO PROPONIT SED DEUS DISPONIT – 'Man proposes, God disposes'. A faint bark greeted my footsteps and, looking up, I saw Slipper wagging her tail.

A door, set into the wooden partition – custom-made to seal off the upper floor during Sir Hugh and Lady Clarissa Trewallyn's time – stood open. With Slipper trailing behind me, I stepped through into a labyrinth of long cavernous corridors.

Slipper took the one to my left, and I dutifully followed. We rounded a corner and made for a faint light coming through an open doorway a few yards farther on.

Slipper pushed the door open and went on in, but I decided to wait outside – partially because I wasn't sure how Topaz would receive me, and partially because I was hoping to eavesdrop on whatever conversation she might be having with Probes.

I had a good view of the sitting room. It was lovely and bright, with huge sash windows overlooking the park.

The wallpaper was made of pale yellow silk and hung with heavily framed family portraits. In front of an ornate fireplace stood an exquisitely embroidered tapestry fireguard. Dark-crimson velvet curtains fell from crested pelmets; a sand-coloured Knole sofa trimmed with gold fringe and enormous tassels was joined by a pair of matching wingback chairs. Bowls of roses in crystal vases sat on several antique occasional tables atop a glorious Persian carpet.

It was a far cry from the tattered Victorian chairs and grime of The Copper Kettle kitchen, and frankly, I felt a little intimidated.

Topaz often pulled the aristocracy card on me, but I usually took it with a pinch of salt. Here, despite her silly lowly waitress act, I realized there really was a class gap between us.

187

At first I couldn't see her. She was standing partially shielded by a large potted palm in a ceramic pot next to another door.

Dressed in a frumpy beige canvas skirt, white short-sleeved shirt, sandals, and pearls, Topaz's short brown hair lay flat on top of her head. On the sofa sat the discarded Jackie O wig.

'It's just not fair!' Topaz shouted through the door. 'Don't you care about the Spat silver?'

'You know as well as I do that this is not the work of the gypsies,' came a muffled voice I recognized as Probes.

There was the sound of a toilet flushing and the loud crack of a lock being drawn across. Probes emerged dressed in plain clothes.

Topaz stood aside to let him pass. 'Annabel said it was the work of a famous silver thief called The Fog.'

'The *Fog*?' said Probes sharply.

My stomach turned over. So this was what Annabel was up to! Was she trying to lure Dad to Gipping-on-Plym? The idea was ludicrous – and yet . . . *not* impossible.

'I'd think it highly unlikely,' said Probes. 'He's still on the run. Interpol has been after him for months, and we'd know if he'd entered the country.'

'But he's supposed to be frightfully clever,' said Topaz. 'That's why he's called The Fog – because he creeps in so slowly and then disappears.'

'The Fog wouldn't dare return to England, let alone Gipping-on-Plym.'

Thank you, Probes. Then I thought, wait – Probes seems to know a little too much about my dad. Naturally, I knew Probes had connections with Interpol, and, yes, it was common knowledge that the reason why Dad had fled the country was because of a botched robbery, but even so . . .

'Did you know that he's one of the top ten famous criminals in the world?' Topaz declared. I couldn't help feeling a tiny bit of pride that Dad was in the top ten and wondered exactly which number.

Probes walked to the window and gazed out over the parkland beyond. 'Why would Annabel think The Fog would come to Gipping?'

'Apparently his specialty is Georgian tea urns.' Topaz flounced over to the Knole sofa, tossed her wig on the floor, and flung herself into the corner. 'Really, this is all so frightfully tedious. I still don't know why you won't let me evict the gypsies today. That eviction service from Plymouth is jolly good and had a last-minute cancellation at five.'

'We searched the wagons. The gypsies haven't done anything wrong, and you know it,' said Probes wearily. 'Where have you hidden the silver, Ethel?'

I'd never heard Topaz addressed by her real name before.

'I told you, I haven't touched it,' she said. 'Why would Uncle Hugh say they could stay here? Why, after all this time, have they come back?'

Up until last night, I had been asking myself the same question, but now I knew the answer. The gypsies were back because Jimmy Kitchen realized he couldn't live without his first love and had come to get her. It was too romantic for words.

'You do know that wasting police time is a criminal offence,' Probes said sternly. 'And if you are thinking of making a false claim on an insurance policy, you could go to prison.'

'An insurance claim?' Topaz brightened. 'I hadn't thought of that. What a frightfully good idea.'

Probes gave a heavy sigh. 'You're impossible.'

Unfortunately, I didn't see the canister of furniture polish left on the ground by Mrs Evans. It made a very loud noise as it rolled across the floor and stopped at Topaz's feet.

Topaz looked up. 'Omigod! Vicky!' she shrieked and leapt to her feet, racing across the room and flinging herself into my arms. 'I've missed you!'

'I heard the news about the silver.' I tried to extract myself from her enthusiastic embrace. 'Your *ladyship*?'

Topaz jumped back and became lady-of-the-manor once

again. 'Thank you for your concern,' she said with a haughty sniff. 'I am quite well, but it was a frightful shock.'

'Oh, for heaven's sake,' groaned Probes. 'Do we have to continue this charade? Vicky knows exactly who you are.'

'What was stolen, Topaz?'

Topaz gave a heavy sigh. 'Obviously, the *priceless* Trewallyn chalice – and some littler knickknacks at the church.'

'You mean the ancient artifacts that have been there for hundreds of years?' I said.

'And the Georgian tea urns, of course,' said Topaz. 'They're the ones that we're really worried about, aren't we, Colin?'

'We would be if they were really missing and not just' – Probes looked me straight in the eye and actually winked – '*mislaid.*'

I was glad to see Probes had more intelligence than I normally gave him credit for.

'Of course they're not mislaid,' said Topaz with scorn. 'The window was smashed. It was the work of a professional, I'm sure.'

'A professional who hurls a brick through a glass window?' said Probes wryly.

'Personally, I think the gypsies are in cahoots with professional thieves.'

So *this* was the angle Annabel was taking!

'Can I see the heirloom room?' I asked.

'Be my guest,' said Topaz. 'You'll see what I mean.' We all trooped down to the heirloom room – as it now seemed to be officially called.

'Are the fingerprint people coming?' I said.

'Colin refused to call them out.' Topaz lowered her voice. 'He's being frightfully difficult about it all.'

'I heard that,' said Probes.

The heirloom room was in chaos. The silver on the refectory table had been disturbed and scattered about.

Having been privy to Topaz's closely guarded list of

190

inventory in the past, I started to count the pieces. Excluding the Georgian urns, the original list numbered thirty-seven items, so it was somewhat startling to find that the number was exactly the same. Even the exquisite silver swan centrepieces were still there, hidden underneath an upturned teapot.

For a fleeting moment, it crossed my mind that Dad could be involved, but then I reminded myself that he always worked alone. Furthermore, he had earned his nickname, The Fog, for a reason.

Dad had never been the smash-and-grab type. Often his victims did not discover the theft for weeks afterward because of the way he only took specific pieces. His method of breaking and entering without leaving a trace was legendary – so much so that his peers have begged him to write a textbook on the art of 'stealth burglary'.

I was now certain that Annabel and Topaz were in cahoots. It was amusing, really.

Probes poked around muttering various comments like, 'I thought that belonged to my mother' and 'Grandfather said this cigarette box was mine.'

Moving over to the sash window, I almost laughed. *What amateurs!*

The lower half had a fist-sized hole in it, but the latch was still firmly shut. In fact, it had been painted over, as had the pulley ropes on either side of the frame that raised the window.

On the carpet lay a large brick. There was a sprinkling of glass on the floor by the skirting board, but peering outside, I saw a pile of shards on the patio. Whoever had thrown the brick had done so from inside this room.

I turned to Topaz, who was hovering in the doorway. 'I'm surprised you didn't hear the glass smash.'

'How would I? This is a frightfully large house, and the heirloom room is in a different wing.'

'I've already warned her she's wasting police time,' said Probes, who seemed to have glided silently to my side. He had a musky scent that I was never quite sure if I found attractive or not. 'My cousin seems to think the focus was on the Georgian tea urns. Why do you think she would say that?'

'I have no idea,' I said quickly.

'Are you two quite finished?' said Topaz. 'I can't stand here all day. I'm busy.'

I closed the shutters, and Probes said he'd return later with some wood to patch up the hole in the glass. 'No point tempting fate,' he said grimly.

After locking the door carefully behind us, Topaz said, 'And don't think I'll be making you any tea. This isn't a café.'

'Let me escort you to your car, Vicky,' said Probes. 'We need to talk.'

'I have no influence over your cousin.'

'Not about Ethel or Topaz or whatever she's called,' said Probes. 'This is about you.'

32

I followed Probes outside, expecting to be taken to my Fiat. Instead, he veered left and took the narrow pathway around the side of the pigsty. No doubt Probes had found out about Topaz sabotaging the gypsies' recycling efforts. I wondered if I should mention that Dora had caught her on camera, too.

We stopped next to the recycling bins, which were still in ship-shape condition.

Probes seemed nervous, jostling from foot to foot and scanning the area. After some moments, he said, 'Sorry to be so cloak-and-daggerish. I don't want us to be overheard.'

'Are you telling me a secret?' I joked.

'You could say that.' Probes's face wore that contorted look that had *anguished struggle* written all over it.

'Is this about the recycling or the silver?' I said, suddenly feeling sick. Probes seemed to know a lot about Dad's movements. 'You know the gypsies didn't take it.'

'Yes, yes, I know all that.' Probes seemed irritated. 'My cousin has nearly ruined everything.' He fell silent again.

Good grief. Spit it out!

Finally, Probes took a deep breath. 'I'm sorry we never got to finish our meal.'

'Excuse me?' For a moment, I was confused. 'Meal?'

Probes turned red. He gave a harsh laugh. 'I see it wasn't as memorable for you as it was for me.'

Realization dawned. 'You mean six weeks ago, when you suddenly rushed out minutes before the main course arrived and left me with two plates of scampi and chips?'

'Yes. And I'm truly sorry,' Probes said ruefully. 'I was called out on a case. I did leave two messages with Annabel Lake. Didn't you get them?'

'She must have forgotten.' No surprises there. Annabel had a habit of forgetting messages intended for me.

'She didn't? I thought you were so annoyed that you decided never to speak to me again.' Probes smiled, showing his neat, sharklike teeth. 'When I saw you with Steve at the Manor—' He thrust his hands savagely into his pockets. 'And now I suppose it's too late. This is embarrassing. I am making a complete fool of myself here.'

Probes's vulnerability was surprisingly touching, and I found myself saying, 'Steve and I are just friends.'

'*Friends?*' Probes eyes widened. 'Do you treat all your friends in such a *friendly* manner?'

Blast! Probes must have seen me kissing Steve at Gipping Manor after all.

I felt my face redden. 'We *were* friends, *then*. But now we're not. It's . . . complicated.' *Good grief, Vicky.* How could you trot out that old cliché!

'I'm a bit old-fashioned,' said Probes stiffly. 'Some call me stuffy, but I'm a one-woman man.'

A one-woman man! How unbelievably refreshing in this day and age!

'Are you seeing anyone?' A trillion butterflies fluttered in my stomach as I realized Probes was actually trying to find out if I was available! Suddenly the area behind the pigsty seemed charged with electricity.

I hesitated. Much as I liked Noah, he was moving on. 'Not exactly.'

'You must know that relationships between police and journalists are frowned upon,' Probes went on. 'It could lead to a conflict of interests. It's just that—' He gave a heavy sigh, and his face turned pink. 'You're not like any woman I've ever met.' He looked into my eyes. 'I really like you, Vicky.'

Golly. This was a real turnup for the books. 'I had no idea,' I said, stunned. 'Honestly – you've always seemed so disinterested. In fact, if anything, you've been a bit standoffish.'

'That's boarding school for you,' said Probes. 'I was sent away at seven and, other than Ethel – Topaz, whatever you want to call her – never had much to do with girls.' *Poor Colin! What an awful example of female companionship!* 'Since my people had a farm in Africa, I was sent out there every holiday, so that didn't help much. Father called me socially inept.' He gave an apologetic shrug.

Golly again! From the very beginning I'd had a soft spot for Probes, but having been brought up to believe that the only good copper is a dead one, the possibility of dating Probes properly was something I occasionally fantasized about, but that was about as far as it went.

Much as I felt flattered, I was also annoyed.

What was wrong with men? Why were *they* only interested when they thought *you* were interested in someone else? Probes only came forward when he thought I was with Steve. Jimmy Kitchen turned up the moment he found out that Barbara was about to marry Wilf.

'I know this venue is hardly romantic,' said Probes, gesturing to the recycling bins. 'Actually, I thought the path led out to a field, but when this is all over, I want us to have a proper date in a restaurant that does not serve scampi.'

195

'Yes, a restaurant,' I said, but my heart began to thump the way it always does when I could sense a story brewing. 'What do you mean, when *this* is over? When *what* is over?'

'There! You see!' cried Probes, exasperated. 'You're asking questions like a newspaper reporter.'

'I *am* a newspaper reporter,' I cried. 'This is about Carol Pryce, isn't it?'

'Goddamit, Vicky!' Probes exclaimed. 'Why do you have to go and spoil things?'

'It was a perfectly innocent question,' I said defensively. 'And I don't see why she should change anything between us.'

'Be quiet,' Probes whispered. 'Don't say that name.'

'After all, according to the police, her death was just an accident.' I suddenly saw Probes back in Mudge Lane on Tuesday night in his pyjamas and had an epiphany. 'Good grief! Was Carol Pryce your *girlfriend*?'

'Enough!' Probes took my arm and pulled me roughly toward him. Redheads had a reputation for fiery tempers, and Probes was no exception.

'What's going on?' said an angry voice. 'Leave her alone!'

Probes dropped my arm like a hot potato and spun around. How long Noah Pike had been standing in the shadows, clutching a white recycling bag filled with plastic bottles, was anyone's guess.

Noah dropped the bag and hurried toward me, sweeping me into his arms. 'Are you all right, luv?'

'Fine,' I mumbled, praying that the ground would open up and swallow me whole.

Probes regarded me with contempt, muttered, 'Unbelievable,' and stormed off, leaving me with the realization that in the space of less than twenty-four hours I'd almost had – and lost – two boyfriends.

'He's a copper, isn't he?' said Noah. 'I can always tell.'

Only last night, as we lay canoodling in Noah's wagon, we'd shared our mistrust of Her Majesty's Police Constabulary. I

196

wasn't sure how much Noah had overheard, and I didn't want to appear two-faced.

'He's a distant cousin of Lady Turberville-Spat at The Grange.' This was true. 'And yes, he's a police officer, and since some of the silver belonged to the family, he is obviously concerned.'

Noah regarded me with suspicion. 'What were you doing around here anyway?'

Think Vicky, think! 'DI Probes was worried that his cousin may have gotten herself into some hot water over the' – I gestured to the row of wheelie bins – 'recycling situation here.'

'Oh, that!' said Noah with disgust. We know the Spat woman is trying to frame us. We've got it on tape.'

'DI Probes and I were wondering what to do about it.'

'You mean, he's wondering how to get her off?' said Noah with scorn. 'But what's that got to do with you?'

Good question. I gestured to all the recycling bins again. 'One of our reporters – Tony – was up here taking photographs of this particular area to illustrate how environmentally conscious you all are and—'

'And that will appear along with my report, I hope.' Dora was standing right behind me, clutching a blue plastic bag – paper products only. Neither of us had heard her approach.

Noah gave a guilty start and sprang back.

Dora's eyes widened as she spotted a litre-sized plastic container marked ACETONE – HIGHLY FLAMMABLE lying on the ground. It must have fallen from Noah's white plastic bag.

The silent warning signal she gave Noah would have been imperceptible to anyone other than me. Dad's anger was legendary, and Mum had perfected various subtle facial expressions that stood for 'Keep quiet', 'Run!' and 'You silly cow.'

'Aren't you supposed to be with Belcher Pike?' Dora said harshly. 'Not chit-chatting around here.'

Noah didn't answer, simply scooped up the offending

197

container, shoved it into the recycling bag, dumped it into the white bin, and scurried off without even saying goodbye.

'Men,' said Dora, all smiles once more. 'Give them something to do, but you may as well do it yourself.'

'Goodness. Is that the time? Best get on,' I said, knowing full well that Dora was going to grill me about her wretched article.

'I'm looking forward to seeing my article on tomorrow's front page,' she said.

'I gave it to Pete Chambers, our chief reporter,' I said brightly. 'He's the man you want to talk to if you have any questions.' I paused, not sure if I should bring up the subject or not. 'You mentioned something about a tape concerning her ladyship?'

Dora nodded. 'That's right.'

'Is this something you wanted to give to the *Gazette*?' I said innocently.

'Do you think I'm blind?' snapped Dora. 'Her so-called ladyship is your friend. You'd never run the story, and anyway, it's too late.' Dora's eyes gleamed with malice. 'What's done is done.'

As I drove back to the office, I couldn't help thinking what a horrible person Dora was. At first she'd seemed so nice, with all her gypsy, activist, want-a-better-future attitude – and environmentally conscious, too – but there was something about her I couldn't quite put my finger on. No wonder Jimmy preferred Barbara.

What could Dora do to Topaz? I'd seen that container marked ACETONE. What if she was planning on burning down The Grange?

My mind was reeling with all that had happened this morning.

Probes had practically declared his undying love, only to be interrupted by Noah, who believed I was under attack. Yet when Dora appeared, he scuttled away like a coward. Was there no perfect man in this world?

Back at the *Gazette*, I let myself in by the side door so as to avoid walking through reception. I'd have more than my fill of Barbara and Olive tonight at the party, and it sounded as if things had already started, judging by the sounds of laughter coming through the walls.

Over the past few months, I noticed that Barbara started having 'Casual Friday Afternoons', which basically meant that with Wilf and Pete putting the paper to bed in Plymouth, the ladies liked to celebrate the end of the week with alcoholic beverages. Word soon got around town.

Upstairs, Edward greeted me with a smile. 'Great. You're back just in time to make my tea. Just kidding. Wait there.' He disappeared into Wilf's empty office and returned with two mugs, having obviously utilized Wilf's personal kettle and raided his tea-bag stash. Whereas we drank PG Tips, Wilf was partial to Yorkshire Gold – a far more superior brand. And I could see why. It was delicious.

'Why do you think gypsies would carry large containers of acetone in their wagon?' I asked suddenly.

'Of course it's highly inflammable, as you know,' said Edward. 'Traditionally, gypsies burned their wagons with all their possessions in it after a death.'

'Not these days, surely?'

'There was a case only recently. It's on the Internet.'

Edward was right. I also found some accounts of incredible gypsy funerals – one, a famous gypsy king from northern England was carried in a white carriage pulled by seven white horses whilst his widow and immediate family travelled behind in silver limousines; another funeral was attended by more than a thousand mourners who walked behind the horse-drawn coffin singing gypsy songs.

Traditionally, floral wreaths and tributes were woven with cherished possessions belonging to the deceased. It all sounded very lovely.

A part of me was sorry that Belcher Pike was leaving and I

199

wouldn't have a gypsy funeral to include in my obituary archives.

For the rest of the afternoon I researched gypsy funerals and studied their traditions. Often, funerals – or wakes – would run for days, if not weeks, so that people from all over the country could come and pay their last respects. Many were undertaken before the gypsy died.

One thing began to really bother me.

If Belcher was such a notorious figure in gypsy life, where was everyone? The gypsies had been at The Grange for at least a week. Perhaps he just wasn't that popular?

I also became increasingly obsessed with Carol Pryce. Probes knew the dead woman, but why all the secrecy? It also occurred to me that Noah hadn't told me anything I didn't already know in the wagon last night.

I searched Google for *sodium hydroxide* and discovered it was used as a drain-cleaning agent for clearing clogs. Years ago it was also one of the main ingredients in hair relaxing products. Among the side effects listed were 'chemical burns'. How could sodium hydroxide have gotten onto Carol Pryce's head?

Steve would know. Hoping the end of our so-called personal relationship had not affected our professional one, I picked up the phone and dialled his number.

It rang for what seemed like ages but then switched into voice mail. I tried again using my mobile – Steve told me he'd programmed a special ring tone for my calls, Abba's 'Dancing Queen' – but to no avail.

With a sinking heart I knew he was avoiding me.

I was beginning to think that Barbara was right. Men brought nothing but heartache.

Tonight was Olive's hen party. With everything that had happened, I couldn't help wondering if Barbara would actually turn up.

33

After inheriting the Larch millions from her overbearing father, the late Sammy K. Larch, Olive couldn't wait to move from her childhood home and had put in an offer for a huge manor house on the outskirts of Pennymoor.

Having lived most of her sixty-plus years as a spinster – a fate that terrified me given my own unsatisfactory status – Olive was certainly making up for lost time.

Leaving my car behind Amelia Webster's white Mini Metro, my heart gave a little leap. Steve's VW Jetta was parked on the opposite side of the street.

Steve was always popular with the older ladies. He had a knack of making them feel young and sexy, but even so, it was highly unlikely he would have been invited to an all-girls hen party.

There was only one reason why his car was parked here tonight.

Me.

Steve was so predictable! Somehow he'd found out about Barbara's party and was determined to win me back.

I deliberately avoided looking in his direction and pretended

I hadn't noticed his car. Now that I knew he was still interested, I wasn't sure if I was that bothered after all.

Olive – wearing a diamante barrette and a long navy evening dress – greeted me at the front door. The dress code had called for 'formal attire'. Fortunately, Mrs Evans had found something for me to wear courtesy of the Gipping Bards costume department – she'd reworked an elaborate black silk ball gown from *The Phantom of the Opera*.

'Quickly!' Olive cried, dragging me inside. 'Barbara is coming with Ruth Reeves, and they'll be here any minute.'

'I thought Barbara already knew about her party tonight,' I pointed out.

'Yes, of course she does. But we're still going to shout "Surprise!"'

Olive was almost beside herself with excitement. 'Florence, go and stand watch from the loo. The window overlooks the street.'

Florence Tossell did as she was told. She looked very nice in a long-sleeved, silver, ankle-length sheath, with clip-on diamond earrings that, to my practised eye, were the real thing.

'Vicky!' commanded Olive. 'Go through into the sitting room and tell them to keep quiet until Barbara arrives.'

I found it hard to believe that the Olive Larch that stood in front of me brimming with self-confidence and shouting orders was the same timid little creature of only a few months ago. Inherited wealth tended to have that effect on people.

'Wait.' Olive peered at my outfit and frowned. 'Didn't Gillian Briggs wear that for the Bards production of *The Phantom of the Opera*?'

'Do you think anyone will notice?' I said, feeling self-conscious. 'I don't own a long dress, and Mrs Evans took out the whalebone bodice.'

'Oh well. Never mind,' said Olive. 'It would have looked better with long kid gloves.'

I headed for the sound of excited chatter and pushed open the door.

Of course, I knew everyone and everyone knew me – and the dress. Despite the fashion faux pas, I was greeted with the usual warmth that members of the public greet the press in the wild hope they might be singled out and mentioned in the newspaper.

Olive's bungalow was stuck in a seventies time warp. The walls were clad in fake wood. A brown shag-pile carpet covered the floor.

Propped on the mantelpiece above a tiled fireplace stood a giant poster of Wilf and Barbara. Each image had been photographed separately but superimposed over a large red heart encompassed by flowers.

Clearly, Olive's newly acquired computer skills extended to Adobe Photoshop.

French windows led to a small handkerchief garden. It was still light enough outside to appreciate the wooden tubs of colourful begonias set at perfect intervals around the perimeter of a crazy-paved patio.

Bowls of peanuts and crisps were placed on various tables throughout the room. A large iced cake inscribed with the initials 'W & B' and decorated with pink roses sat on a plate of paper petals atop the teak sideboard.

It was very touching, and had I not known differently, I would have been very excited for Barbara and her new life.

There were fifteen of us all dressed per Olive's instructions and even a few pieces of antique jewellery that had probably not seen the light of day for a very long time.

Annabel was not coming. Never one of Olive's favourite people, her invitation had been given in a very offhand manner, using the 'don't feel you have to come' and 'I won't be offended' ruse.

However, I'd been surprised and a little hurt for Mrs Evans on learning that she'd only been invited to 'do the dishes' rather than attend as a guest. Twice I had to spring to Mrs E.'s defence on overhearing her being accused of losing cheques.

'I told her the money had cleared through my bank,' grumbled one.

'I did, too!' said another. 'And she still insisted on seeing a copy of the cheque!'

'Frankly, I think Bill Trenfold might have something to do with it,' declared Florence Tossell. 'Is it just me who noticed that he seems to have his own collection schedule? Someone should complain to the post office.'

Barbara arrived with the appropriate fanfare of shouts and whistles closely followed by whispers of incredulous consternation given that Barbara's version of formal attire was a long cotton dirndl skirt and white ruffled blouse with a plunging neckline. She wore her long grey hair loose, large hoop earrings, and armfuls of gold, jangling bracelets.

There was a momentary pause of shock amid comments of 'What is she wearing!' and 'She looks just like one of those gypsies!'

Olive was the first to rally round and stepped up to clip a white veil onto the crown of Barbara's head. 'There! Now you look bridal,' Olive declared. 'Let's find you a drink.'

'Are you okay?' I whispered to Barbara.

Barbara held her head high. 'Let them talk,' she said defiantly. 'They'll soon have something far more shocking to talk about than these clothes!'

Barbara may still be engaged to Wilf tonight, but it looked like his days were numbered after all.

'Put on Frankie!' shouted a voice. Moments later, the dulcet tones of Frank Sinatra's 'Fly Me to the Moon' joined the excited chatter of Barbara's friends.

Amelia Webster, dressed in a plum velvet ensemble piece, emerged from the kitchen with a tray of sherry glasses filled with an orange liquid that looked vaguely familiar.

'There's plenty more coming.' Amelia giggled. 'Let's just see how *special* these cocktails are!'

There was a murmur of excitement as glasses were snatched off the tray. I took a sip, and just as I was trying to place the unusual taste, Frankie's 'Fly Me to the Moon' was abruptly cut short and replaced by Donna Summer's 'Hot Stuff'.

The kitchen door flew open. Steve sashayed in wearing nothing but a frilly white apron. There was a united gasp of horror followed by cheers, then laughter.

Underneath that frilly white apron, Steve was stark naked. His flesh was white as marble, and his solid thighs and firm calves ended in nicely shaped feet with neat toes.

I was stunned. Clearly, Steve had not been laying in wait for a chance to woo me back. He was Olive's featured entertainment – her butler in the buff!

Steve had obviously been studying the various dance routines from *The Full Monty*, although, thankfully, his apron stayed firmly in place throughout. However, the occasional twirl afforded us a bird's-eye view of dimpled buttocks, which caused squeals of shocked delight.

I even found myself cheering along with the rest of them and couldn't help thinking what a good sport Steve was. He had an excellent sense of rhythm and was very funny. Barbara seemed to be back to her old self, leading the chant of 'Apron off! Apron off!'

Luckily, Steve did not oblige. He also did not look in my direction once, and although I was relieved to see that he had obviously not killed himself on my behalf, I was surprised at the speed with which he'd recovered from our breakup. Mrs Evans was right.

After Steve had danced to the entire soundtrack of *The Full Monty* – even running up the wall and doing a backward flip – he disappeared into the kitchen, only to emerge a few moments later with a tray of salmon pinwheels and sausage rolls.

Passing them around the room, Steve put up with the

occasional slap and tickle from the ladies with his usual good humour.

Steve's popularity made me wonder if I'd made a mistake in pushing him away. These older women had far more experience than I in the romance stakes. Mum always maintained that eventually the fireworks fizzle out and that what mattered most at the end of the day was companionship and someone to make you laugh.

Mum had a point, and Barbara was living proof that passion only brought heartache and misery.

At last, tray aloft, Steve headed in my direction. My stomach gave a funny jump. I braced myself for a torrent of compliments about how I looked. 'That was a great performance,' I enthused.

'Salmon pinwheel?' said Steve with a polite smile.

'They look delicious.' I took one but found I'd suddenly lost my appetite. 'You were wonderful.'

'I'll do anything for good old Babs.' And with a nod, Steve just turned away. I couldn't believe it!

'Wait!' I reached out to touch his arm, and yes – there it was, that *tingle*. 'Is everything all right?'

'Never been better, Vicky,' said Steve. *Vicky?* Not *doll*? 'The weather looks like it will hold for tomorrow's Morris Dance-a-thon.'

The *weather*?

I struggled to find something to say but could only manage, 'Thanks so much for talking to your friend at Plymouth morgue. It really helped.'

Steve frowned. 'Not sure I follow.'

'Your friend? The one who told me about Carol Pryce? I might have a couple more questions for him about the sodium hydroxide?' A sudden burst of laughter from Barbara reminded me that I wanted some information on Mildred Veysey's death, too. 'I also wondered if you had access to old coroner reports. From the sixties?'

Steve shook his head. 'Sorry, Vicky. You're talking to the

206

wrong guy. Don't you know a few people in the police force? I am sure they could help you.'

Blast! So he was taking the passive-aggressive path. How childish! I felt intensely annoyed but more than a little bit scared. Steve had always been *there*. Maybe I had really blown it.

'It's not for me,' I pleaded. 'It's for Barbara.'

'Why?' Steve said sharply. 'Is she in some kind of trouble?'

'Possibly,' I said. 'I know you care about her. I thought you might be able to help.'

'You're right. I do,' said Steve. 'I'll go and have a word with her right this second.'

'No!' I cried. 'Don't do that' *Good grief!* That would be disastrous. 'In fact, I'd rather she didn't know about this for the time being.'

'Nice try, Vicky,' he said quietly. 'But I know what you're trying to do, and it's not going to happen.'

'What do you mean?'

'The days of using me just for information are over.' Steve shook his head with sorrow. 'If you'll excuse me, I've got some ladies to attend to.' And, with a short bow, Steve – and his white, dimpled buttocks – disappeared into the kitchen.

So that was that.

To my astonishment, my eyes began to sting with tears.

A sudden commotion signalled that more excitement was in store for Barbara, but I just felt numb. I couldn't stop thinking about Steve. I'd never *really* wanted him in the first place, so why did it bother me now? Was I one of these awful women who were only interested in a man I couldn't have? Wait! Didn't I just accuse men of the exact same crime?

Madame Dora and Ruby – clutching a canvas bag – strolled into the room. Both were dressed remarkably like Barbara – a fact that did not go unnoticed by several of the ladies present. Barbara's expression was stony. Things were about to get ugly.

'Tonight's readings are on the house!' cried Olive.

There were yelps of excitement along with 'Clever Olive!' and 'Maybe she can tell us who stole the church silver!'

Whilst Dora stepped out into the garden to 'ready her mind' for the evening ahead, Ruby helped Olive set up a collapsible card table and two chairs in the middle of the room. She put the canvas bag on the floor and pulled out a pack of tarot cards, the crystal ball – wrapped in a velvet tablecloth – and some tea lights.

'How's your husband's charm working?' asked Ruby. 'Ronnie, isn't it?'

Olive turned pink. 'He's not my husband. Yet.'

'Don't forget he's got to keep that dung on his head for twenty-eight days.'

At last all was ready. The curtains were drawn closed.

Candles were lit. Dora reappeared from the garden, settled into the chair, and placed her hands on the table.

'Where's the bride-to-be?' demanded Dora.

'Here!' shouted Olive, but Barbara dug her toes in.

Olive pushed Barbara forward. 'I told you, I don't want to.' Barbara threw off Olive's arm.

The others let up a chorus of 'You must!' and 'Madame Dora is so good.'

The look on Barbara's face was nothing short of murderous as she was forcibly manhandled into the chair. I hurried to her side, whispering, 'It's all rubbish; you do know that, don't you?'

The overhead lights were switched off, leaving just the tea lights to cast an eerie glow. The ladies sat where they could, and a hush descended over the room.

Dora placed her hands over the crystal ball and closed her eyes. She was quiet for what seemed like an hour but was probably all of two minutes. Suddenly she began to sway in her chair, becoming more and more agitated, and then – her eyes snapped open!

'I see blood!' she gasped. 'A lot of blood! Blood on your shoes!'

Barbara shrieked and tried to stand, but Olive – with remarkable strength – grabbed her shoulders and held on tight.

'Where? Whose blood?' called out Florence Tossell, who was told in no uncertain terms to sit down and be quiet.

'A lane. I see water. Lovers kissing,' wailed Dora. *'Death!'*

A shiver ran down my spine. The gypsy was certainly putting on a good show. Olive kept Barbara locked firmly in her chair.

'It's that woman in Mudge Lane,' whispered Amelia. 'Maybe she could help police like that psychic person on the telly.'

'I see two men,' Dora boomed. 'Dishonesty! Lies! One is not being true to you. He is not free. He is not for you.'

'I'm not doing this!' Barbara jumped to her feet, practically tossing Olive across the room. 'I'm just not.'

She sped straight for the kitchen, leaving a buzz of speculation in her wake.

'I'll go after her.' My eyes met Dora's, and I didn't have to be psychic to see triumph reflected there. It was obvious who had sent Barbara the shoebox.

Olive followed me into the kitchen, but there was no sign of Barbara or Steve.

'Where is Barbara?' said Olive. 'She can't leave yet. There is still one more surprise.'

'I thought she drove here with Ruth Reeves?' I said. 'And you know she won't get far on foot with her ingrown toenail.'

'You're right. Go and search the garden. She's probably hiding.' Olive pawed at my arm. 'Do you mind taking care of her? I really must get back to my guests. This is my party.'

I decided not to point out that it was supposed to be Barbara's.

But Barbara wasn't in the garden. She was standing under a streetlight outside Olive's front gate being comforted by Steve – now fully dressed.

I hurried over to join them. 'Is she all right?'

'Not really,' said Steve. 'We can't have the bride-to-be upset by some silly gypsy.' He put his arm around Barbara's shoulders and gave her a squeeze. 'Let Steve get you home, luv.'

'Let's take her home together?' I suggested. 'Maybe grab a nightcap. Or something? I really want to talk to you. Please?'

'I'm happy to walk,' said Barbara in a dull voice. 'You two youngsters go ahead and enjoy yourselves. What are you waiting for? Life's too short.'

'Steve won't hear of it,' said Steve. Our eyes met, and I thought I saw a flicker of renewed interested captured in the streetlight's yellow glow. 'I suppose we could always come back for your car, doll?'

'Or I could follow you?' I suggested.

Headlights swept into view, and a sleek black Mercedes drew up alongside us.

The window buzzed down, and Phil Burrows leaned out. 'Hey brother! Where's the party?'

'What are you doing here?' said Steve coldly. 'We're just leaving – unless you want to stay now that the *celebrity* has arrived, Barbara?'

Barbara shook her head. 'I'm tired.'

'I'll keep an autographed headshot just for you,' Phil said, adding with a frown. 'I've only brought fifty. Do you think that's enough?'

'Why don't you go on inside, Phil?' I said. 'They're all waiting.'

'Vicky!' cried Phil. 'I didn't recognize you. Love the dress. Very dramatic. You look stunning. Doesn't she look stunning, Steve?'

'Thanks,' I said, stealing a glace at Steve. As I feared, his expression was hard.

'We had fun last night, didn't we, Vicky?' Phil grinned. 'How did you like that champagne?'

Steve's jaw hardened. 'Come on, Barbara, let's go.'

'Phil's making it up!' I said. 'Wait!'

But it was too late. Steve seized Barbara's arm and fairly

210

propelled her up the street to his car, with no heed to her ingrown toenail and whimpers of pain.

Furious, I turned to Phil. 'Why did you have to say that?'

Phil laughed. 'Steve's so easy to wind up.'

'Well—' I said. 'Don't.'

'Where are you going?' said Phil. 'Don't leave me with all those boring old biddies.'

I looked at him with disgust and, without another word, strode off to collect my Fiat. I was beginning to understand why the men disliked Phil so much.

Back at my car I discovered that Ruby's VW camper had practically boxed me in. It would take ages to ease my way out.

It was the last straw. A lone tear trailed down my cheek.

Was I actually crying over *Steve*? Or perhaps even Probes or Noah leaving town? Maybe it was my dad or missing my mum? Then there was Topaz, who now had a new friend. God, I sure had plenty to cry about.

How *pathetic*! I was quite sure that Christiane Amanpour didn't allow her personal life to get in the way of her job.

Angrily, I wiped away my tear and threw back my shoulders. *Pull yourself together, Vicky!*

I was over men and their games forever. My parents lived in Spain, and I wasn't a child anymore. As for Topaz and Annabel – they deserved each other.

What really mattered was solving Carol Pryce's murder. Who was she? What really happened?

But most of all – who killed her and why?

211

34

I woke up to the soft sound of rain pattering on my bedroom window.

It was typical English weather for any outdoor summer event that had been planned months ahead. I could already picture the waterlogged showground, cars stuck in mud, damp tents, and fraying tempers.

As I strolled into the kitchen, it would seem that Mrs Evans's temper was equally frayed.

'That Mrs Pierce practically accused me of being a liar,' she cried, dentures clicking into overdrive. 'That's twice this week that I've been told I've already cashed my cheques! I'm beginning to think I'm going round the bend.' She seemed close to tears. 'I suppose everyone was calling me a thief at Olive's grand party.'

'No,' I lied. 'They were too interested in seeing Steve Burrows turn up as Butler in the Buff. Other than an apron, he was completely naked.'

'*No!*' Mrs E.'s jaw dropped. 'Well, I never!' She started to laugh, as I hoped she might. '*Naked*, you say?'

'Steve even did a dance routine to *The Full Monty* soundtrack,' I said. 'He must have been rehearsing for ages.'

'That sexpot Steve,' said Mrs Evans with a chuckle. 'Can't keep his hmm-hmm in his trousers, but you've got to love him.'

Yet another person who loved Steve! 'Olive booked Madame Dora to come as well.'

'Really?' Mrs Evans brightened. 'Was anyone asking for her fidelity potion? I always thought that Ruth's John had a wandering eye.'

'What fidelity potion?' I asked. 'The dung?'

'Dung? The notion!' Mrs Evans looked toward the kitchen door and lowered her voice. 'Well, that potion she gave me for my Lenny is already working. Madame Dora told me it cured her husband, too.'

'You mean Jimmy Kitchen?'

'She said he was a hard dog to keep on the porch. Those were her very words – "a hard dog to keep on the porch." Toast?'

'Two pieces, please.' I didn't have the heart to tell Mrs E. that judging by Jimmy's rendezvous with Barbara the other night, Dora's cure had been very short-lived.

I suddenly felt fiercely protective toward Barbara. How dare Jimmy Kitchen just come back and play with her feelings? Maybe it was Jimmy who was driving the night they discovered Mildred Veysey lying dead in Mudge Lane? Maybe it was Jimmy who forced Barbara to take the blame, and because she was so infatuated with him, she agreed. Prisons are filled with women who will do anything for love.

Maybe something had been going on between Jimmy and Carol Pryce? Perhaps Jimmy had lied to Barbara when he said he was estranged from his wife, and Dora found out?

When I was younger, I never understood what made a woman stay with a man who betrayed her over and over again. One day Mum explained that in spite of all of Dad's infidelities, she loved him more than life itself and knew, at the end of the day, he would always return to her.

Annabel sauntered into the kitchen wearing her pink silk

robe. She had wet hair and looked all scrubbed and clean. 'Where's today's *Gazette*?'

'Lenny doesn't like anyone to touch it before he does,' Mrs Evans declared. 'Did you enjoy your shower?'

Annabel looked surprised. 'Yes, thank you.'

'You smell nice. Is that a new shampoo?'

I looked up sharply. Mrs Evans oozed with insincerity.

Annabel blushed. 'It was a gift from a . . . friend.'

From Mrs Evans's husband, I wanted to say. It must have been shampoo that was wrapped up in pink paper.

Annabel joined me at the kitchen table and poured herself a cup of tea.

'Ah!' said Mrs Evans. 'How handsome you look, luv!'

I did a double take. Even though I'd seen many posters and even watched several short clips on YouTube.com, nothing prepared me for the sight of Mr Evans dressed in the green multihued uniform of the Gipping Ranids.

'Look at his little bells!' squealed Annabel. 'Aren't they darling?'

'Did you *buy* those knee pads?' Mrs Evans said suspiciously.

'Don't start your nagging, Millie,' snapped Mr Evans, giving Annabel a wink.

'I just spent hours sewing those bells on by hand,' Mrs Evans said. Actually, she was wrong; I had. 'We've got boxes of bells lying about doing nothing but wasting space.'

Annabel scratched her head. 'If you need the money, you could always sell them on eBay.'

'eBay? *eBay*? I don't want to sell them on eBay!'

'Don't be like that, Millie,' said Mr Evans. 'She means well, don't you Annie, luv.' He reached out and ran his hands through her wet hair, accidentally pulling out a small clump. 'Jesus. You're molting.'

Annabel leapt to her feet, mortified. 'It must be that new shampoo you bought me.' She scratched her head again and pulled out another clump. 'Omigod! Excuse me,' she shouted, and darted from the room.

'Shampoo?' Mr Evans shrugged and sat in her chair. 'What's she talking about?'

'Tea?' said Mrs Evans swiftly, handing Mr Evans the newspaper. 'Quite a front page we've got this week.'

It wasn't one of the *Gazette*'s better efforts. Page One was split vertically down the middle. A large photograph of the Gipping Ranids and their frog mascot was featured on the left-hand side, with photographs of the Georgian tea urns and Trewallyn chalice on the right.

Both had headlines in equally heavy font: RANIDS READY TO ROCK! and SILVER SWIPE SHOCKER: TOWN REELS FROM DOUBLE WHAMMY!

Underneath a minuscule photo of Annabel in the bottom right-hand corner was the caption – TURN TO PAGE 2 FOR HOW YOU CAN HELP STOP CRIME!

'I pulled out the programme.' Mrs Evans passed me the centrefold that listed today's attractions, which included both hedge-cutting and hedge-jumping displays, a snail exhibition, and a bottled-jam boil-off.

A quarter-page advertisement carried a colour photograph of the Trewallyn Trio with the announcement that work would start on Monday.

'I thought we'd never raise enough money for that stained glass window,' Mrs Evans went on. 'It's been years since the night of the great storm.'

'Millie, come and see where they stuck old Phil Burrows,' chortled Mr Evans, pointing at the fine print in the left-hand corner of the front page. 'Page eleven, ON THE CEMETERY CIRCUIT WITH VICKY!'

'Serves him right for leaving town!'

'You won't get any of us leaving Gipping,' said Mr Evans. 'Why would you want to go somewhere else? Everything you need is right here. Right, Vicky? You moved from a big city to come to Gipping-on-Plym. What does that tell you?'

More than you could ever believe.

'Not only did Phil abandon the Ranids,' said Mrs Evans, 'but he left his brother, Steve, to take care of their dying mother.'

'*Valerie* Burrows?' I said, alarmed. 'I thought she was still alive.'

'She's been dying for years,' said Mr Evans.

'Attention seeking,' Mrs Evans chipped in. 'And, of course, if you say anything, she'll toss the "I'm dying" card, and no one can argue with that.'

Mr Evans turned to page two and frowned. 'Read this, Millie. What's Annie talking about?'

Following a bulletpoint list on how to keep your home burglar proof, Annabel had given her e-mail address promising 'absolute privacy' should anyone have any information leading to the recovery of a pair of priceless Georgian tea urns and the Trewallyn chalice from St Peter's Church. The article stressed that the gypsies residing at The Grange had already helped police with their inquiries and were not involved. However, she welcomed comments on her Facebook fan page.

'Load of rubbish! Of course the gypsies have stolen the silver,' said Mr Evans with disbelief. 'She needs her bloody head examined.'

'I thought the same thing, Lenny.' Mrs Evans's voice held a note of triumph. 'Annabel just doesn't think things through.'

The story went on to say that it was feared an international silver thief could be in the area and that he was highly dangerous. I had to read that sentence twice.

'International silver thief! What's that famous one called, Lenny? Something to do with the weather?'

'The Fog,' said Mr Evans. 'Though I can't imagine why he'd come to Gipping.'

My thoughts entirely!

Annabel returned having blowdried her hair but still in her pink robe with a rolled-up copy of the *Plymouth Bugle*.

'This just came through the letterbox, and I know how you

216

like to read – Omigod—' Annabel turned pale. She scratched her head, and another clump of hair came away, but this time she didn't notice, seemingly too preoccupied with whatever horror lay on the front page. 'What a stupid, stupid cow!'

'Give it here, silly lass,' said Mr Evans, taking the newspaper from her. 'What's happened? Aliens arrived in Gipping?'

'Nothing, nothing at all,' Annabel said brightly. 'Excuse me, I have to get to The Grange.' Tossing the *Plymouth Bugle* onto the kitchen table, Annabel ran out of the door and thundered up the stairs.

'She sounds like an elephant,' grumbled Mrs Evans.

Mr Evans picked up the *Bugle*. 'Bloody hell! Will you take a look at this?'

'Well I never!' said Mrs Evans. 'That's The Grange for sure!'

Splashed across the front page was a series of grainy photographs of a figure dressed from head to toe in black. Headlines screamed TOFF TOSSES TRASH! GYPSIES BLAMED!

The first image showed a tidy courtyard with a row of recycling bins. Each subsequent image showed the contents of said recycling bins scattered on the ground until the area resembled a tip. Even more telling was a link to a YouTube clip of the incident that I resolved to take a look at when I could.

An interview with gypsy human rights activist Dora Pike claimed that it was none other than the owner of The Grange, Lady Ethel Turberville-Spat, who was determined to get the gypsies evicted. Her ladyship could not be reached for comment.

'I can't believe her ladyship would do such a thing,' protested Mrs Evans. 'She's upper class.'

'No one takes any notice of this newspaper, Mrs E,' I said – although Annabel had seemed very upset about it.

I wondered if the recycling sabotage wasn't the only thing that her new friend Topaz was involved in. Dora had proven to be adept with a camera. What else had she been filming – a burglary or two, perhaps?

I fully intended to find out.

35

Rain had given way to a light drizzle, and all roads signposted to the Morris Dance-a-thon were choked with cars, bicycles, and pedestrians.

Along the narrow lane that led to the main gate, traffic was at a standstill, and when it was moving, it seemed to be at a snail's pace.

I must have double-checked that my homemade PRESS card was visibly displayed on the dashboard at least a hundred times.

As I edged my way up the drive, I saw the reason for the holdup. Someone had erected a STOP! HIGHWAY ROADWORK sign next to an open gate that led into the field allocated for public parking.

Standing at the entrance was my ex-heartthrob, Lieutenant Robin Berry, carrying a bus collector's old-fashioned ticket machine. Dressed in neatly pressed jeans, a white shirt, and a fiat tweed cap, Robin wore a red band diagonally across his chest emblazoned with PARKING £5.

This demand was excessive and seemed to be garnering a *lot* of complaints. A few cars had even managed to execute eleven-point turns and were causing a massive jam as they tried to return to the main road.

One driver stopped and wound down his window. 'You're press, aren't you?' It was snail-racing fanatic Bernard J. Kirby and his wife, Lily. 'Daylight robbery is what this is. There's nothing in your paper that said we had to pay for parking.'

'We've never paid before,' chimed in Lily.

Without even waiting for an answer, which was just as well, since I didn't have one, Bernard floored his Ford Kia, sending a torrent of muddy water over an entire family, who had been walking by on foot.

It looked like today was off to a bad start.

As my Fiat edged closer to Robin, my stomach gave a flutter of anticipation. He was handsome in that chiselled, man-cologne advertisement kind of way but – as I'd found out – not a very nice person and always looking for ways to make a profit.

Robin peered into my open car window. 'Five pounds. Cash only, please.' He gave a start of recognition. 'Vicky! Where's that little moped of yours?'

'I bought a car.'

'You should have told me,' he said. 'For a small fee, I would have happily helped you find a bargain.'

'Very kind. I hope you're not going to charge me – as in the press.' I pointed to the sign on my dashboard. 'And since when have people had to pay for parking around here?'

Robin shrugged. 'I'm just following her ladyship's orders.'

It didn't surprise me that Topaz had found another way to make money, but I was surprised that Robin had agreed to help. I made a mental note to ask her. I was beginning to have a very long list of questions for Topaz Potter.

Robin directed me to take another gate further up the drive between a marquee and a bank of blue Port-a-loos to the VIP entrance.

I was relieved. As I feared, the field allocated for the public was already a quagmire and claiming a few victims. I could make out four figures in matching hoodies pushing cars out of deep ruts, and the day was still young.

The drizzle stopped, and a watery sun peeped through the clouds. I was pleased to see that the showground looked really professional, with a plethora of coloured flags and bunting.

A rousing sound of military music drifted on the summer breeze. Barry Fir's cover band – Hogmeat Harris and the Wonderguts – had swapped their leather and fake tattoos for the scarlet, gold-buttoned jackets and white trousers of a traditional brass band. Accompanied by several members from St Peter's Church Youth Group, the band was seated on a raised covered podium and sounded surprisingly good as they belted out 'Coronation Bells'.

Set above the showground at the top of the bank adjacent to The Grange's vast patio stood Mary Berry's traction engine. Instinctively, I searched for Steve's ambulance and was reassured to see his white vehicle marked with a red cross and parked next to the bottled-jam boil-off tent – no doubt needing to be close to the unpredictable portable gas range used for this highly volatile competition.

Steve emerged from his ambulance and was mobbed by two young teenage girls. He made them laugh, and I felt ashamed. I realized I'd judged Steve because of the size of his body, not the size of his heart.

As I drove on by, I noted that the makeshift bleachers were already filling up with spectators.

The Devon Morris teams – or *sides,* to use the correct term – were assembled in brightly coloured groups, headed up by mascots ranging from dragons and rams to dogs and lions. Some dancers were warming up, tossing sticks back and forth. Others were doing squats and lunges. A banner listed the participants:

GIPPING RANIDS, TARKA MORRIS MEN, BLACKAWTON MORRIS, HARBERTON NAVY, DARTMOOR BORDER MORRIS, GRIMSPOUND BORDER, PLYMOUTH MORRIS MEN, DARTINGTON MORRIS MEN,

AND A SPECIAL GUEST APPEARANCE BY PHIL BURROWS OF THE TURPIN TERRORS!

The official Dance-a-thon wasn't due to start until eleven and was expected to run for at least six hours. There were two main categories – Side and Individual. Sponsors could rout for a side or an individual and had been given specific coloured ribbons to show their support when they originally signed up. A dropped stick or handkerchief merited instant disqualification even if the dancer could have kept on going all night.

I found a good parking spot far beyond the Port-a-loos, which backed onto a small copse and next to another five-bar gate that would afford me a quick exit. The gate was padlocked, but locks had never deterred me.

Donning my Wellingtons, I started back toward the arena when I heard the sound of an angry voice coming from behind the Port-a-loos. Creeping around the side, I went to eavesdrop.

To my astonishment, I found Jimmy Kitchen pinning one of the Gipping Ranids against a tree. I could only hear snatches of conversation but managed to catch 'pillar box', 'church window' and 'curse'.

Jimmy stepped aside to reveal Bill Trenfold!

I couldn't believe it. What could Bill Trenfold and Jimmy Kitchen possibly have in common? I knew I had witnessed something significant but didn't know what. However, I intended to find out.

I darted back to the front of the Port-a-loos just as Jimmy walked past, followed by a very worried-looking postman.

I hastened to join him. 'Hi, Bill,' I said. 'How are you?'

'Fine,' he mumbled. 'Excuse me but I'm in a bit of a rush.'

'That's okay,' I said. 'I'll walk with you.'

Bill set off at quite a fast pace, which was surprising, given his bandy legs. I had to hurry to keep up.

'What's all this nonsense about a pillar box and being cursed?' It was a wild stab in the dark, but as Mum says, *'nothing ventured, nothing gained.'*

221

Bill stopped dead. He turned pale, which against his green uniform gave him a ghoulish pallor. 'Lawd have mercy,' he whispered. 'How did you find out?'

'It was obvious.' I had no *real* idea what he was up to, but his reaction indicated I was on the right track.

Bill grabbed my arm, clearly frightened. 'I only left them open an hour or two, I swear to God. That's all I did. Nothing else.'

'Calling all competitors! Calling all competitors!' blasted the public address system. 'The Morris Dance-a-thon will be underway in five minutes. *Five* minutes!'

'You'd better go.' I'd hunt Bill down later. 'Good luck! Break a leg!'

Bill scuttled off, leaving me with a puzzle.

Dad says to look at what a man does for a living, what use he can be, and what kind of Achilles heel or secret he may have. Bill Trenfold was a post office worker who, by all accounts and purposes, was heavily in debt. If there was a service he could offer the gypsies, what could it possibly be? What could he have 'only left open an hour or two?'

Did it have something to do with the new collection times? Had the pillar boxes been deliberately left open? And why mention the church window?

One way or another, I was determined to find out.

36

A cacophony of feedback and screeches from the public address system was followed by an eruption of percussion instruments and the jingle of a trillion bells. The Morris Dance-a-thon had begun.

I headed toward the thick wall of people pressed against the ropes, applauding and cheering on the competitors.

Apart from Phil Burrows, who was standing on a special raised podium, all I could see were a series of leaping hats and waving handkerchiefs. Every so often the top hats and blackened faces of the Grimspound Border Morris dancers leapt into my line of vision, but frankly, after ten minutes I began to feel bored. Tony was welcome to report on this for the next six hours.

The snag was that I still wanted to talk to Steve about the sodium hydroxide but since I hadn't finished questioning Bill, I daren't leave this spot in case he darted off.

Reverend Whittler materialized by my side. 'Vicky, a word?'

Whittler's face was etched with worry. What's wrong?' I said.

'Did you post that letter?'

223

I was filled with a ghastly premonition. 'Of course,' I said. 'Why?'

'Where?'

'At the post office.' I felt terrible lying to a man of God but just couldn't bring myself to tell him that not only had I forgotten but when I *had* remembered, I'd dropped it in a pillar box.

Whittler gave me a piercing stare. 'Straight after Gladys Trenfold's funeral?'

I couldn't look him in the eye. 'Yes.'

Whittler wrung his hands. 'Windows of Wonder has not received the cheque. They have refused to start work on Monday.'

'I only posted the envelope on Wednesday,' I said. 'Maybe give it a few more days?'

'It had a first-class stamp.' Whittler shook his head. 'It should have arrived yesterday at the very latest. What if it's lost?'

Or *stolen*? *Good grief!* I had a startling epiphany. Hadn't I heard Jimmy say 'church window' and 'pillar box'? What would he have to do with either? It was obvious. The gypsies were in cahoots with Bill Trenfold. Somehow they had persuaded him to be an accessory to the crime. Bill Trenfold wasn't being forgetful about leaving the post boxes unlocked. He was doing it deliberately!

'What am I going to do?' said Whittler. It would certainly cause a scandal of almost Enron-like proportions in this community. I'd lost count of the number of times Mrs Evans had complained about donating money to the Trewallyn Trio and her concerns about Reverend Whittler's capabilities.

'Get the bank to trace the check when it turns up.' And what was the betting that the payee would have a different name!

'That's far too late,' groaned Whittler. 'What if we never get the money back?'

But I was only half listening. I wasn't my father's daughter for nothing. I knew all about cheque washing.

It was actually quite a simple process and could be done with household chemicals like acetone or bleach, even paint thinner. After erasing the payee, one simply wrote in the name needed, adjusted the amount, and deposited the cheque. A fake ID would secure a new bank account. With central banking and overseas call centres being the norm, by the time a rogue cheque was traced, it was too late. Money would have been withdrawn, the account closed, and the scam team moved on to pastures new. It was sheer genius. With Dora's flashy Winnebago, it was obvious that the actual process happened in there. What a scoop!

'I don't know why you are smiling,' Whittler scolded. 'This is very serious.'

'I'm smiling because I'm quite sure there is nothing for you to worry about,' I said. 'Do you trust me?'

'Of course, Vicky dear.'

'Can you stall them?'

Whittler brightened a little. 'I'll go and phone them right this minute.'

As he hurried off, my spirits fell. Did this mean that Noah was embroiled in the scam, too? What was I to do? Go to the police? Had I decided to stay and work in the family business, wouldn't I be doing exactly what Noah was doing now?

Once again, I saw how easily love could get in the way of my career. What a horrible dilemma!

A sudden blast of a car horn brought me back to reality. A Westward TV white Ford Transit 2.4 TDCi with the usual rooftop antennas and satellite nosed through the crowd.

My dilemma was forgotten as I was consumed with a horrible gnawing feeling of envy. Annabel was about to be on the telly. Annabel was soon going to be propelled to instant stardom.

The crowd's focus shifted away from the Morris dancers and seemed to move as one, away from the arena, much to the consternation of the competitors, who leapt even higher in an effort to keep their attention.

Confronting Bill Trenfold had now lost its urgency, and I found myself trailing after the news van along with everyone else. There was some problem as the line of customers outside Madame Dora's tent refused to move to let the vehicle through – for some reason, Dora had decided to pitch her tent in an area that was supposed to be left clear for emergency vehicles.

The news van had to take a detour around the perimeter of the arena until it reached the bottom of the flight of steps that led up to the patio of The Grange.

I had no trouble pushing my way through to the front. 'Let our Vicky by!' cried one. 'Break a leg!' and 'Here's the star!' called out another. If only that were true!

As Topaz began to regally descend the steps, there was the odd speculative comment referencing 'her ladyship's' appearance in the *Plymouth Bugle*, but this was instantly squashed by a general sense of disbelief.

Eavesdropping on various conversations, I realized that Topaz was held in the same high esteem as our own Queen Elizabeth II. It occurred to me that if Topaz's ridiculous pranks were ever exposed – throwing recycling around, stealing her own silver, and impersonating a lowly waitress – the town might never recover.

Today, Topaz wore a large straw hat and a pale blue linen suit – I was glad to see she had finally taken my advice and worn some magic knickers to control all that padding. Even from twenty feet away, I could see that her face was heavily powdered. She wore two bright spots of blusher on each cheek and a pale pink lipstick.

Standing ramrod straight, Topaz carried a square handbag with a snaffle-bit clasp. She paused on the bottom step, staring loftily across the crowds with a superior look that plainly said, 'These are my people.'

Annabel appeared, looking stunning in a forest green silk dress and white denim jacket and carrying a new Kate Spade handbag. In her hand she held a sheaf of notes and was laughing with a burly cameraman sporting a heavy beard whom she kept calling Rock. 'Rock, you are funny!' and 'Rock, I don't believe you!'

The two other members of the crew were Crispin, who reminded me of a ferret and was presumably the actual producer, and a very pale girl of around my age, who was dressed from head to foot in black and sported a large nose ring. She placed a sturdy metal cosmetic box on a collapsible table, then retrieved a plethora of cosmetic products and brushes from the box.

I scanned the growing crowd of admirers, waving at Mrs Evans and noticing – with relief – that Barbara stood next to Wilf, her arm linked into his. Hopefully she'd come to her senses – especially now that I was about to expose her lover's illegal business dealings.

Annabel waved me over. 'I'm so excited,' she gushed. 'All my life I've wanted to be on television.'

'And here you are,' I said with a tight smile.

'Have you met Cherish?' Annabel turned to the makeup artist. 'Cherish has connections with the BBC.'

'My brother works in the cafeteria.' Cherish gave me a sweet smile. 'Can I just finish you up, Ms Lake?'

'*Ms* Lake,' giggled Annabel.

Cherish took a large powder brush and loose powder pot and began to dab large puffy white clouds all over Annabel's face.

I thought I was going to die of envy. Pete pushed through the crowds and readjusted the collar of her denim jacket. 'You look good, Annie.'

Another *Annie*. I groaned. *Anyone* could look good if you had a full-time makeup person and the right lighting.

Cherish closed the lid of her sturdy metal box and put it on the ground. With a heavy-toothed comb and wire hairbrush in hand, she stepped up onto it and began to backcomb Annabel's hair.

Suddenly, there was a united gasp of horror.

'Omigod!' Cherish turned even paler than she was already and fell off her makeshift stool.

227

In her hands she held a huge clump of hair, as if she had just taken a scalp in the Wild West.

'What's the matter?' asked Annabel. There was a deathly hush.

Annabel's hand flew up to the crown of her head, her eyes widening in confusion. She spun around and, with a look of utter horror, saw her own hair dangling from Cherish's comb.

'Omigod!' She backed away, then turned tail and tore up the steps toward the house, her screams gradually receding into the distance.

'She never told me she had hair extensions,' cried Cherish. 'Honest to God.'

I caught Mrs Evans's eye and saw a flicker of what I knew to be guilt. Someone began to laugh, and then everyone was laughing.

However, Topaz's expression remained a mask of aristocratic indifference, and there, plain for all, was the difference between the upper and the lower classes. The former stayed cool and aloof in any situation, even if it was facing almost certain death by a thousand Zulus in deepest Africa, and the latter dissolved into hysterical disorder.

'Will you give this back to her?' said white-faced Cherish, offering me an auburn clump of hair the size of a fist.

'Put Vicky on camera!' Pete shouted.

It all happened so fast I didn't have time to react as Crispin swept forward and pulled me out of the crowd. Within a matter of minutes, Cherish had *very* carefully brushed my hair and applied a coating of makeup and powder.

Topaz materialized at my side with just a curt nod of acknowledgement. A hush descended on the spectators.

Crispin handed me an earpiece and a cordless mike. 'You do a general intro. The focus will be on her ladyship. We'll have to feed you Annie's questions.' *Does everyone call her Annie?* 'There will be only one take.' Crispin patted my shoulder and returned to the news van.

At last I was going to be on telly! I was euphoric! Instant nerves made my head clear and my mind sharp. Cherish helped me adjust the earpiece.

'Put in a word for the Olympics!' called out Dave Randall.

'Quiet!' ordered Cherish, who had exchanged her powder brush for a clapperboard. 'Ready to rock, Rock? Aaaaannnd . . . action!'

'Welcome to Gipping-on-Plym in deepest Devon and today's spectacular Morris Dance-a-thon,' I said smoothly. 'There are *many* Morris sides dancing here today, including a guest appearance by celebrity Phil—'

'Good morning, viewers,' said Topaz, snatching the mike from my hand. 'Welcome to The Grange, my ancestral home. The Turberville-Spats can trace our family tree to the War of the Roses—'

'Phil's participation' – I snatched the mike back – 'in this prestigious event has already raised money—'

'Which is why today' – Topaz took it again and started walking away, closely followed by Rock and his camera – 'I am making a nationwide appeal for the return of a pair of priceless Georgian tea urns that were given by George III when he visited Gipping in the summer of 1810, shortly before he was diagnosed with a bipolar disorder.'

Try as I might, I couldn't grab the mike back. 'There have been rumours that the Romany gypsies who are *guests* on my land are responsible,' Topaz went on in a lofty voice. 'However, we now know this is not true, and it's thought that because these Georgian urns were crafted by Hester Bateman – now dead but frightfully famous – these thefts can only be the work of an international silver thief called The Fog.'

The Fog? I thought I was going to faint. A murmur of excitement mixed with fear swept through the crowd. Topaz thrust the mike back into my hand. 'Vicky Hill is going to tell us all about this dangerous person.' I stood there like an idiot.

229

'*Tell them about The Fog*,' came the order through my earpiece.

'Yes, The Fog.' I struggled to think of something to say. 'Isn't he supposed to be in Brazil? I can't imagine why he'd come to Gipping-on-Plym.'

'*We don't want your opinion*,' growled the voice in my ear. My mind literally went blank, and as I searched for something to say, I saw Probes watching me intensely.

'Good question and one I was anticipating,' said Topaz, taking the mike back once more. She seemed to magically produce a photograph out of thin air and held it up to the camera lens. It was a mug shot of Dad looking violent, taken at his last admission to Wormwood Scrubs prison. 'This is whom we must be on the lookout for.'

'*Is he armed and dangerous?*' urged the voice in my ear, but I was speechless with shock.

Suddenly, the music in the background stopped, and apart from a few stray bells, a deathly hush descended on the showground.

A lone voice cried out, 'It's out of control!'

The crowd around Topaz and me now swarmed back to the arena. Someone began to scream.

Rock darted up the steps, camera rolling. I followed and, from our vantage point, witnessed something I hoped never to see again.

The Gordon traction engine came trundling down the slope without a driver. Mary Berry slithered down the bank, having desperately tried to clamber into the empty cab but fallen. A cry of terror swept through the crowd, but luckily, Mary rolled away from the deadly wheels.

The traction engine began to pick up speed; it broke through the rope and bunting and into the arena, heading straight for Phil Burrows's podium. Phil seemed rooted to the spot.

There were screams for him to 'Jump! Jump! For pity's sake!' and it was only as the giant wheels seemed to be upon him that he dived out of the way. The podium disappeared under the machine, reappearing seconds later as flat as a pancake.

Widespread shrieks switched to an eerie silence as it became apparent where the rogue machine was headed next.

Breaking through a flimsy post and rail fence, The Gordon plowed into Madame Dora's tent with a sickening crunch. It went straight through and out the other side, continuing on its trail of destruction until it pitched forward into a drainage ditch and stopped.

It began to rain.

37

It had been an hour since Dora Pike had been whisked away in Steve's ambulance. Having suffered from internal injuries beneath The Gordon's giant wheels, her condition was described as 'critical'. She was not expected to survive.

DI Stalk had shown a different side to his usual brusque nature, taking Ruby and Noah – who were completely hysterical – into his own car directly to Gipping Hospital.

I looked everywhere for Jimmy but assumed he must have been left with the awful job of informing Dora's father, Belcher Pike.

Following their dramatic departure, accompanied by a bevy of sirens and flashing lights, the Morris Dance-a-thon fell flat – no pun intended. Officers from Gipping Constabulary declared the event cancelled and sent people home. Tents were struck, merchandise was loaded up into Land Rovers, and there was the general feeling of shock mingled with euphoric fascination that always follows any tragedy. People demanded answers. Who was responsible? Was Mary Berry drunk? Was this an accident or manslaughter?

A rumour began to spread of potential lawsuits and insurance claims. The traffic division moved in with their various tape measures, sticks, and piles of stones to measure the trajectory of the vehicle, depth of tires, and skid marks. Special attention was paid to the condition of the ground.

I joined forces with Tony, jotting down eyewitness accounts. Tony told me that Annabel was seen driving off in her silver BMW with a paper bag over her hair.

Topaz retired to her rooms without even offering me a cup of tea and slice of cake. She seemed particularly unsympathetic to Dora Pike's accident, simply remarking that 'the gypsy woman was told she couldn't put up her tent in the emergency fire lane, but she wouldn't listen. It was her own fault.'

From the shelter of an overhanging oak tree, I watched the park empty out and a police minibus move in. Six officers disembarked – wearing riot gear and carrying shields – along with two German shepherds, terrifying dogs for someone like me. The coppers splashed through puddles, trying to keep their balance over fields slick with mud.

I managed to corner DC Bond. He was guarding Dora's partially collapsed tent behind a perimeter of crime scene tape.

'What's going on, Officer?' I said, gesturing to the riot police. 'Are you expecting trouble?'

The young copper's eyes filled with tears. 'We just got word from Steve Burrows. Dora Pike died on the way to the hospital. This place will be heaving with gypsies in the next few hours.'

Poor Steve. He'd taken Dora's death personally, of that I was sure.

'I am sorry.' I couldn't help but steal a glimpse at the partially flattened tent where I spied a solitary wooden leg from the same table I'd sat at only days ago. 'Have you seen Detective Inspector Probes?'

'He's down at the station helping take statements,' said DC Bond. 'We don't know if it was an accident or manslaughter—'

'It was neither,' said a familiar voice. 'It was an attempted murder!'

I turned to find Phil Burrows, still wearing his tricorn hat and highwayman mask, looking surprisingly cheerful. 'That engine was meant for me.'

'That's a very serious accusation, sir,' said DC Bond, whipping out his notebook.

'Vicky?' said Phil. 'You were there at Gipping Manor. Go on, tell him.'

My mind flew to John Reeves's threat in the bar on Thursday night and to Jack's secret meeting at the abandoned factory with the Swamp Dogs. Phil could be right, but why should I support his claim?

Frankly, Phil wasn't one of my favourite people. He was arrogant and conceited, not to mention the way he had deliberately sabotaged any sort of relationship – if I had wanted one – with Steve.

There was also the matter of alienating my readers. Those very people who had threatened Phil Burrows were also my friends.

'I think a lot of the men here are just jealous,' I said. 'I don't think they meant anything by it.'

'Oh really? Just take a look at this.' Phil retrieved a white envelope from inside his red tatter jacket and withdrew a piece of paper. 'Here, read that.'

The letters had been crudely cut from newspaper and stuck on with glue, LEAVE GIPPING OR YOU'RE A DEAD MAN.

'That's a death threat all right,' said DC Bond, peering over our shoulders.

I was shocked. 'Where did you get this?' I suddenly thought of TURPIN TERROR TERRORIZED!

'Gipping Manor,' said Phil. 'I found it under my hotel room door first thing this morning.'

'Did you ask the night porter?'

'No one saw anything.'

'Do you have any enemies?' DC Bond asked.

'A man in my position always has enemies,' boasted Phil.

'Can I look at the envelope?' I gave a start of recognition. EXTREMELY CONFIDENTAL – the exact spelling as that on Barbara's shoebox. For a moment, I was confused. I was positive that Dora had sent the shoebox to Barbara, but why would she threaten Phil Burrows?

'I saw them do it, you know,' said Phil.

'Who?' I said sharply.

'Those kids. That gang.' Phil shook his head. 'Kids today!' He snorted with disgust. 'I even gave them four of my tricorn hats for free.'

I was incredulous. 'You can't mean the Swamp Dogs?'

'I was dancing, and I like to pick a point in the crowd to help me focus – especially on the more difficult numbers,' said Phil. 'My spot was the traction engine on the bank. Three of the boys distracted the old biddy in the orange boiler suit, led her away on some pretext, whilst the fourth fiddled with something in the cab. Next thing I know, the thing comes down the bank at a hundred miles an hour.' *A slight exaggeration.*

'Those kids are a menace to society,' said DC Bond.

'Can I just have a word, Officer?' I pulled him to one side. 'I know these boys. They're not bad, just high-spirited, but could be easily led astray. I'd like to talk to them first because I have a feeling that someone put them up to it.'

'Sorry. This is now an official police matter.' He turned back to Phil. 'Would you go down to the station to make a statement, sir?'

Phil looked at his watch. 'I'll have to talk to my agent in LA first,' he said with a frown. 'I'm not sure if attempted murder is good or bad for my image. I'll be in touch.' And with that, he said goodbye and walked off.

'I'll speak to my superior officer and issue a warrant for the boys' arrest.'

'At least give them a chance to explain,' I said.

'No can do.'

With disgust, I left DC Bond to it, determined to find the Swamp Dogs first.

In the thirty-five minutes it took me to collect my Fiat and head for home – post-show traffic was terrible – the police were already swarming around the abandoned warehouse.

It would seem that the Swamp Dogs had vanished.

38

The moment I stepped through the front door at 21 Factory Terrace, I heard Annabel's heartbreaking sobs coming from upstairs.

As I passed her bedroom door – still bearing the traces of angel stencils despite Mrs Evans's attempts at removing them with acetone – another wail of grief stopped me in my tracks.

I refused to feel sorry for her. Even though it was hardly likely that Dad would watch the interview – Westward TV was not broadcast in Spain – there were enough of his cronies who lived in England who would. Dad would find out soon enough. He always did.

'Oh, oh, I want to die,' she sobbed.

It was no good. I wasn't that heartless. Maybe her hair would never grow back.

Gingerly, I tapped on the bedroom door. 'Can I come in?'

'Go away,' cried Annabel.

'At least let me take a look,' I said. 'And stop being so dramatic. Did you hear that Dora Pike died on the way to the hospital?'

There was a pregnant pause, then, 'Good.'

'Phil Burrows thinks the traction engine was meant for him. He said he's been having death threats.'

'Really?' I detected a glimmer of interest. 'Who sent them?'

'Apparently he had a lot of enemies.'

'Wait a minute.' Annabel blew her nose with a violent trumpeting sound and unlocked the door to her Hello Kitty-themed boudoir. 'It's obviously one of the Ranids,' she said with a sniff.

Annabel was wearing a pair of Juicy Couture plum-coloured sweatpants and a matching hoodie. Her face was a mass of blotches and streaked with mascara. A cotton bandana was wrapped around her head.

On the dressing table sat clumps of auburn hair.

Annabel's face crumpled. She sank onto the edge of her bed. 'My life is over,' she said miserably. 'I'll never be a Westward TV anchorwoman.'

'Mind if I take a look?'

'My head hurts.' Ignoring her feeble protestations, I removed the scarf and gasped. Annabel's scalp was covered in patchy livid whorls.

'Men will never look at me now.'

A peculiar feeling swept over me. Steve – oh Steve, how I need you now – had mentioned chemical burns caused by sodium hydroxide on Carol Pryce's head. Even though I'd only caught a glimpse that night in Mudge Lane, I had a feeling these were similar.

'I think it's something to do with your shampoo,' I said.

'Lenny bought me an expensive bottle especially for long hair.'

And in a flash I just knew! It wasn't Mr Evans who had bought the new shampoo but his wife. Hadn't she mentioned purchasing a 'fidelity potion'? Was it possible that Carol Pryce had been the victim of such a potion, too? In which case, the two women were linked. And if Mrs Evans's attitude toward

Annabel was anything to go by, they were linked by one thing. Jealousy.

'Where is the shampoo bottle?'

'In the bathroom. Why?'

'I want to look at the ingredients.'

'Why?'

'Perhaps you've had an allergic reaction?'

'To *shampoo*?'

'Ask Mr Evans where he bought it?'

'Oh no! I couldn't. Just couldn't.' Annabel looked utterly miserable. 'When Lenny got home earlier, I hoped he would comfort me, but instead, he was very unkind. He . . . he . . .' she gulped. A tear trickled down her cheek. 'He told me that he'd rather wait until my hair grew back and that we should lie low for a while.'

Men! Annabel had only been attractive to Lenny when she was a potential trophy mistress. Mum says that when a relationship is based on sex – though in this case, I shuddered to think of them reaching that level – the slightest physical deformity can end even the most passionate affair.

'What if it never grows back?' said Annabel. 'Or by the time it does, Lenny has found someone else?'

He's married to Mrs Evans, I wanted to scream, but instead had one of my clever ideas.

'I bet it's also the water here,' I said. 'A buildup of chlorine reacting with the Nice 'n Easy chemicals in that hair dye you use. Coupled with your new shampoo . . .'

Annabel frowned. 'I've never heard of that happening before.'

'Perhaps it's something to do with the factory across the street,' I went on, warming to my theme. 'The water is probably filtered through their old system. Copper pipes. Maybe even asbestos poisoning! You should stop colouring your hair.'

'Stop colouring my *hair*? Are you mad?' Annabel seemed appalled. 'I've never told you this, but . . . I went prematurely grey at sixteen from the shock of— no, I don't want to talk about it.'

'Oh dear. Poor you,' I said. 'What on earth are you going to do?'

'I don't have a choice, do I?' Annabel's bottom lip began to quiver. 'I'm going to have to move out.'

'Might be an idea,' I said, barely able to disguise my triumph. 'Why don't I remove that shampoo for now, though – just in case you accidentally use it again.'

I found Mrs Evans downstairs chopping carrots in the kitchen. She was humming quietly along to the radio, seemingly oblivious to the sounds overhead of drawers opening and slamming shut and the squeak of luggage wheels.

'Recognize this?' I said.

Startled, Mrs Evans spun around, vegetable knife in hand. Her eyes widened when she saw the shampoo bottle in my hand.

'No,' she said, but a faint flush covered her face. 'Whose is it?'

'Come along Mrs E,' I chided. 'Is this something to do with that fidelity potion?' There was still no answer other than a few clicks of her dentures. 'Pity. Because I thought it might be working.'

'What do you mean?'

'Hear that?' I pointed to the ceiling as the banging of drawers continued. 'Annabel is moving out.'

Mrs Evans burst into a grin so wide that I could practically count every single one of her false teeth. 'I can't believe it! I just can't! Fancy that!'

'Did you buy this shampoo from Dora Pike?'

'That poor woman,' said Mrs Evans. 'Dreadful. I was close to the ambulance, you know. When Steve loaded her onto the stretcher, her arm flopped out. It didn't look at all flat. I thought it would—'

'Mrs E.,' I said sharply. 'Where did you buy it? It's really important.'

'I don't remember.'

240

'If you don't tell me, I might have to mention the shampoo to Mr Evans.'

'You wouldn't *dare*!' Mrs Evans's dentures clicked into overdrive. 'It's too late. I threw away the bottle.'

'Good.' I marched over to the row of mini recycling containers on the draining board and went straight for the white bin (plastic bottles). 'You mean this?' The black plastic bottle was labelled MAN-STAY. I needed to get this analyzed as quickly as possible, but naturally I'd have to ask Steve, and, of course, he'd refuse.

'Please don't tell my Lenny,' begged Mrs Evans.

Mr Evans flung open the kitchen door. 'Come quickly! We're on the telly!'

We hurried into the sitting room just in time to watch The Gordon begin its descent down the slope, accompanied by a ticker-tape warning at the bottom of the screen rolling by on a loop: '*What you are about to see might be disturbing to some viewers.*'

The camera managed to capture the orange boiler-suited figure of Mary Berry desperately trying to climb aboard the runaway engine; Morris dancers scattering in all directions; and Steve bursting through the crowd, his mouth open in a long drawn-out 'Noooooo!'

The lens even zoomed in on a horrified Phil Burrows frozen with fear on his podium with the tagline TURPIN TERROR TERRORIZED.

'Oh bollocks,' muttered Mr Evans.

As the massive traction engine plowed through the ropes and rolled into Dora's tent, demolishing everything in its path, Mrs Evans clung to her husband's arm, shrieking, 'Is that her leg? It's her leg, isn't it?'

The last shot cut to Steve loading Dora – arms dangling off the side of the stretcher – into the ambulance.

'You see? She doesn't look at all flat.' Mrs Evans sounded disappointed.

WIDESPREAD RIOTING PREDICTED ran the ticker tape as DI Stalk warned folk to expect repercussions following Dora Pike's tragic death. He went on to say that the police had 'someone helping with inquiries' and that if she were found guilty, she could expect to face criminal charges of manslaughter.

'That would be Mary Berry,' said Mrs Evans. 'I saw her being driven off in a Panda car by young Kelvin.'

Stalk added that they were hoping that four lads – 'you know who you are' – would step forward to answer questions down at the station.

'Oh bollocks,' said Mr Evans again. He got up and left the room.

'Don't you want to see the rest of it?' shouted Mrs E.

'Got to make a phone call,' Mr Evans shouted back. And I had a very good idea to whom. I was going to have to have a word with Mr Evans about his rendezvous with Jack Webster.

There was no mention of Phil Burrows's death threat, though twice I saw him jumping around in the background, trying to attract the attention of the cameraman. Each time he was dragged away by Cherish and her clapperboard.

Stalk went on to wax lyrical about the dangers of drunk driving before being cut midsentence to Crispin, standing with Topaz at the bottom of the steps leading up to the patio.

Crispin looked grave. 'And that's not all that Gipping-on-Plym has had to endure this past week. Let's hear what reporter Vicky Hill from the *Gipping Gazette* has to say about one of Britain's top ten wanted criminals . . .'

Mrs Evans congratulatory strike across my back took me by surprise. I watched numbly as Dad's mug shot – so thoughtfully provided by Topaz – filled the screen.

As I spoke directly to the camera, the ticker tape switched to running details of Dad's most spectacular robberies – specifically the botched job in Bond Street, which resulted in a critically injured security guard – and that he was last known to be hiding out in Spain. A revolving slideshow of stolen silver antiquities – mostly Georgian tea urns – flashed to the right of my head along with their value.

I thought I was going to be sick.

Mr Evans returned and hovered behind the sofa: 'Got to go out in a tick, Millie.'

'Be quiet!' she admonished. 'Our Vicky's on the telly.'

My segment ended abruptly and cut to the studio for an 'extended report' on The Fog's crimes, mentioning the price tag of a hundred thousand pounds on his head.

A clip with Topaz – clearly taped before the afternoon's tragedy, since she was filmed sitting on her Knole sofa – claimed that her ladyship was convinced The Fog was responsible for the theft of the 'priceless Spat tea urns' because there had been a sighting of him in Gipping. The thought of Dad being here in Gipping was too much to take.

A short interview followed with criminal psychologist Skip Tanner, who explained how Harold Hill had earned his nickname because of his unique ability to seemingly come from nowhere and just as mysteriously vanish.

'The Fog's in Gipping, all right,' declared Mrs Evans. 'They have plastic surgery nowadays. Look at the Great Train Robber, Ronnie Biggs. He's had it done.'

'Your name's Hill,' chuckled Mr Evans. 'Any relation? We could do with a hundred thousand pounds, couldn't we, Millie?'

'She's got relatives in Spain, Lenny.' Mrs Evans cocked her head. 'Marie and Derek, isn't that right?'

'Very funny, Mrs E.,' I said, laughing just a little too heartily until Skip Tanner mentioned the distinctive sapphire blue eyes.

'Well I never,' she declared. 'Just like yours.'

'You know I wear contact lenses, Mrs E.,' I protested. 'In fact, they're really bothering me. Will you excuse me? I must go and take them out.'

I pushed past Mr Evans and darted from the room and tore upstairs.

I threw myself onto my bed in shock. Had Mrs Evans guessed

the truth? She often questioned me about my family. When I'd told her that my parents had been eaten by lions in Africa, she was very upset, saying, 'poor little mite' over and over again and insisting I regard her and Lenny as my adoptive parents.

Seeing Dad's face on the telly and Dora Pike's body on that stretcher had truly shaken me. I had to get a grip.

Dora Pike had definitely known Carol Pryce, and it was my belief that her estranged husband had been indulging in a little affair – hence the use of MAN-STAY. Was Carol Pryce murdered because of this – or was it something to do with the cheque-washing scam? I was beginning to see that perhaps justice was being served in the gypsy community, and I'd never know the truth.

Even though I knew Steve no longer wanted to talk to me, I left a message for him all the same – mentioning that I physically had the source of Carol Pryce's chemical burns and desperately needed it analyzed. I was ashamed to admit that I added a quick 'I miss you' as I ended the call so that when my phone rang mere minutes later, I felt a tiny grain of triumph.

But I was wrong. It wasn't Steve. It was one of the Swamp Dogs.

'Vicky, it's Malcolm! We didn't mean to kill her. You've got to help us.'

Begging me to meet them up at Ponsford Cross phone box, I quietly slipped out of the house.

There wasn't a moment to lose.

39

When I got to Ponsford Cross telephone box, there was no sign of anyone. The place was deserted. Located high on Ponsford Ridge, the location was bleak.

I stood around for several minutes until I heard a *'Pssst'* coming through a hole in the hedge, followed by, 'are you alone?'

'There's no one here but me,' I called out.

Moments later I joined them on the other side of the hedge in a field full of sheep.

They all looked deathly pale apart from Brian, whose face was blotchy, as if he'd been crying.

'What happened?' I said.

The boys all talked at once: 'accident', 'not our idea' and 'Jack Webster threatened to blackmail us about stealing some cutting equipment – which we never touched!'

'We only meant to scare him,' finished Mickey.

'Him?' I was confused. 'I thought this was about Dora Pike?'

'It's bad luck to kill a gypsy,' wailed Brian.

'No. Mr Webster wanted to frighten that celebrity, Phil Burrows.'

'It was just a trick,' piped up Ben.

'She wasn't supposed to be there,' said Mickey. 'She refused to move her tent. Least, that's what I overheard Steve Burrows say. He said she was creating a safety problem blocking the emergency lane.'

'And Jack Webster put you up to it?' I said. 'Did he pay you?'

'It was supposed to be twenty-five pounds each, but now that the woman is dead, he's pretending he doesn't know what we're talking about.'

'It's our word against his,' said Malcolm. 'No one will believe us.' He was right. Everyone knew that Jack had a personal vendetta against the Swamp Dogs.

'Just to be clear,' I said, 'one of you released the brake on the traction engine whilst the others distracted Mary Berry?'

'Yes,' mumbled Mickey. 'That's about it.'

'But how did you know The Gordon would roll down the hill in the right direction?' I said.

The boys all looked at one another. 'Go on,' Malcolm said, 'tell her.'

'Mr Webster wanted me – because I'm good at physics – to calculate the basic mechanical units of mass, length, and time,' said Mickey.

'You're losing me.' I had never been good at physics.

'The weight of an object is the force of gravity on the object and may be defined as the mass times the acceleration.'

I still didn't have a clue as to what he was talking about. 'Okay. So what you're saying is that all those little stones and drawings in the dirt the other day had something to do with this?'

The boys nodded in unison.

'That's really silly,' I said. 'Didn't it occur to you that people would jump out of the way?'

'The gypsy woman didn't,' said Malcolm darkly.

'What about the anonymous letter?' I said. 'Did you send that to Phil, too?'

'No!' they chorused.

'Spell *confidential*.'

Brian stepped forward. 'C-o-n-f-i-d-e-n-t-i-a-l. Confidential!'

'That's right.'

'Of course that's right. Brian's the best at spelling.'

If the boys hadn't sent the note, chances were that Jack Webster had, and he could have left trace evidence. We might at least be able to prove that Jack was involved.

Ben started to cry. 'Dad is going to kill us—'

'We're going to jail—'

'What we're going to do is go down to the police station,' I said firmly. Ignoring the chorus of protests, I went on, 'I saw Jack Webster leave the abandoned factory the other night, remember?' I also remembered seeing Jack Webster call on Mr Evans and only hoped he hadn't enlisted him into the bargain.

'I'm staying here. I'm going back to the Land Rover.' Ben turned on his heel and started walking away toward what looked like a camp built into the corner of the field and covered in a khaki tarpaulin that I hadn't noticed up until now.

In a flash, I just knew what was under there.

Moments later I had pulled the tarpaulin aside to reveal the hood of a green Land Rover. A further inspection revealed a safari rack and overhead lighting. Trembling with excitement, I traced my fingers along the scrapes of blue paint that ran the length of the driver's side panel.

I had found the Mudge Lane mysterious Land Rover at last.

On the front passenger seat was a copy of *Romany Ramblings*.

'How long has this been here?' I was euphoric. The fact that it had been hidden away was a sure sign of guilt. The question was, who had been driving?

'Dunno,' said Ben. 'When we saw all the police arrive in that minibus, we got scared and were looking for somewhere to hide.'

Promising Ben that it was highly unlikely they were going to prison for life, we rejoined the others.

The day may have started off badly, but – without meaning to sound callous – things were certainly looking up for my next Vicky Hill exclusive!

But first I had to sort out the Swamp Dogs. I loathed police stations at the best of times, but I wasn't about to let four young lives be ruined.

These boys would need all the help they could get.

40

Half an hour later the four boys and I were sitting on a hard wooden bench in the waiting room courtesy of Gipping Constabulary. On arrival, the desk sergeant had taken one look at my charges and said, 'You lot are going to jail,' which made Ben cry again.

It was getting late, yet the place was still heaving with people eager to give eyewitness accounts of the afternoon's tragedy.

One hour later, we were still sitting there. The boys were fidgeting and had started to pick fights with each other. I was beginning to get irritated myself. This was not how I'd planned my Saturday evening.

I wanted to return to The Grange and attempt to break into Dora's empty Winnebago before Ruby and Noah returned from the hospital. I'd been doing a lot of thinking and come to the conclusion that the cheque-washing equipment had to be in there or in Belcher Pike's wagon.

'I'm thirsty,' snivelled Ben. 'Can I have a coke?'

I set off in search of snacks and soon regretted my generous offer. Standing next to a vending machine packed with cans of Coca-Cola, soft drinks, and crisps was Lieutenant Robin Berry.

Blast! I'd forgotten about his mother being arrested. Of course he'd be here – and most likely his odious aunt, Eunice Pratt, too.

I darted back around the corner, but Robin had seen me. 'I thought that was you. Can you spare three pounds? I don't have any change, and Auntie is hungry.'

'Sorry, I need the change myself.'

He watched whilst I pressed the various letters and numbers and heard the reassuring clunk of four cans of Coca-Cola drop down, one after the other.

'That's very kind of you, Vicky,' said Robin. 'But I wished you'd checked. Auntie doesn't drink Coca-Cola. She'd rather have a cold orange juice.'

'Actually, these are for the Swamp— never mind.'

'You were going to say Swamp Dogs, weren't you?' Robin's eyes narrowed. 'I don't believe it! They're the ones responsible for putting my mother in here! My God! Are you actually buying them refreshments?'

'The police gave me the money,' I lied. 'How is your mother?'

'What do you expect?' snapped Robin. 'It's a blatant case of ageism. Stalk believes no one over the age of sixty should be driving. He even accused her of being drunk! Auntie is going to start one of her petitions. As a matter of fact, perhaps she should write a piece for your newspaper?'

'Great idea! She should phone our chief reporter, Pete Chambers,' I said. Let him handle her. 'Must dash. Bye.'

When I got back to the boys, DI Stalk was waiting for me along with DC Bond. The younger twins were now crying hysterically. The elder pair was just looking sullen.

'I've got their parents in interview room two, but they begged me to wait for you,' said Stalk.

I handed the boys their drinks. 'Can I have a quick word, Inspector? In private?'

Stalk glowered but gave a curt nod. 'All right. Two minutes.

Officer Bond, take them to their parents.'

Briefly, I told Stalk about Jack Webster hiring the boys. I mentioned that they were good students at school – well, at least two of the four had brains. Stalk listened but just said he'd 'take my comments into consideration' and that the boys were 'old enough to know what "malicious intent" meant.'

I felt disappointed, but what else could I do?

'You're saving me a trip,' said a voice I knew all too well. 'I heard you were here at the station.'

DI Probes handed me a plastic cup of tea. 'Milk and one sugar if I remember correctly?' He was dressed in jeans and a sweatshirt. 'We didn't really ever finish our conversation behind the pigsty, did we?'

I felt my face redden as I remembered Noah rushing to my rescue. 'I think there was a misunderstanding.'

'Don't worry, I've forgotten about that,' he said. 'I really need to talk to you. It's very important. Follow me.'

It was an order. Probes set off with his long, quick strides, with me hurrying after him, trying to keep up.

He ushered me through a door marked INTERVIEW ROOM 3. 'Take a seat.'

It was a stark place with drab green walls and a mirror that I knew disguised a one-way window into an adjoining observation room. Two surveillance cameras were set high in opposing corners. In the centre stood the usual metal table and four uncomfortable plastic chairs, with a tape recorder plugged in and ready to go.

As a young teenager, I'd sat on the wrong side of a table such as this one many times and instantly felt defiant and on the defensive. The cops in Newcastle used to call me Little Vicky Light-Fingers. Perhaps that was why I felt empathy for the Swamp Dogs. Once the police know your name, you get a reputation that is almost impossible to shake off.

I dragged out a chair and sat down, mentally preparing myself for some kind of interrogation.

Probes did not sit down. Instead he used his chair to stand on and switched off both surveillance cameras. Then he pulled the blind down over the one-way window.

My mouth went dry, and my stomach began to churn. What did he want to talk to me about? Topaz? The missing silver— oh God . . . *Dad*?

Probes sat down and clasped his hands in front of him on the table. 'This is completely off the record,' he said firmly. 'This is not for the newspaper.'

I nodded but, of course, wouldn't take any notice.

'Operation Pike has collapsed.' I must have looked puzzled because Probes gave an exasperated sigh. 'Come on, Vicky, you can't really believe that we would deliberately let the murder of one of our own go unreported?'

'Carol Pryce was a *cop*?'

'One of our best undercover policewomen from Scotland Yard,' said Probes grimly.

How could I have been so blind! It made perfect sense. My hunch had been right all along. Carol was a gypsy – but not a real one. It explained why the gypsies pretended they didn't know her and why the police didn't seem to care.

'But how did Carol manage to befriend them?' I said. 'They're a close-knit community, naturally suspicious of gorgers.'

'It took her six months to gain Noah's trust,' said Probes. 'She met him on the road, posing as a scout for a gypsy folk festival.'

'How old was she?' I asked, surprised to feel a small twinge of jealousy.

'Why? Is it important?'

'It will be when I write the story.'

'I told you, this is off the record, and I will explain why in a moment,' said Probes. 'I really felt we could still pull it off until my ridiculous cousin started meddling and stealing her own silver, trying to get them evicted. We had to play it down, keep it quiet—'

'Which is why you moved Carol Pryce's body to Plymouth morgue and tried to hush the whole thing up?'

'Naturally your editor and chief reporter knew,' said Probes.

'Wilf and Pete *knew* about all this?' I was stunned and more than a little upset.

'They had to,' said Probes. 'We couldn't afford for anyone to go digging – but you still did it anyway. When are you going to learn to do as you're told?'

'Excuse me?' I said hotly. 'I was doing my job! Some poor woman was murdered, my Fiat was hit by a getaway car, and you expect me to *ignore* it?'

'Well—'

'And what were you doing in Mudge Lane anyway?' I asked. 'You just materialized from thin air.'

'Carol was on her way to see me.' Probes's voice was riddled with anguish. 'She left me a message that she'd found something out about Belcher Pike. The autopsy came back saying she was knocked unconscious by a blunt object and drowned—'

'By the man in the Land Rover fleeing the scene,' I said.

'We *have* been looking for that Land Rover, Vicky, but can't find it anywhere.'

'That's bad luck.' I was still fuming about being kept in the dark. 'And why were you wearing your pyjamas in Mudge Lane?'

Probes gave a wry smile. 'My grandfather left me Mudge Cottage in his will. There is a footpath that leads to the ford through the sunken garden.'

'Oh. That's nice,' was all I could say. How was I to know?

'Carol was a good cop, and she deserves justice,' said Probes. 'It's over. There's no way to connect her with the gypsies now.'

'There is, actually,' I said slowly. 'Didn't the autopsy report say she had chemical burns on her scalp?'

Probes frowned. 'How do you know that?'

'I can't tell you.' Quickly, I outlined Annabel Lake's experience at the hands of the fidelity potion.

253

'*Man-Stay*?' said Probes incredulously. 'But why?'

'My guess is that one of the women – Dora or Ruby – didn't like Carol getting close to their men. It was a warning.'

'What difference does that make now?'

'My landlady bought a bottle from Dora Pike. I have a sample. The lab could analyze it. At least it would connect her with Carol Pryce.'

'Both are dead, Vicky.' He stood up and started pacing around the room. 'This is all so hopeless.'

'Why *was* Carol Pryce working undercover?' I said. 'Is this anything to do with the cheque scam?'

Probes jaw dropped. 'How did you guess?'

Jeez. Did I have to do all the work for the Gipping Constabulary?

'I'm very close to the community,' I said modestly. 'Not much passes me by.'

'Clearly not,' said Probes, though I detected admiration in his voice. 'Dora, Ruby, Noah, and Jimmy – last name Kitchen but still married to a Pike. Ninety-nine per cent of gypsy crimes involve the entire family.'

He could say that again. It was the same in Dad's world – except I was the only one who refused to do it.

Probes filled me in. Apparently it starts with an advance party. He or she moves to a town – usually at least one hundred miles from the last – and studies the local newspapers. The goal is to get a feel for the area, find out what kind of fund-raisers or appeals are going on. A bank account is also set up using a fake ID.

In Gipping, there would have been a lot to choose from, ranging from the stained glass window appeal to the Naked Farmer support fund. The gypsies never stay long – a maximum of three weeks so as to avoid detection.

'I assume you've checked Dora's Winnebago?' I said. 'She has a ton of high-end printers and scanners in there.'

'All above board,' said Probes. 'We searched all their wagons the first time the silver went missing. The moment Stalk took Ruby and Noah off to the hospital, we made a thorough search and came up with nothing. We've looked everywhere—'

'Except Belcher Pike's wagon, which you can't touch,' I said. 'It's off-limits. Human rights. Race relations. You name it. Dora certainly knew the law.'

'Our laws are now making it easier than ever to conduct illegal business dealings,' Probes declared. 'Hiding behind a front of respectability.'

'Yet they always need help from the inside,' I pointed out. 'Like Bill Trenfold.'

'The postman?' Probes nodded slowly. 'But how to get him to confess?'

'Legally, he's doing nothing wrong,' I said. 'Forgetting to close the pillar box door is hardly—'

'A criminal offence—'

'Unless we can prove he's doing it for monetary gain.'

'Have you ever considered becoming a detective?' said Probes dryly.

'I suppose an investigative reporter *is* a detective!' I said.

'Vicky, we need your help,' said Probes. 'You seem to get along with them – or should I say, Noah – pretty well.'

'I'm sorry. I don't understand.'

'We need to get inside Belcher Pike's wagon. Find some evidence. Anything.'

'Presumably you went through the recycling bins?' I recalled Dora's wide-eyed panic when Noah dropped the plastic bag containing an empty bottle marked ACETONE. I had assumed he'd had far more sinister reasons – like burning down The Grange.

'We will now,' said Probes. 'Will you help us?'

The truth was, I liked Noah. We had much in common, both trying to escape our families. Deliberately befriending Noah would amount to a betrayal, and I didn't think I could do it, to say nothing of the obvious – a Hill? Helping the police with their inquiries? I didn't think so. And yet here was a chance to snag one of the biggest scoops of the year – a real undercover exclusive.

I stood up. 'Sorry. I'm not a spy.'

'We really need you, Vicky,' said Probes. 'A policewoman was murdered. Jimmy Kitchen is a very dangerous man.'

'Sorry,' I said again. 'I can't.'

'This isn't snitching on a rival crime family about some missing Georgian tea urns, Vicky.' Probes's voice was hard. 'This is serious.'

I felt dizzy and had to clutch the edge of the table. 'I really don't know what you mean.' But I did! Probes knows! Oh God! He knows who I really am! He knows about Dad.

My mobile phone suddenly rang. Relieved, I fumbled to get it out of my safari-jacket pocket. 'Yes?' I croaked.

It was Olive.

'Barbara's run off,' she shrieked. 'She's gone with that gypsy, Jimmy Kitchen. You have to stop her!'

'I have to go,' I said to Probes. 'This is an emergency.'

'Take this,' Probes handed me his business card. 'In case you change your mind.'

'I won't.'

256

41

Dusk was falling as I drove as fast as I could to The Grange.

With Dora out of the way, Barbara must have had a change of heart. I thrust all thoughts of cheque scams, missing silver, and Dad out of my head. I had to get to Barbara. Probes had warned that Jimmy was a dangerous man. She'd be making a terrible mistake.

As I drew closer to The Grange, I was stunned to find the place heaving with caravans, old wagons, and campers.

Women were setting up communal cooking areas. Some men secured tarpaulins and plastic sheeting to add undercover living space to their caravans, whilst others marked out their own individual pitches with knee-high posts and rails. A group of youths were digging a trench and putting in standpipes. Another large truck was offloading hardcore directly onto the grass.

News of Dora's death had travelled fast and was clear evidence of the Romany phone tree – vurma – in action.

To my relief, I saw Jimmy's and Noah's painted wagons and Ruby's VW camper still parked by the hedge.

Leaving my Fiat, I clambered over the fence and set off

across the grass. Fortunately my presence was ignored, as the newcomers seemed too absorbed in setting up their own camps.

I half expected to see Barbara's pink bicycle leaning against the rear.

All three vehicles were deserted. Standing outside Jimmy's wagon, I began to have second thoughts. What exactly was I hoping to achieve? When had Barbara ever listened to me anyway? Hadn't I just used Olive's phone call as an excuse to run away from Probes and the terrifying possibility that he knows who I really am?

Noticing that many gypsies seemed to be heading in the direction of Dora's Winnebago, I did, too.

No doubt Jimmy would be there – but wait! That didn't make sense. Even if he and Dora *were* estranged, would Jimmy really flaunt Romany custom and blatantly parade his new woman the very night his wife had died? Something was off.

Up behind the stable block, a candlelight vigil was being held in front of Dora's Winnebago. Even though her body still lay in Gipping morgue, the Winnebago was slowly being transformed into a shrine, as people laid down flowers, jewellery and colourful shawls.

There was no sign of Jimmy. Presumably Noah and Ruby were still with Dora's body, if gypsy custom was anything to go by. Although I'd had my fill of gypsy research recently, I wasn't clear on what happened if someone had met a sudden and unexpected death and made a mental note to find out.

This scenario was so different from the other Pike, who was still awaiting the Grim Reaper in Trewallyn Woods. It got me thinking: wouldn't these mourners want to pay their respects to Belcher, too?

A young couple no older than me walked up. He wore a flat cap, jeans and a denim shirt, and was carrying a small cardboard box full of colourfully painted fir combs; she was heavily pregnant, with beautiful dark hair falling down to her waist. In her hand she cradled a Royal Crown Derby milk jug.

258

'I was looking for Dora's husband, Jimmy Kitchen,' I said. 'Have you seen him?'

'Why?' The man's eyes narrowed. 'You're not one of us. Go away.'

The woman gently pressed his arm. 'Hush, this is no time for anger.' She turned to me with a smile. 'I'm Elaine Pike, and this is Seth. Who are you?'

'Vicky Hill. I work for the *Gipping Gazette*—'

'The papers,' said Seth, barely disguising his contempt.

'Dora and I were friends,' I said with exaggerated sadness. 'I'm actually going to write her obituary.' If I played my cards right, perhaps Elaine might help me with the names of the mourners. 'She was a wonderful woman. *Wonderful.*'

'She was. Always looking out for her kind,' said Elaine.

Seth, seemingly overcome with emotion, set down the box of fir combs on top of the Winnebago steps. He snatched off his cap, head bowed.

'Dora gave us the fir combs for our first Christmas tree,' said Elaine. 'This milk jug was our first wedding anniversary present.' She gave a heavy sigh. 'But Dora needs them now to take on her journey to the new world.'

'What happens to all these things?' I said.

'They'll be put in the Winnebago and burned,' said Elaine. 'We do what we can these days to keep our traditions alive. We are put onto caravan sites and told not to fight fires, but how can we bury our dead with dignity if we can't light a fire?'

It must have been difficult for Dora to speak out for gypsy rights and to demand equality yet at the same time insist on the preservation of ancient customs in the face of progress.

I gestured to the growing number of mourners, hoping for a glimpse of Jimmy and Barbara. 'Are you all Pikes?'

'For the most part,' said Elaine. 'We marry our kind.'

'I suppose you'll be paying your respects to Belcher, too.' I pointed in the direction of Trewallyn Woods. 'His wagon is over there.'

259

The girl frowned. 'Who?'

'Belcher Pike?'

'Belcher?' said Elaine with surprise. 'Are you talking about Dora's dad? He's been dead—'

'Elaine!' said Seth sharply as he rejoined us. 'Let's go back to our caravan.' Glowering at me, he took her arm and led her away.

I stood there like a fool. How could I have been so blind – and I called myself my father's daughter?

Belcher Pike was just a front. The wagon was obviously being used for some other purpose, and I had a jolly good idea what that could be.

Pushing past a group of oncoming mourners, I decided it was best to take the animal track through Trewallyn Woods to Belcher's wagon. With Ruby and Noah presumably still with Dora's body at the morgue, it was highly unlikely they'd be there, but it was best to be on the safe side. Ditto Jimmy. And if he were, he'd be with Barbara. And that's when I got worried. Did this mean that Barbara was going to get swept up in this mess, too?

Three of the six policemen – who I noted weren't Gipping regulars – and the two German shepherds were hanging around the pigsty. With their riot shields and helmets tossed aside, the coppers were chatting and playing cards, using the top of an oil drum as a makeshift table.

DC Bond had been wrong when he said that Dora's tragic death would result in trouble. With nothing to do, they were just frittering away taxpayer money.

Even if I had been tempted to enlist their support, the sight of those dogs made up my mind. Giving a friendly wave, I hurried on by, acknowledged only by growls from both German shepherds.

When I reached the clearing, the place seemed deserted, the barbed wire had been taken away, and the sign – GORGERS KEEP OUT – removed.

After counting to five hundred, I decided to take a chance and darted across the grass and up the three short steps to the door. Of course it was locked, but when had any lock stopped me?

Deftly using my lock pick, I let myself inside and shut the door behind me. It was dark. I brought out my Mini Maglite and found a light switch.

With a click, the wagon was filled with dazzling overhead fluorescent lighting.

This may have been a traditional wagon at one time, but not anymore. The casement window at the back and the high narrow windows on both sides had been covered with some kind of coating to keep out sunlight.

Two artist's tables, with a giant magnifying glass on hinged brackets affixed to each, stood side by side, with two three-legged stools. A scanner, laminating machine, laptop computer, and high-end printer were set on one counter, along with various tools – gel pens, box knives, tongs and rulers. On the other stood various liquid-filled pans, an industrial-sized bottle of acetone marked HIGHLY FLAMMABLE and a half-eaten ham sandwich on a china plate. Someone had left in a hurry, no doubt on hearing news of Dora's death.

Above me, three cheques were pegged to a piece of washing line that was hooked from corner to opposite corner. I took them down, fairly bursting with excitement.

The account holder of the first was none other than ST PETER'S PARISH COUNCIL, C/O THE VICARAGE, CHURCH LANE, GIPPING-ON-PLYM. The cheque was for five thousand pounds, but instead of being made out to Windows of Wonder, the payee was now Danny Stone.

Immediately I thought back to Phil Burrows calling Noah 'Danny' in Gipping market square.

How could I have been so naive? Of course Noah would be involved. He's family. Even though I understood, I felt a stab of acute disappointment. I'd hoped he was different.

Forcing myself to focus on the matters in hand, I took down the other two cheques. Both were made payable to Danny Stone, but I suspected they were intended for poor Mrs Evans.

One was from Margaret Pierce; the other, from Lady Turberville-Spat with a London address. The latter was for a huge amount – one thousand pounds. Presumably the gypsies had thought she could afford it and wouldn't notice.

Spying a heap of empty gunnysacks in the corner, I recalled seeing Jimmy with one flung across his handlebars. *Very clever!* I'd thought him off poaching – which in a way he was – yet if I'd really stopped to think about it, poaching goes on at night. Not in broad daylight.

Didn't Dad always say that the most successful operations were usually carried on right under people's noses? I was losing my touch and should have known better.

I had to say I was impressed with this scam, which had been brilliantly planned and perfectly executed.

Belcher Pike had proved to be a very effective front, particularly using the 'isolated wagon' ruse of a dying gypsy. No one would dare upset the applecart for fear of legal reprisals.

Using Dora's celebrity-activist status was sheer genius. She'd exploited the Human Rights and Race Relations Acts to the extreme. Even her passion for recycling had presented this small gypsy family as one trying to live in peace and not make waves.

As Probes had said, the gypsies never stayed long, cherry-picked their victims, and didn't get too greedy. Cheques went missing, but not enough to attract media attention. If it hadn't been for Dora's unexpected death, no one would have been any the wiser.

The gypsies were pure opportunists, and I had to applaud them. Suddenly the door flew open.

'What the hell are you doing in here?'

It was Jimmy Kitchen.

42

'I was looking for Barbara,' I said desperately, hoping my friendship with the love of his life might save me. Usually in this kind of situation, I'd either bluster my way out or run. This time I could do neither.

'You shouldn't be here.' In his hand he carried a heavy gas can and was blocking my escape.

'Where, is she?' *Talk of Barbara, Vicky! Focus on Barbara.* 'What have you done with her?'

'What do you mean?'

'Barbara,' I said. 'Where is she?'

Jimmy all but threw the heavy can onto the ground with a thud. He grabbed my shoulders and shook me hard. 'Why would she be here? Tell me.'

'She . . . she . . . told Olive Larch.' My heart gave a sickening jolt. 'Aren't you running away together?'

All the colour drained from Jimmy's face. 'Running away? We can't run away! Not now. Not ever.'

I started to feel frightened. 'Then . . . what's happened to her?'

'Come out with your hands up!' a voice boomed, followed by

263

a chorus of frantic barking. 'You are completely surrounded; I repeat; you are completely surrounded!'

'It's the police!' I said, startled. Those card-playing coppers must have been paying attention after all.

Jimmy seized the gas can and unscrewed the cap. 'Get out!' he cried, throwing me aside. He moved swiftly to the back of the wagon, sloshing the liquid over every surface.

'What are you doing?' The stench made me gag. 'It's too late. The police know everything.'

'We're coming in!' boomed the voice. 'We have dogs, and they will attack!'

I thought I'd faint with fear. 'We've got to leave! Now!'

'No, I must do this.' He turned to me, his voice cracked with emotion. 'I think Ruby has my Barbara.'

'*Ruby?* Why? Where?' I grabbed his arm. The sound of dogs barking drew nearer. 'Where would Ruby take her?'

Jimmy pulled a box of matches out of his pocket. 'Our special place. The kissing bridge in Mudge Lane.' He paused, his face etched with sadness. 'Tell her that she's always been the one.'

I ran out of the door, hands held high in surrender. Twenty yards away stood the three policemen, cowering behind riot shields, with the dogs straining on their leashes, ready to attack.

'Wait! I'm Vicky Hill!' I shrieked. 'Run! Stand back, he's got—'

But it was too late. There was a huge explosion that picked me up off my feet and hurled me to the ground.

The wagon was engulfed in a giant ball of flame. Numb, I watched it burn with such fierce intensity that, within minutes, all that was left was a blackened shell.

'He's alive,' shouted one of the policemen from behind his riot shield. He pointed to a ragged figure crawling toward the undergrowth. 'Clever bugger must have jumped out the rear window.'

Jimmy had also destroyed all the evidence.

A police officer ran toward the fallen gypsy. 'Call for an ambulance!'

'Find Barbara,' gasped Jimmy. 'Hurry.'

I only hoped it wasn't too late.

43

It was dark by the time I reached the entrance to Mudge Lane. I'd come in from the other side this time. The road was just as steep, narrow and twisty. I only hoped I wouldn't run into Ruby's VW camper coming from the opposite direction.

Switching off the headlights, I slowly eased the car downhill, praying I would be able to find a place to leave it. A field would be perfect.

I'd had some time to think on the drive over and realized I would be dealing with an irrational female who had just lost her mother and believed she was about to lose her father, too.

To my relief, a five-bar gate loomed out of the darkness. I jumped out, dragged it open across the mud, then returned to my car. The field was practically a bog. Thank heavens for four-wheel drive!

Donning a black balaclava and changing into my Wellingtons, I took off on foot, feeling a weird sense of déjà vu. Wasn't I doing just the same thing last Tuesday?

With my Mace Screecher in my pocket along with a pair of handcuffs – courtesy of www.handcuffworld.com – I felt as ready as I would ever be. I'd also had to swallow my pride and send Probes a text. Only an idiot would tackle a killer alone, and besides, this was no longer about me. It was about saving Barbara's life.

Rounding a corner I stopped, stunned at the strange sight below me and for a moment, I felt disorientated. The ford was lit up by a row of dazzling bright lights – just as it had been on the night of Carol Pryce's murder.

Drawing nearer, I realized that they came from the overhead safari rack atop the very same Land Rover that had been hidden along Ponsford Ridge – the same one that had hit my car.

Hugging the hedge, I crept closer and only now saw Barbara's mangled pink bicycle lying in the stream. I froze in a silent scream. Was she dead?

'Keep looking,' shouted Ruby. She was standing on the kissing bridge, looking out into the darkness beyond. 'She can't get far with that bad toe!'

I almost cried with relief. Barbara was alive! Crouching low, I scuttled toward her and under the kissing bridge, hiding in the shadows.

'She's gone,' I heard Noah shout back. I felt sick to my stomach. So it was true. Noah was involved right up to his neck. 'I say we leave her,' he said. 'She'll not survive the night out here. She'll fall into a bog and drown.'

Noah emerged from the far side of the ford, flashlight in hand. He shielded his eyes from the headlights' glare, saying, 'She's hardly going to come out with all these lights on.'

'I hope she dies,' cried Ruby. 'It's all her fault. Mum would still be alive if we hadn't come to Gipping. Why did we have to come here?'

Ruby started to cry. Noah hurried over and put his arms around her shoulder. I had a perfect view. They couldn't be more than ten feet from where I crouched.

'At least we've still got each other,' he said.

'Ruby turned toward him. 'What about that stupid newspaper reporter?'

267

Automatically my stomach clenched. *Please don't say anything unkind about me.*

'She was a gorger, Ruby,' was all he said. 'I just wanted information.'

'I was worried,' said Ruby. 'You won't leave me, will you?'

'What do you think? We're friends, right?' Noah kissed the top of her head.

'Yes, friends.' Ruby turned to look at him with longing in her eyes. I could see she hoped for more.

'Let's go,' said Noah. 'We've got to pretend everything is normal. We'll move onto a new place next week and start again.'

'What's the point? Mum's dead,' snivelled Ruby. 'You go back. I'm staying here. As long as that bitch Barbara is still around, Dad will always want her. You know she found him on Facebook, don't you?'

'Don't, Ruby,' said Noah. 'You've already got Carol Pryce's blood on your hands.'

My heart caught in my mouth. It was Ruby who had murdered the policewoman. Not Jimmy, not Dora, and, most of all – thank God – not Noah.

'She found out what we were doing. She lied to you, and she made a fool out of Dad,' cried Ruby. 'I saw them down by the lake, you know. *Kissing.*'

'Forget all that,' said Noah. 'That's past. People are coming from all over England to pay their respects. You've got to pull yourself together.'

Ruby whispered something in his ear. I strained to hear over the noise of the water sloshing around the wooden bridge supports but could only make out 'stay' and 'pretend'. He handed her the flashlight and headed for the Land Rover.

'Okay,' said Ruby in a very loud voice. 'I know you're right.'

Opening the passenger door first, Noah slammed it hard, then returned to the driver's side and got in – slamming the door a second time. Switching off the overhead lights, he turned over the ignition, and the diesel engine burst into life. He eased the vehicle forward through the stream and around Barbara's bicycle, leaving it lying there, partially submerged.

The lights of the Land Rover gradually faded into the distance. A strange mist came down. All was silent save for the sound of the ford, trickling across the lane.

I hardly dared breathe. I knew Ruby was there, but not where. Moments later I heard her footsteps overhead. Then silence. It was now or never.

I double-checked that my balaclava was in place, took off my cumbersome Wellingtons, and crept out from my hiding place, grateful for the darkness. Just wearing socks, I tiptoed up the short flight of steps to the bridge.

I could just make out Ruby standing there in the mist with her back to me.

I pounced, flinging one arm around her neck, hooking my right foot in and around her right leg, and threw my weight forward. Unfortunately, Ruby was stronger than I thought. She flung herself upright and we both fell backward, screaming, over the edge and into the water.

Winded, freezing cold, and soaked to the skin, I tried to recover but Ruby was too fast. In a trice she was on top of me, raising the flashlight high and ready to strike. She cried out on seeing my mask but brought the flashlight down hard. I threw my head aside and managed to roll her underneath me, splashing, choking as the water filled my eyes and lungs.

As I clamped her small body between my knees, Ruby fought like a wildcat. We wrestled for the flashlight. I got it, but she knocked it out of my hands and into the water.

Twice I almost reached my Mace Screecher, but each time she reared up, biting down hard on my wrist, making me cry out in pain.

And I was underneath her again. Ruby's face was a mask of pure hatred. She tore off my balaclava. 'You!' she spat and punched me full in the face.

I fell back into the water, head spinning, unable to move.

'Stop it!' I panted, working the Mace cylinder into my fingers, which were practically numb with cold. 'Your dad's badly injured, Ruby. It's over.'

'Liar!' she screeched, and flew once more at my head.

I flipped the button.

Pepper spray hit Ruby full in the eyes as an ear-splitting whistle exploded through the night air, over and over again. Ruby fell backward and plunged her face into the water, moaning, crawling to the side of the road, shivering with pain. The alarm went silent.

I staggered to my feet and was engulfed in warm, sturdy arms. 'I've got you, dear,' Barbara said. 'You're safe now.'

I burst into tears. 'Oh! I thought . . . I thought . . . you—'

'Goodness, it would take much more than a little gypsy trollop to get the better of me,' she scoffed as Ruby's moans continued.

'But how—?' I stammered. 'When I saw your bicycle—'

'Yes, I'm not very happy about that,' she said. 'I may not be as young as I was, but believe me I can still move when I have to. Although my toe—'

'But they were *searching* for you!' I wailed.

'Not far from here is a sunken garden,' Barbara said wistfully. 'There's a hidden grotto. Jimmy and I used to meet there. It was all such a long time ago.'

A pair of headlights came over the brow of the hill. I grabbed Barbara's hand, terrified. 'Oh God. It's Noah's. He's come back!'

'I think you need your eyes checked, dear,' said Barbara with a chuckle. 'Look again.' A convoy of flashing lights was streaming down toward us from both directions. 'I do believe the cavalry has arrived.'

44

'I've been robbed! My Georgian tea urns have gone!' shrieked a voice on the other end of the phone. 'I *knew* that would happen! I *knew* those gypsies couldn't be trusted!'

I grabbed my watch and groaned. Six thirty this time! Why did Topaz always call so early? 'Don't try that one again,' I said coldly. 'It won't work.'

'But I swear to God—' she sounded hysterical. 'Honestly—'

'Talk to your cousin. I'm sure he'll help.' I hung up the phone and tried to get back to sleep for one more precious hour, but then it occurred to me that perhaps it was best to get an early start.

Today was the day.

It had been over a week since Dora had died, and Gipping-on-Plym had been invaded by literally hundreds of gypsies, who were pouring in from all over England for what promised to be Devon's biggest funeral ever.

Now that I saw bona fide Romanies grieving, I realized how easily we had all been duped.

As I headed for the bathroom, I realized I still hadn't gotten used to having it all to myself again. Now that Annabel had moved out and into a tiny terraced house close to the office, I found I quite missed her. She'd also had to cut off all her hair and taken a last-minute three-week trip to a private health spa, presumably to recover from the after-effects of MAN-STAY.

Needless to say, the church silver, Trewallyn chalice and Georgian tea urns had all been returned to their rightful places, with no reward being claimed. Later, Topaz admitted that although she had masterminded the first burglary, the second was all Annabel's idea.

When I pressed for reasons why they'd picked Georgian tea urns, Topaz just shrugged, saying that Annabel would do anything to get on the telly.

Topaz had decided to stay at The Grange, having come to an arrangement with the new gypsy council. If they promised to leave directly after Dora's funeral, she had offered them a deal – a daily rent of three pounds per caravan, paid in cash. They all agreed.

At the *Gazette* it was business as usual. I was glad to see Barbara back at her post. Later, she'd told me privately that she and Jimmy had realized it could never work between them, saying she wished she'd kept their magical romance exactly where it had been – back in the past.

'But why did you go to Mudge Lane?' I asked.

Barbara shrugged. 'One last kiss perhaps? He left me a note telling me to meet him there. Now that I think about it, it didn't look like his handwriting – though he'd never been good at spelling.'

I didn't want to, but I just had to ask. 'Who was driving the Land Rover?'

'I couldn't see. It came from behind, dear,' she said. 'Jimmy was a terrible womanizer. A hard dog to keep on the porch.'

'So I heard.'

'He made that poor Dora so unhappy,' Barbara said. 'Why would he treat me any differently?'

272

Whether she had decided to go ahead with her wedding was still up for debate.

'I'm not sure I'm really ready for that big commitment,' Barbara said, admitting that it had been her idea to look for Jimmy and lay a ghost to rest. 'It was Annabel who had told me all about Facebook,' she went on. 'Do you know she has over four hundred friends?'

Wilf agreed to a long engagement, saying he just wanted her to be happy.

With Olive becoming more of a fixture in reception, Wilf agreed to give Barbara an agony column to run alongside Gipping Roundup on page seven. It was called 'Dear Babs'. Readers were invited to e-mail her with their relationship problems for 'no frills' advice.

By the time the police found Noah's abandoned Land Rover, his horse and his green-and-yellow-painted wagon had vanished. I couldn't help but feel glad. Falling for rogues seemed to run in our family.

Both Jimmy and Ruby had been hospitalized – Jimmy for third-degree burns following the explosion, and Ruby, suffering from the after effects of having Mace sprayed in her eyes.

Rumour had it that she would be allowed to attend her mother's funeral before being moved to Dartmoor Prison to await sentencing. With one count of first-degree murder, two of attempted murder, and counts of forgery and grand theft up the gazoo, Ruby would most likely be detained at Her Majesty's pleasure for some time to come. Jimmy faced lesser charges, but basically, the future for both looked bleak.

Dora's funeral procession started at The Grange in Upper Gipping and along the main Plymouth road to St Peter's the Martyr.

Traffic was at a standstill. People came out in droves to watch a white hearse drawn by seven white horses with plumed feathers and hundreds of mourners on foot go by.

Ruby was escorted by a plainclothes policewoman, who

walked with her behind the hearse. There was no sign of Noah, but given that there was a warrant out for his arrest, it was hardly surprising.

Fortunately, Elaine Pike – the young woman who had so conveniently told me there was no Belcher Pike – helped gather the names of the mourners by circulating a notebook around the site. The total this morning was seven hundred and ninety-two, but more were expected. It was a far cry from Gladys Trenfold's funeral of one vicar plus two.

Since Church Lane was packed with gypsies and non-gorgers alike, Reverend Whittler broke one of his rules and allowed me to leave my car at the vicarage nearby.

I was struck by the pungent smell of cooking meat. Entering the car park I was startled to see an enormous fire pit had been dug and a whole pig was roasting on a spit. At the far end, someone had driven Dora's Winnebago, where it sat in a sea of spectacular flowers, glittering gold jewellery, cases of china and mounds of clothes. Wildflowers covered the lych-gate. Floral tributes in designs ranging from horse heads to giant teapots flanked the herringbone path all the way up to the church porch.

Whatever role Dora had played in the Pike cheque-scam operation, she seemed to have died with her political reputation intact. Questions about Jimmy, Ruby and Noah's illegal dealings were met with blank stares and not even a 'no comment'. True to form, the gypsies had closed ranks.

Standing in the porch, I was pleased to find Reverend Whittler grinning from ear to ear.

'It's quite something, isn't it?' he beamed. 'Of course, they won't all get into the church.' He went on to say that Barry Fir had loaned him some of the band's audio equipment so that the service could be heard outside.

'What's the Winnebago doing here?' I asked.

'They'll set fire to that after the ceremony.' Whittler rubbed his hands with relish. 'Many years ago Romanies used to burn

274

the caravan *and* the body together. You'll be glad to know that I've found a nice little spot in the southeast corner of the cemetery for poor Dora.'

Noticing that scaffolding with the sign Windows of Wonder had been erected against the east wall, I asked, 'When do they start work?'

'Monday,' Whittler said. 'Thanks to Olive Larch's generous donation of five thousand pounds. She really is a saint!'

I only wished Olive could have made a donation to my landlady, who felt she'd been ripped off, not just by her employers but by the justice system, too. From now on she insisted that Doing-It-Daily was a cash only deal.

Topaz arrived dressed from head to toe in black, carrying a black bag and wearing an enormous picture hat and veil. Without so much as a greeting to either the vicar or myself, she grasped my elbow and steered me behind a stone buttress, where presumably we wouldn't be overheard.

'Something frightful has happened.'

'I've already told you what I think about the missing tea urns,' I said firmly.

'Urns? This has got nothing to do with *urns*,' said Topaz. 'This is much, *much* worse!'

With shaking hands she struggled to undo the clasp of her handbag. Retrieving a stamped envelope, she thrust it into my hands. 'The postmark says Gipping. It's dated over a week ago and must have gotten lost with all this dreadful post business.'

Inside was a good quality photocopy of a birth certificate. I studied it, confused. 'This says Robin Cuthbert Berry.'

'I know,' Topaz said. 'Look at his . . . his . . . *father*. Oh God.'

'Good grief!' I had to read the name twice. In the box marked FATHER was – 'Sir Hugh *Trewallyn*?'

Topaz snatched it back. She seemed closed to tears. 'It must be a fake.'

'Possibly.' But I wasn't so sure. From the dim recesses of my memory, I seemed to recall some hint of hanky panky

275

between Mary Berry and Sir Hugh years ago, plus hadn't Dora Pike mentioned that Sir Hugh might have exercised his rights as lord of the manor? Why else had Mary Berry been granted a lifetime tenancy at Dairy Cottage?

'And to think I've allowed Mary Berry and that ghastly Eunice Pratt to live on my land scot-free.'

'Did you have any suspicion?'

'You mean, did I know that my uncle was a frightful Casanova?' Topaz said. 'Auntie used to say he was one for the ladies, but actually it is quite normal for the upper classes to take a mistress or two.'

Not just the upper classes. Was there no man in England who was faithful?

'Do you realize what this means, Vicky?' cried Topaz. 'Lieutenant Robin Berry is the direct heir to The Grange. Not me! It's too humiliating for words.'

'Who else knows about this?' I said. 'Apart from Robin's mother.'

Topaz bit her fingernail. 'Wouldn't someone have tried to blackmail me by now?'

'Yes, you're right. They would.' The odious Eunice Pratt for one and Dora Pike for another had she not been mown down by Mary's traction engine. 'I think you should burn it.' Though I wondered where the original could be.

Topaz gave a heavy sigh. 'Really. This is most inconvenient.' She swept back down the path, acknowledging 'her people' with a gracious bow as they parted for her like the Red Sea.

As the solitary bell tolled in the Norman church tower, accompanied by the various screeches and feedback from Barry Fir's public address system, the gypsies filed into the church, and those who could not fit sat on the grass outside.

I moved to the rear of the crowd mainly because the awful audio system was giving me a headache.

To my delight, Steve was waiting for me at the bottom of the path with a manila envelope in his hand. My heart gave a little jump for joy. Perhaps I'd finally been forgiven for breaking his heart, and we could now be friends.

'Can we go and talk somewhere quiet?' he said. 'Away from all that noise?'

'Of course!' He *had* forgiven me! I followed him out into Church Lane. 'Where's your car?'

'I followed the procession on foot.'

'It's nice to see you again,' I said. 'Doesn't the pork smell delicious?'

'Got something for you, Vicky.' Still no 'doll'. 'Would you give this to Barbara?'

He handed me the envelope – *gosh*, everyone seemed to be giving me envelopes this morning! 'It's the coroner report you were asking about.'

'Thank you,' I said. 'Maybe we could have a drink so I could thank you properly?'

'I don't know.' Steve regarded me with his blue puppy-dog eyes. 'Are you saying you want us to get back together?'

Looking at his earnest, honest face, I hesitated. Was I afraid of love and just using my parents as an excuse not to get close to anyone? Did I want to be alone forever? 'Can I think about it?'

'Take all the time you need,' said Steve. 'You can let me know in the morning, okay?'

Steve walked off with a spring in his step. My heart sank. What had I just done?

I tore open the envelope, glad to find the coroner report from 1963. It stated that Mildred Veysey had suffered an aneurism before her body hit the ground. The tyre marks over her legs were caused five hours later. The only thing Barbara and Jimmy had been guilty of was failing to report and leaving the scene of an accident. I couldn't wait to give Barbara the good news.

'You've got quite a job cut out for you here with all these mourners,' said Probes, startling me. I hadn't heard him creep up. He was beginning to do that quite a lot. 'Very nice front page exclusive by the way.'

'Thanks,' I said modestly. In fact, my story – HILL DOES IT AGAIN: SCAM SCANDAL SOLVED! – had run for four pages in last Saturday's *Gazette,* garnering me a prime-time interview on Westward TV as well as coverage in all the national newspapers. Naturally I gave some credit to the Devon Police Constabulary, with a special mention to DI Probes's part in the successful denouement of Operation Pike. Bill Trenfold turned witness for the prosecution and revealed that Jimmy, Dora, Ruby and Noah had actually infiltrated the national postal system, offering small kickbacks in exchange for leaving the pillar boxes unlocked for an hour or two.

With regard to Dora's coveted special report, Pete decided to run it alongside her obituary, which would come out in this Saturday's edition.

'I thought you'd like to know that Jack Webster has been arrested for manslaughter for his part in persuading the Swamp Dogs to release the brake on The Gordon showman traction engine,' said Probes. 'Apparently John Reeves was involved, too.'

'Stalk *believed* them?' I said, stunned.

'No, Mr Leonard Evans stepped forward and said that Jack Webster had told him all about his plan to frighten Phil Burrows,' said Probes. 'Speaking of Phil Burrows. We were able to get a sample of DNA from the anonymous note he received. The strange thing is that the DNA is very similar to his own. Quite possibly a family member? We want to run more tests, but apparently Phil has gone off to America. Something about being on a television show.'

'I shouldn't worry in that case.' I'd suspected that Steve might have been responsible for that note. Was Brian Baker the only person who could spell *confidential*? Apart from me, of course.

Probes started to fidget and clear his throat. 'Vicky,' he said, 'I don't know how to say this, but you can't run forever—'

'I don't know what you mean,' I said, laughing heartily and

278

swiftly changing the subject. 'Whatever happened to Mary Berry?'

'She's had her driver's licence taken away – for heaven's sakes, why do you do that?' Probes sounded exasperated. He took a deep breath. 'I don't care who your father is. None of us can choose our parents—'

'My parents are dead,' I said, far more coldly than I intended, but truthfully, I was scared. 'Excuse me. Is that the time? I really must go.'

'Vicky! Wait!'

But I couldn't. I just had to get home. Probes's words had shaken me to the core. How could he *possibly* know?

With everyone at the church, I was hoping the house would be deserted. When I pulled up outside 21 Factory Terrace, a red post van drew up alongside. It was a new postman – clean-shaven, bright-eyed, and with a big smile. 'Got a package for a Vicky Hill?'

I joined him at the rear of his van as he handed me a tall box wrapped in brown paper. It was big and quite heavy, with my name and address written in a black Sharpie and marked CONFIDENTIAL.

I stared at it for several moments. It wasn't my birthday, but maybe it was a gift from Steve – the get-back-together kind.

Up in my bedroom I tore into the wrapping with scissors. Inside were handfuls of packing straw. Delving down into the depths of the box, my fingers met something cold and hard.

I saw the gleam of a silver top. Then – a second one. I burrowed deeper, tossing out the paper straw. And there they were.

Topaz's Georgian tea urns.

Inside one of them was a note.

'*Welcome back into the fold, kiddo. Thanks for the tip-off. Will be in touch regarding the enclosed. Love D.*'